DARK DISASTERS

A Dark Dozen Anthology

Uncomfortably Dark Horror

Print ISBN: 9798866794218

eBook ISBN: ASIN: B0CLKZ2LK1

First Edition 2023

Cover Art for digital, paperback, and hardcover editions by Don Noble of Rooster Republic

Interior artwork by John Kostov

Edited and formatted by 360 Editing (a division of Uncomfortably Dark Horror).

Editors: Candace Nola. Darcy Rose. Mort Stone.

PRAISE FOR DARK DISASTERS

"This anthology is every weatherman's nightmare and every reader's dream. Each story is its own forecast for countless sleepless nights." — Clay McLeod Chapman, author of WHAT KIND OF MOTHER and GHOST EATERS

"Dark Disasters is a book like no other. Twelve gripping tales of fire, flood, storm and other tragedies. Fear, destruction, and death abound in these stories of humanity under siege. Sometimes it's the storm that gets you. Sometimes it's the supernatural. And sometimes, the people you're locked inside with are the most terrifying of all..."—Jill Giradi, author of HANTU MACABRE

"The only thing disastrous about Dark Disasters is the impact it will have on readers. In these pages, you will find devastation of all kinds, but it's the emotional or psychological devastation that will have the most lasting effects. There were no drills in school to prepare me for what I experienced in these pages. Nola has done it again...lightning strikes thrice, which is fitting, considering the subject matter."-Nikolas P. Robinson, author of INNOCENCE ENDS

CONTENTS

Dedication

To the usual suspects: the kitty, the puddin', and the sir.
For Mom.

For all the readers, reviewers, fans, and incredibly talented authors that support Uncomfortably Dark.

For every author that has taken part in a Dark Dozen Anthology.

For Christina- for reasons too many to list.

And always for the Unicorn.

Content Warning

This is an anthology of extreme and graphic horror. Natural disasters of all kinds take place within these stories, including hurricanes, wildfires, blizzards, and volcanoes. Also, contains graphic descriptions of violence against men, women, and children. Trigger warnings include cult practices, domestic violence, and childhood trauma and abuse. Please proceed with this cautionary warning in mind.

Our Darkness: An Introduction

By Patrick R. McDonough

There's darkness in all of us. It isn't the absence of light, nor is it the shadowy corners in our hearts. Rather, this darkness is a feeling. It's an invisible vise grip that constricts your throat and forces your heart into quick and irregular rhythm.

Darkness is fluid, it ebbs and flows within us as we face our fears, our demons, our disasters.

All twelve contributors have shared a piece of their darkness and offered compelling experiences with disaster: natural disaster in this case. Every story is uniquely written, fantastically executed, and beautifully curated. *Dark Disasters* is a reflection of you and me, of us and them. It is the internal storm built over grueling time versus external catastrophes sprung on you in the blink of an eye.

When a natural disaster forces you to participate in its game, it's not a matter of how you can beat the disaster. It's a matter of how you use your darkness to help you survive.

When faced with literal life-or-death scenarios, do you come out as the hero or the villain? Everyone likes to think they know what they'd do, but the truth is, none of us knows until we're faced with disaster. My heart wants to believe most of us would rise to the awful occasion, but my gut, sadly, doesn't feel the same way. *Dark Disasters* is full of pain so realistic you'll find *your* darkness slinking out from its hiding place; it's whispering for you to be a good little reader and play along with the characters.

Whispering to help that sweet old lady, or to stab that nice old man. Cut deep and hard, because nice people die here, too.

No person is entirely good or evil. Stories that expose the checkered layers of an individual are tales worth exploring. Books like this are lessons in understanding each other. Well-written characters build empathy, and it's in the character's actions that we feel the darkness trying to manipulate us with its hushed suggestions.

What is your darkness whispering to you right now? Is it about love or hate? Does it tell you to do things that make you smile and cause others to weep?

When Candace Nola puts together an anthology, darkness whispers throughout every damn page. She has a magic about her; a way to frame every disconnected story by a string of emotion. Like her first anthology, *Baker's Dozen* (read that book after this one, seriously), the moments of extreme violence are anything but random and sporadic. The violence within the pages of this third anthology explodes like a volcano and chills the flesh like a New England winter.

It is through storytelling that we can experience everything this world has to offer. Some of it's good and some...well, you get the point by now. May the whispering not be a burden and your heart remain strong throughout the uncomfortably dark and disturbing.

Good stories stick with you, but great stories... destroy.

The darkness in this book will absolutely destroy you.

—Patrick R. McDonough
South Jersey, November 4th 2023

THE SLEEPWALK SOCIETY

BRENNAN LAFARO

1

THE SLEEPWALK SOCIETY

By Brennan LaFaro

A BARE BRANCH SCRATCHES at the window of the Grant Road Lodge and makes Peter clench his teeth. It reminds him of chalk catching a blackboard at the wrong angle and unleashing a hellish shriek. The unpleasant noise seems to bounce around the stone walls of the small two-room lodge before being swallowed by the weathered floorboards.

Beneath a lifeless bulb with expired filaments, a fire crackles and sparks at the hearth. The only source of light or heat since the storm took out the electricity nearly an hour before. As Peter warms his hands a careful distance from the flames, he takes in the silence of his companions. Nearly the entire Sleepwalk Society waits for Peter to call the meeting to order.

Dan's face droops in a perpetual frown in contrast to his posture, broomstick-straight and exuding a sense of authority. He's the kind of man who could wish you a happy birthday without meaning the first word. Richard scarcely tears his eyes from the sole window in the room. Only a puff of bushy gray hair above a charcoal-hued courtroom suit gives him away. His curls shine oddly bright when compared to the dark rain slapping against the window, a steady enough deluge to make one think the fire department had loosed a hydrant and turned the stream against the glass.

Older by a few years, John returns Peter's stare, the corners of his mouth slightly upticked in the unwitting smile of someone who's lived their life in customer service. "Can I get anyone a drink?" he asks, raising his cloud-like eyebrows. Peter returns a half-hearted grin and turns back toward the comforting light of the fire.

No one else places an order.

"Getting colder," says Richard, though his gaze remains fixed outside. The wind roars in agreement and somewhere nearby, a tree crashes to the ground with a dry snapping sound. "And the rain. It continues to fall."

Peter bites back a snide comment.

Dan has no such compunctions. He straightens his tie and allows his right hand to brush past the place on his hip where his sidearm used to hang. "Yet here we sit, the annual meeting of the Sleepwalk Society, and our de facto leader has yet to elaborate on why we must convene in the midst of a Nor'Easter."

"The worst Nor'Easter in thirty years," adds Richard, extending a finger but still refusing to grace the group with his full attention. "Perhaps terrible enough to warrant a sobriquet when all is said and done."

Peter glances toward the secondary room and tries to make out the outline of the door. The shadows fall over his face and hide his grin. Sleepwalk Society. A name more than forty years old. Only a group of men in their early twenties could have assigned such a title. A group that meets solely at night and becomes so familiar, so ingrained in the lives of its members, they could find their way there even in dreams.

Dan clears his throat and Peter spins to face the restless crowd. "Richard makes a good point, Peter. Why, with this impending storm, did you insist we keep the meeting only to make us sit in cold, stony silence?"

Peter draws a gold pocket watch from his coat. His eyes skate across it, barely lingering long enough to register the time. "Paul is not here yet," is all he says.

"And with the wind moving at these gusts, I daresay he won't be joining us." Richard turns to the other three men. Surprise dances in his eyes as though he had expected to find himself alone. "Worse yet, perhaps he is stuck somewhere. Myself, I felt as though the storm chased me all the way here from the firm, barely allowing me in the front door before unleashing its full fury."

"He'll make it," says Peter. "He always makes it. Forty years of gathering and he's never once let us down."

"Nonetheless," says Dan. "Maybe we should begin and allow Paul to join as he may."

John offers a ghoulish smile. His face is gaunt, but Peter sees the sturdy young man that lives in his memory. A towel slung over one shoulder; eyes fixed on the patron even while he wipes down the top of the bar. "Where are you in a rush to be, Daniel?" asks John.

Dan opens his mouth to reply, but a crash keeps his words from escaping. A terrible grinding sound, like a car slamming into a stone wall. The building seems to reverberate in harmony with the sudden noise, but then again, the wind has been making the tired wood and stone of the lodge dance to an unfamiliar song all evening.

"Another tree, I suspect." Richard's voice wavers ever so slightly.

"Or Paul has arrived." The grin slips on John's face but does not disappear entirely.

The wind screams at the accusation and rattles the windowpane like an empty wine glass dropped in a sink.

A shiver runs up Peter's spine, the breath of the cold wind trying to break into the room. Or maybe something else. He nods at Dan. "I suppose we can begin."

Dan reaches beneath his chair and brings out a small box lined with black velvet. Setting it on his lap, he takes off the lid with a sense of reverence and sets it down soundlessly. The box teeters at the edge of his withered knees.

Even the sound of the storm seems to disappear for the space of a moment, as if the box contains a vacuum.

John's chest rattles as he sucks in a deep breath. Too many years breathing in the second-hand smoke of the less considerate. His words arrive in a rasp, clawing their way out of his concave chest. "The forty-first meeting of the Sleepwalk Society is hereby called to order." The noise of the clattering rain returns, crackling back into existence like a needle dropped on a record player.

Dan removes a small bag and pours a stingy dusting of black powder across his palm. "We have order. All members present and accounted for?" The men give no answer. They know the ritual too well.

With a grunt that bemoans his arthritis, Dan casts the powder into the flame. Ribbons of fire burst from the hearth and Peter jumps in his seat. Forty-one times he's witnessed the chemical reaction of the black powder and still he believes one of these times, the fire might continue past its limited confines and wrap its loving arms around him.

"I, Daniel Pollock, am an aye," says Dan, removing a sepia-colored bit of paper from the box. "John Finney?"

"Aye."

Dan scratches a mark with a weathered-looking pencil. "Richard Bryant?"

"Aye." Another scratch.

"Paul Fairchild?"

The wind blusters and a twig taps at the glass, begging for admission. In Dan's hand, the pencil trembles slightly, unsure how to break four decades of precedence.

"Absent," says Richard, absently.

Dan nods, visibly relieved to have the decision taken from his hands. "Peter Sturgeon?"

For a moment and only a moment, Peter wonders what the others would do if he remained silent. Arms crossed, he sucks his teeth and voices a soft, "Aye", almost lost to the chaos on the other side of the sturdy barrier between a warm hearth and cold death.

Another crash sounds from outside the lodge and the pencil slips from Dan's hand and leaves a graphite scar across the ancient attendance ledger.

"That one sounded positively metallic," says John. "Hinges on a door, unless I'm mistaken." Without another word, John struggles to his feet. "Go on and get started, I'll be right back." Outside, the racing gales groan as if to lament his disappearance into the dark of the other room.

"We can wait," says Dan, laying a protective hand on top of the box.

Peter shakes his head. "I'd like to get started if it's all the same to you."

With a small nod, Dan dangles the pencil over the sheet of paper. "The honor belongs to you tonight, Peter. What is the name of your story?"

Richard loses his gaze out the window once more.

"I call it 'The Cost of Fidelity'."

"Very well." Dan scribbles on the parchment, then closes the lid of the box with a nearly lost click and lays it under his chair.

Leaning forward, Peter casts one more glance into the tangible darkness. No sign of John. "Somehow, the stories that make their way to these gatherings every year turn out to be ghost stories, more often than not. If you'll have it..." A smirk sneaks onto his face as he says the four words meant to trigger the purpose of tonight, their reason for joining. "If you'll have it, I present to you a story about a ghost that has yet to realize its circumstances."

"We'll have it," comes the response. Richard and Dan in unison. Peter almost believes he hears more voices join the chorus from somewhere in the dark.

"It starts as a game," begins Peter. "Two children making eyes at each other from across a crowded classroom. Perhaps the boy only does so because his friends dare him to. It's seventh grade, after all, and he's never so much as held the hand of a member of the fairer sex."

Dan wrinkles his eyebrows. "Does the boy have a name in this story?"

Peter grimaces. Once a story has begun, there can be no interruptions. "For the purpose of the story, we will simply call him, 'the boy'. For now." He waits to continue, fixing Dan with a look to let him know further interruptions would be unwelcome.

"The girl is a marvel, and more than that, she returns his gaze without a show of repulsion. Later in the halls, they converse with excessive shuffling and no eye contact, eventually entering an agreement to attend a school dance together. The night arrives, a wonderful night where the boy places his hands on the girl's waist and worries his fingers will melt into the smooth fabric of her dress. When the night ends, he thinks about kissing her, but decides against it. Neither is it right the next time they are alone. But he is patient and so is she, and the dance continues, so to speak, winding through formative years. Kisses sneak in along the way, alongside other explorations in various states of dress. College separates them in body, but not in spirit. Late-night phone calls and countless miles driven on weekends see to that. It is after graduation, however, that the boy faces his greatest challenge yet."

Dan opens his mouth to speak, but catches himself.

"It starts as a simple evening out," says Peter.

"A bit drafty in here," says Richard. The others ignore him. From the opposite side of the lodge, a door opens and shuts. In that space, the wind screams.

"The boy finds himself at a favorite tavern surrounded by friends. The officer, the lawyer, the bartender, and the writer. Countless drinks deep. Enough so that his legs threaten to abandon him with every trip to the bathroom. But he's happy. He's celebrating. Because he's asked for the girl's hand in marriage. And she's said yes." Peter allows the sound of the wind to fill the room. "She always says yes."

Peter sighs, looks around the dull gray of the lodge, letting his eyes rest on the empty seats for a moment. "Nothing bad could possibly happen surrounded by friends, celebrating the metaphorical eve of the end of his boyhood. All it takes to dampen the joy is a spilled drink and loose lips. Exchanged words spiced with vinegar escalate to fists. The boy sees double and his challenger is in no better shape. Everything tinged red with rage. Shapes blur, thunder cracks, and blood drips. Pain explodes in the boy's head, his hands. The face of the challenger floats before his eyes, unfocused features, eyebrows drawn in anger give way to confusion, fright. The features slacken as the boy wraps his hands around the other's throat. Squeezes. The world spins and the boy is pulled to his feet by friendly arms, surrounded by anxious murmurs. It's only after that the boy—perhaps now is the point in the story where we must refer to him as the man—learns he has taken a life."

Footsteps echo through the air, approaching, knocking like a cane rapped against a solid oak door. There is something in that sound that sets the hair on Peter's arms standing up. His heart gallops as a shadow forms out of the darkness and he wishes the lights would come back.

Outside, branches flutter across the siding of the lodge and the wind laughs, jeering at him. As it climbs, the laughter starts to sound more like a scream before it abruptly cuts off.

With a shaky voice, Peter continues, "While the man recovers from a series of knocks and bruises coalescing around a minor contusion, the others go to work like a well-oiled machine. In a manner of speaking, they save his life. The bartender, sporting a nervous smile, locks the door while the anxious murmurs turn to plotting. The officer uses the rotary phone on the wall to dial trusted comrades. He reports the incident by the dictates of the law, but maintains control over who arrives first on the scene. The lawyer peppers the atmosphere with questions, adjusting the answers as they trickle in, and tweaking the events like a pilot at the controls of a complex aircraft. The writer sits and observes. His role will come into play later, a combination of manipulating words in the local newspaper to minimize the role of his friend and relegating the story to a forgotten page. No small feat when writing about a murder in a small town mostly unfamiliar with the concept."

The other men pass uncomfortable glances. Peter holds up a hand.

"Misdemeanor battery. When the verdict is read and the man understands he will serve no prison time, he feels a rush of emotions. Gratitude for his friends, their protection. In that moment, he swears he will never let them drift away, never let a year pass without their presence. Hope overcomes him, as well. A second chance and the opportunity to leave this indiscretion behind before his wedding day. A clean slate, except he hides the old markings from her. The woman knows the bones of the story, but not the marrow that lies within."

"I thought this was supposed to be a ghost story," says Paul, stepping out of the shapeless dark of the other room. The dying firelight gleams off a beige jacket with leather patches on the sleeves and unveils a pencil tucked behind Paul's ear. He never goes anywhere without that pencil. His clothes drip, creating rivulets between the cracks of the floorboards that remind Peter of blood tunneling through a vein. Paul's shoes clack against the slats as though one or both are made of sterner material.

"Your slacks, Paul." Dan narrows his eyes. "They're torn. Looks as though they've survived a brush with a wild animal."

Paul's eyes crawl over the room, landing on one of the two empty seats. Without further acknowledgment of his state, he drops into a chair with a creaking noise and motions for Peter to continue. In the darkness of the other room, something scurries across the scratchy wood floor.

John. What is he doing in there?

"A clean slate," Paul prompts with the flicker of a smile.

"Yes." Peter collects his thoughts and continues. "And within six months, the man and the woman are wed. They buy a house, nothing gaudy but a fair piece of property with woods at the back. Not long after, there are children. A little girl and then her younger brother two years later."

"Abigail," says Paul.

"And Owen," says Dan.

Peter shakes his head, quick enough to make the blood rush and the muted dark gray of the lodge go blurry. "It's a story," he hisses through clenched teeth. "Just a story."

"Please," says Richard. "Continue."

"A few years pass before the nightmares begin, as though up to that point the man had lived in a safety bubble. What sets them in motion? He can't imagine. They visit at least a few times a week, leaving him gasping for air in the middle of the night, soaked in cold sweat, and staring mistrustfully at the shadows gathered in each corner. In the dreams and in the shadows, he sees the face of the man he killed, obscured yet angry. Finally frightened. The eyes lively, then suddenly dull.

"The woman dutifully sits up with him until he gets his breathing under control. She rubs his back, digging her nails in just enough to make her presence known. There is no pain. But there is judgment in her eyes. The first time he sees the look, he hopes it is his imagination, but her narrowed eyes, her thin lips climb out of sleep all too often. Soon enough, he notices the way she puts herself between him and the children."

Peter licks his lips. "How much does she know? How much more does she suspect?"

A breath catches in Peter's throat. With glistening eyes, he turns to judge the captivity of his audience. "A man who has experienced such loss of control knows the cost," he says. "Knows the toll it can take. So the man resolves to swallow his medicine, no matter the bitterness, and aims to improve. He breathes deep and counts before family interactions, always taking care to speak in soft, measured tones. He visits with a counselor at the officer's recommendation. It feels fruitless, contemptible even, but somewhere along the way, the nighttime episodes reduce from four to three times a week, from three to two. In rare instances, the number is one. But never zero. Every time, the woman wakes with him, but her fingernails grate rather than comfort. He cannot bear to look her in the eye for fear of what he might see. The end of a marriage, a family, a legacy."

Peter lets the last word hang in the air. Outside, the wind caterwauls against the rain, two bitter foes locked into a battle for the ages. Tree branches fight each other like sparring partners, the sound of clattering wood dancing between raindrops. In the comparative silence within the cold stone walls, no one speaks. A squealing creak like worn leather emanates from the low shadows drifting along the floor. The darkness drifts over the tops of Peter's shoes, encouraging him to continue. But he is afraid. Both to finish the story and to leave it untold.

"Through primary school, secondary, and even into the children's college and early adult years, the man and woman perform this perilous tango. Conversations never dip their toes past the surface. What the man initially thinks of as a soothing way of speaking, the woman tells him is patronizing. She refuses to elaborate. Refuses to see reason. So the man stops counting before he speaks. No more bludgeoning the blow. There are only two pieces of information to give. Everything or nothing. More often, he chooses the second, because when the man unleashes everything, he does so with a calamitous fury the likes of which beat down like the storm upon the roof of this very lodge."

The fire crackles, pops, and dims, relegating more of the room into darkness. The remaining flames paint the four men in a picture of purgatory. A light tapping skitters across the floor, so close Peter feels it brush the cuffs of his pants.

"What—" Dan starts to ask. A wet squelching sound cuts his question off at the legs and his eyes go glassy. Embers of light dance across their surface, but Dan has nothing more to add. His right hand dangles lazily by his hip, reaching for a weapon that is not there. The sound of breath in the cozy room diminishes and the flickering shadows throw strange shapes across Dan's face, like jungle vines questing beneath his skin. Peter's throat feels dry. So dry. He wishes he'd taken John up on that drink.

But the story must be told.

"Hair goes gray," he gulps, "and wrinkles take hold. The man and the woman build a house of secrets. Walls of silence occasionally broken down with bricks of rage. An angry young man inhabiting a body too old for such impulsiveness. Outside, they wear smiles like Halloween masks. The children, though..."

"Abigail and Owen," says Paul.

"Shut up!" A single bead of sweat drips down Peter's temple. He counts one-two-three and continues.

"The children. No matter how loyally the man and the woman don their masks on evenings and weekends, the children see through the ruse. The man uses the bathroom and he returns to whispers. Changes his clothes. Whispers. Always whispers. They've taken her side, the man thinks. And he notices the bruises along her forearm, the ones collected during gardening. Except the way the children look at the dark purple splashes and then turn accusatory eyes on the man, it tells him everything he needs to know."

The outer dark takes on a purple hue, the same shade as the bruises in the story.

"Oh my," whispers Richard.

Spiderwebs spread across the glass as a sharp, nosy branch pushes its way through. The intruding wind whistles in through the cracks. Something nips at Peter's shin, then withdraws. A miniscule offering of blood rolls down into his sock. A tear rolls down his cheek.

"Decades of fidelity swirl the drain," says Peter. "The children spirit their mother from the house, glaring even as the car backs out of the driveway. Their black sedan races around the corner and the man braces against the doorframe and screams. Screams until his throat tastes of salty blood, until the capillaries in his eyes swell to look like fat worms, until his breath runs short and his legs cry 'no more'. Then he sits in silence. And he counts."

"My friend," says Richard. "My deepest apologies. I had no idea Helene had left you."

Peter stares daggers but says nothing. Richard's eyes are still fixed on the window. The cracks expand as the storm sneaks inside. The fire dims and the shadows swallow Richard. From their dark pocket, a soft scratching noise gives way to a gurgling and Richard is silent before he can offer to draw up divorce paperwork. Peter imagines his eyes staring sightlessly into the murky precipitous flurry.

"Go on," says Paul, and Peter hears his friend dragging breaths into his lungs, a ragged sound like a current rattling through a sea of broken glass.

Paul lays an encouraging hand on Peter's thigh and those nibbles begin again, something injected in his bloodstream. It should hurt more, but a numbness overtakes him. He remembers a shot of benadryl he once received, so tame in its pill form, but like liquid fire in a syringe. He remembers the instantaneous burn as the nurse depressed the plunger.

This is different.

It scrapes. Infinitesimal splinters race through his leg, scraping the walls of veins and arteries. Each and every time it happens, Peter grimaces. He feels it now. The isolated splinters group together, a growing sapling coursing through the veins of a living thing. A shriek escapes Peter's mouth and his throat goes raw. It sounds familiar. It's the sound from the other room before John vanished. His leg feels heavy and sweat pours down his forehead.

Paul removes the hand. "Finish the story, Peter."

Sucking in rapid, shallow breaths, Peter presses on. "Three weeks. That's how long she was gone. I... the man calls her. Five times a day. Often more. She never answers. One day, he gets a pre-recorded message. Her number has been disconnected. She refuses to answer. Because of what they both know. She will say yes. She always says yes."

Peter sobs. The sapling hollows out his leg, replacing muscle, bone, tendons with leaves and wood. It moves at the frenetic pace of the wind outside and takes aim at his abdomen.

He speaks faster.

"The nightmares wake him. They come every night. Leave him paralyzed. Terrified. She's done something to make them worse. Except they haven't changed. Not one whit. Without her calming touch. His demons roam free. The terrors keep him awake at night. Drain his skin of color. His mind of rationality. With the woman avoiding him, he turns to his children. 'I need to see you,' he says to his son. The son makes excuses. But this is his father. He was raised better than to disobey his father. They set a time and the man waits. He does not count."

Dan's still form falls from his chair to the floor and it sounds like a heap of kindling dumped unceremoniously. His gnarled hand, a light shade of oak brown by the remnants of the fire's glow, sticks out of the shadowy mist roiling across the floor.

The branching tendrils ravage Peter's other leg, quick as a flash freeze and then thread through his pelvis, dragging and scraping against bone. He digs his fingers into the arms of the chair as a barbed thread of vine twists through his urethra and bursts from the end. Glistening with blood, they burrow into the exposed skin of his stomach.

"It hurts."

"It's what you've earned." Paul's voice no longer sounds like Paul. Inside his words, waves crash and electricity crackles and thunder booms.

"What I've earned." The words dribble out of Peter's mouth as the jagged branches, riddled with thorns, wind through his chest, riding an icy wind. Fireworks of agony erupt before Peter's eyes as the writhing wood impales vital organs.

I should be dying, he thinks, but the storm inside refuses to let him. Paul, or the thing that used to be Paul, holds his gaze. He must finish the story.

"The son arrives. Waits outside the car. Stares around the yard. The house where he grew up. Like he doesn't know the place. The man is patient. When the son comes inside, the man hangs his head. Shoulders low. Defeated. The son lets down his guard. The man springs. He... he doesn't mean to hurt him. He just wants to talk. Wants to keep him from leaving. Even then, things could be salvaged. The man rolls off the son. Brushes himself off. The son doesn't move. A crimson puddle spreads from beneath the son's head. The obtuse corner of the countertop protrudes with guilt. The man counts. Then an idea strikes him. A final gambit."

The tendrils are inside Peter's arms now, snaking down toward his fingertips, seeking control. He digs his talons deeper into the arm of the chair, freeing white clouds of stuffing from their velvet prison. Needle-thin chips of pine eke out from under his fingernails, sending waves of white-hot pain to Peter's brain, the only area of his body not yet overtaken. Outside, the storm reaches its zenith. Air so cold it feels laced with microscopic razors pours in through the shattered glass scratches at every pore for admission. Branches torn from their trunks slither through the jagged hole like snakes escaping from a zoo.

How can air create so much sound just by moving?

The thought distracts him from the staggering pain as the storm takes up residence inside him, forcing its way in like a 747 navigating a subway tunnel.

"What does the man do next?" Paul enunciates every syllable, forces them through the shrieking gales invading the lodge.

"The phone," Peter chokes out. The tendrils of branch tickle his windpipe, threatening to squeeze. "The man sullies the son's still-warm body. Digs through pockets until he finds a cell phone. He winces. Hates himself. Holds it up to the son's gawk-eyed face, anyway. It unlocks. And there it is. Mom's new number."

"And what did you write?"

"It's a story."

"Even you don't believe that anymore."

Peter closes his eyes and tries to remember the exact words while something scratches at his spine. "Come to Dad's house now! He's not breathing!"

"He's not breathing," Paul repeats. The fire gives a dying gasp and illuminates the room like a camera's flash. Tree limbs, both large and small, spread through the room like cables on a movie set. Parts of Dan, of Richard, lay motionless on the floor, reaching out of the mire like drowning men. The branches spire lovingly up Paul's legs and rest on his lap like a sleeping cat.

"She says yes." Peter tries to suck a breath up through ruined lungs. It tastes of sap and insects. "The woman arrives in fifteen minutes. She sees the son's car. Never hesitates. She flies in the door. Eyes wide and expectant. She finds the man holding up placating hands. But not her son's body. He's still thinking clearly enough to have moved it. The pool of blood is gone. Cleaned up hastily. But not the smell. Whether or not she picks up on it, she is aware. The man can see it in her eyes. Fear seizes her. She clutches her purse tight. What's inside? A gun. Pepper spray. He never finds out."

The vines squeeze at Peter's throat, almost tenderly, but he feels contempt radiating from them. Malice. The end of the story is so close and when he arrives, they won't wait.

"'No. No, no, no,' says the man. The woman freezes. Body still as glass. Her eyes rove the room like she's watching a tennis match. 'Where is he?' Her voice is a whisper. The son, she means. Of course, the son. She's come to protect the boy. Not because she cares about the father. A snarl escapes from the depths of his being."

Peter remembers the sound like a song on the radio. The same low growl the wind makes as it circles the ceiling, watching over him and Paul as they wrap up what is likely to be the final meeting of the Sleepwalk Society.

"The man doesn't remember crossing the room. He doesn't remember raising his arms," Peter sobs. "He doesn't remember pressing his thumbs into her windpipe. He squeezes as he gently strokes her skin, the same way she did for him all those nights. He helps her sleep. He just wanted to help her sleep."

The inky mist begins to clear from the floor, shadows retreating. From a tangle of briar patch, Dan's glassy eyes stare up in accusation. Peter can almost hear him asking, "how long, my friend?". Mere feet away, Richard lies crumpled in his chair, eyes turned away as if the waning storm holds more interest than the sordid lives of the men seeking shelter. As the firelight touches the other room, Peter sees John's corpse, a tangle of branches laced through his skin like a pincushion. He stares out with a rictus grin etched on his face.

"I had to hide the cars. Neighbors see them. Neighbors talk. They couldn't stay."

"How long?" asked Paul, giving voice to the voiceless.

Peter opens his mouth to speak and a tooth drops free, a molar replaced by a wriggling root. Pressure builds in his head as the other offshoots prepare to break free. Any moment now. More teeth wrench free and Peter spits them to the floor, where they rattle like dice thrown across a game board. "Three days. I parked the cars in the woods out back. Sooner or later, they will be found."

"And Helene? Owen?"

"In the basement, hidden beneath a tarp. Already the scent is climbing the stairs. The daughter—"

"Abigail."

"Yes, Abigail. She's called so many times. Once she even came by the house. I pretended not to be home. It's only a matter of time before she returns. With the police. They'll drag me away. Maybe that's a good thing."

Suddenly Peter realizes the pain has become almost bearable, borders on comforting. "Yes. A good thing." The vines at his throat begin to squeeze, gentle but firm. Peter's eyes bulge as he struggles to draw breath.

"So you leaned on your friends." Once again, Paul places a hand on Peter's knee. There is no bite this time, no feeling of any kind, really. "Of course you did. They got you out of a bind once before, changed the course of your life."

Peter tries to shake his head. The vines hold him still, stroking his face like a wife's caress.

"Oh yes," whispers Paul. He looks around at the scatter of bodies. "Now you think you've killed them, but you haven't. They bought this fate long ago. You see, Peter, these men didn't simply dismiss a drunken homicide. They changed the course of your life. Your wife, your son. They are dead because of these men and their perversion of justice. They gave you life and, in doing so, allowed you to continue to take. They created this storm. And now, we all must pay the price for it."

Paul takes a deep breath and for the space of a second, the sheen in his eyes disappears, replaced by fear as he studies his surroundings.

"Peter," is all he says before the twist of flora on his lap springs upward, covering his frightened features in a layer of writhing bark and dragging him to the floor.

A faint scream sounds then fades to nothing as a sharpened twig darts into Peter's ear, racing through eardrum and then gray matter like an archer's arrow.

I have become the storm, he thinks before all goes dark.

Outside the shattered window, the storm rages on, watching over the mausoleum. The Sleepwalk Society concludes its final meeting.

A TASTE OF IT

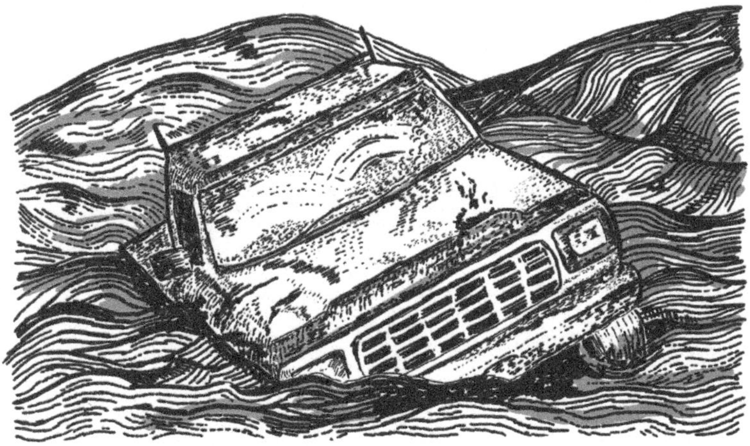

JUDITH SONNET

2

A TASTE OF IT

BY JUDITH SONNET

Ain't Nothin' But The Rain

IT STARTED WITH RAIN. Constant, thick, and quilting. The rain fell in sheets, and Porter couldn't help but suppose—as he pressed his face against the window so he could watch the parking lot flood—that this must have been how Noah felt. He'd stood in safety on his Ark, and he'd watched the world outside as it was made soggy, then stifled by God's wrath.

Psssh. God ain't got nuthin' ta do with this. It was the damned Pelham. That Pelham river's done flooded up our town every rainy season, and ain't nuthin' that no one can do about it. We knew that it was eroding the mountainside... we knew it was getting' out a hand. But the dam can only do so much. Least we's up on a hill. Should be safe up here. Should be.

Porter McKinny's thoughts were snarky. He was well known in town for holding a derisive tongue. Especially when it came to the younger generation—or, in his terms, "whippersnappers." Even forty-year-olds were nothing but petulant children in Porter's eyes, and he could make them feel low all the same.

He'd been about to do just that at Kutty's Grocery before everyone's doo-dad went off in their hands and pockets. The phones burped and gurgled, announcing a harsh weather alert. Everyone looked at their phones as if they were perplexed. But everyone had known it was going to get bad. That's why Kutty's was full. People were stocking up, just in case they got flooded into their houses.

The man Porter had been arguing with looked at his own doo-dad, totally forgetting he'd been in the middle of a heated and spontaneous debate over gun rights.

Porter didn't own a doo-dad. Didn't see the point. Those little devices did nothing but distract drivers and melt teenage brains. Around Christmas, Porter's son had bought him a Trac-phone, and Porter had personally escorted him back to the store so he could get a refund on the blasted thing.

"I don't mind you spendin' money on a gift fer me, son," Porter had said. "What I mind is you wastin' yer money. I won't have it."

"Yeah. Sure. Sure, Dad," Carrey had said, glumly.

Hope Carrey had the good sense to stay in the house. This rain... it's real bad, Porter thought as he watched the water sluice over the pavement and blast around the sides of the parked cars. *Ain't no use drivin' in weather this hostile. No sir.*

"Aw, Christ, Port," Josh said, showing his phone to the older man. "We might oughta table our conversation. Looks like the mountain done gave."

Porter took the phone and squinted. The brightness was up, and the text was so big, it almost pushed out of the phone's hard boundaries.

"Mudslide? Shit. Knew it'd happen."

"Apparently it's creamed Essex and Harlow."

"Creamed?"

"Flattened 'em places. Took them houses down."

"This gizmo tell you if there's a body count?"

"Nah."

"Well, at least it'd be headin' away from us. Right?" Porter asked.

"Sheee-yit. Forgot you done flunked geometry."

"Geology?"

"Geography. Geography, what I done meant an' you know it. But nope. It should be coming round and hit us here."

"Well, ought we leave?"

"Where too? Roads is flooded." Josh snorted and pocketed his hands. Despite being twelve years younger than Porter—who was in his sixties—Josh was just a scrawny little kid in the older man's eyes. A scrawny kid who didn't know nuthin', or next to. "You see that water rushin' down? 'Bout a foot deep, I'd bet. Knock a grown man to his ass. Shit. Maybe even deeper."

The grocery store employees had locked the only door on the front, and the water was sweeping over the glass, as if it was an over-eager hound pushing to get in. Porter imagined the water turning muddy, like running shit. Then he imagined it growing hard and thick, like moving concrete. It'd blow easily through the glass walls of Kutty's.

"So what? So we just hope for the best?"

The manager hopped up on a step-chair and addressed the crowd of worrying shoppers. Checkout girls and bag boys stood around him like pimple-faced sentries. They seemed, already, to be relishing what little authority the situation had afforded them.

"Folks, Imma need y'all to listen up here, 'kay?" the manager shouted. He was a portly man with shoe-polish hair and deep acne scars. His beady eyes were peppered with cataracts, and his lips looked like they'd never once been dry. He had a little stubble, but Porter doubted that the man had ever grown a successful beard.

"What we gonna do?" a redneck with a MAGA hat shouted, looking like he was about to piss his overalls. Porter couldn't help but smile at the man's anxious knee-knocking.

"The way I unnerstand it, this here is a 'mergency. If it weren't for the rain, there'd be helicopters to pick us up. If it weren't fer the mudslide... there'd be trucks. But we're in a good place here, folks. We're up elevated on a hill, and even though the water is thick out there, that mud is gonna be encouraged to go 'round us and head down toward inner Pottsville. What I've been told is... now, Mr. Colton. Just cuz this here's a 'mergency don't mean you got right ta steal. You put that outta yer pocket and back on the shelf."

Porter heard Colton Hicks grumble as he returned a candy-bar to its proper place.

"Now, we've got us our backroom, and it's got concrete walls and a concrete roof. Two ways in and out. One of them leads back here, and the other leads to that little gravel lot where all of us here park." He indicated his employees. "It'd be a bit cramped, but it's safer than standin' by the glass."

The lights blinked out. The earth shook. Porter braced himself against Josh's shoulder. He'd been so frightened he had almost jumped out of his skin.

There was a quick moment of panic, but the manager—his name was Lenny, Porter remembered—hushed them down. And being mild-mannered country folk, there was no backlash or bum rush. Although Porter suspected that Colton might have taken the opportunity to re-pocket his candy.

Ain't no reason not to. No one's gonna check inventory after the mud comes.

Porter and Josh had been standing by the window, looking out on the dark mess that was overtaking the parking lot. The rest of the shops in this district had been closed for the day, and they'd been wise to do so.

The real wise ones hitched up and scrammed.

Hope Carrey is a'ight.

After everyone had calmed, Lenny spoke up from his pedestal. "Okay, folks. Okay. We gotta do this smart or we ain't doing it at all. I've already sent Chad down to the back and he's got the door open. He's gonna make a headcount too, or at least try to. So that means we all go in as easy as we can. If we rush and crowd, someone's liable ta' get hurt. No one wants that, yeah?"

The crowd murmured. It was a small group. Porter wagered that there were only around twenty-five to thirty folks in the grocery store, including the four check out girls and the three bag boys—Chad being one of the latter.

They'd be easy to manage if no one got it in their heads to act out.

"Yep. Single-file now," Becky—the loudest and oldest of the check-out gals—shouted. "C'mon, you heard the man!" She sounded like a drill instructor trapped in the body of a college student. Her face was clownish with makeup, but in the dim light spearing through the glass windows, she just looked like an amorphous blob with bright red lips.

In order, the patrons moseyed toward the back of the store, where Chad was waiting. He used the flashlight on his cellphone as a beacon, and like a cop at a traffic stop he shined the spotlight onto each face that walked by him.

"I dunno, boss," Josh muttered to Porter. "I don' like tight spaces."

"You'll be fine, buddy," Porter said, clapping his pal on the back. Much as they could get on each other's nerves, when push came to shove, Porter considered Josh to be a great friend. Sure, he was gullible as all get out, and he believed some awful screwy things when it came to politics, but cripes! What was the point of having friends if they were just mirror-images of oneself?

Maybe the storm is just putting things in perspective fer ya.

Should give Carrey a call. Borrow Josh's phone. He's got one of them.

Sigh.

Should've just accepted the doodad when Carrey gave it to ya.

It was a nice gift.

Thoughtful.

You didn't have to drag him back to the store once Christmas was over and make him give it back.

In fact, that was right cantankerous of ya, Porter. Awful thing ta do.

Once all this business is through, you'll apologize to your son and let him know you 'ppreciate him.

Porter stepped through the door that led into the back area of the store. There were high pallets, topped with merchandise. When the ground shook, so did the towers.

Precarious.

Guess there's nowhere better ta go.

Wish this place had a basement.

Is basements safe in mudslides?

Dunno.

Never dealt with sumthin' like this 'fore.

A lot of folks had their cellphones out. Spears of light swayed up and down the pallets and investigated the ceiling. Someone gasped when a cooing pigeon took flight.

Christ!

When Lenny came in at the rear of the herd, he shut the door behind him and clicked the lock.

Doubt a locked door will hold back half a mountain. But good effort, Len. You gave it the ol' college try!

Porter wished he could turn his internal dialogue off. He was getting tired of his own voice and its snappiness.

Lenny's jus' tryin' his best, Port. You got a stick in your craw?

He was scared. That was it. The weight of the situation was heavy on his chest, and he felt as if his bowels were doing the mashed potato. He'd seen mudslides before, but never anything that could take out a house, much less a neighborhood if Josh's doodad could be trusted. Usually, mudslides tore up the road and at worst knocked a car sideways. There'd been some damage on Old Hickory Bridge a few summers back, but Hickory had been in long need of reparative attention before the mud hit it.

When he was just a child, Porter had once got caught on the mountain during a gully-washer. The steepness of the mountain became a conduit for thick streams, and the streams carried mud and gravel with them. Porter had scuttled up a tree and sat in its crotch, and he'd looked down in horror as the water grew thicker and darker and meaner. By the time the storm was over, Porter came down the tree with a shaking cold. He was dismayed to see that the shaft of the tree had tilted, and if the storm had gone on any longer, it would've tumbled and carried him down the mountain.

Momma done tanned my hide fer going out an' actin' reckless, but I could tell she weren't cryin' cuz she was angry. She was relieved. She thought I'd died by acting a fool and running out to play on the mountain when I knew a storm was brewin'. She was praisin' Jesus I'd come back in one piece, even as she laid her wooden spoon against my butt.

Porter sighed. He missed his momma. She always knew what to do. He'd figured, as a young 'un, that he'd gain that wisdom naturally. He hadn't. Even well into adulthood, with children and grandchildren of his own, Porter still felt like a whelping pup. He felt as if everyone around him had it all figured out, and he was left in the dust blinking away confused tears. Even his son, who'd been a rebel since birth, had it all sorted. He owned a big house, took care of his kids without spoilin' them *or* whuppin' them, and he knew how every doodad worked, even if he'd never once set eyes on it before.

Porter sighed. His son definitely inherited his good sense from his mother.

Darcy had died in childbirth, and Porter missed her dearly.

She smelled like cinnamon, even when she didn't wear perfume—

"Porter, you hearin' me?" Josh interrupted Porter's thoughts. The older man exhaled and returned to the present. He was standing in the crowded backroom of Kutty's, and it was starting to smell like sweat and nervous gas. The cinnamon was drifting off and away.

"Sorry, son. What was that?" Porter asked.

"Jeez. You actin' like you flew off with that pigeon!" Josh snickered.

"Har-har. Yuck it up. What was you sayin'?"

"Askin' you if you think these walls will hold," Josh said, pointing toward the nearest concrete wall. It looked thick enough, but the mud could become a battering ram if it was strong enough to overcome the hill. It all depended on what angle the mudslide was coming from.

"Either they will, or they won't," Porter muttered. "We'll find out when we find out."

"I reckon yer right, huh?" Josh said. "I dunno, Port. I'm a construction worker. I'm not used ta sittin' 'round and doing nuthin' about sumthin'."

"Ain't nuthin' you can do."

"Right. But it don't *feel* right!"

"I know what you mean," said the redneck with the red cap. "Wilbur Pryce."

"Josh Simpson."

"Porter McKinney."

"I think I saw you fellas at Packard's last week, didn't I?"

"Yeah. We drink there every once in 'while," Porter said.

In the scant light of Josh's cellphone, Wilbur removed his cap and wiped his sweaty brow. His black hair was a mop, and his face was sandpapered with stubble. He was a younger man, and his body was taut with muscle. "I didn't even catch that the storm was gonna get so severe. Came over to Kutty's for a hangover cure. Guess that's good luck. My trailer is in Poverty Gulch. Bet that place flooded up right quick." Wilbur grimaced. "Bet my goldfish have croaked. Or maybe not. Could be having a heckuva time with all this water!"

Porter didn't know whether to laugh or offer sympathy.

"Anyways, I'm glad we ain't alone, ya know?"

"I hear ya," Josh said. "Loud and clear. I ain't seen weather like this since I was little. Even then, I think my mind is only exaggerating how bad it was back then."

"Minds got a funny way of doin' that. I was done 'memberin' getting trapped up that mountain as a kid just now," Porter squawked. "Seemed like life or death but couldn't've been that bad. It didn't even tear down the tree I'd scrambled up."

"This one's bad, all right. That's a fact." Wilbur looked at his cellphone. "Yeah. No signal no more either. Bet it ain't even the clouds causin' that. Bet the muds knockin' cell towers over like bowling pins!"

"Can we all think a little more positively, please?" A librarian-like voice hissed. The men turned and saw Becky scowling at them. Her mascara was running, betraying her tough exterior.

"Sorry, ma'am," Josh said, like a child caught gabbing during a test.

"Sorry, hun," Wilbur said. "You know how us old men get."

Becky turned her nose and strolled away, looking for another conversation to insert herself into. When she was out of earshot, Wilbur rolled his eyes. "Fuckin' bitch."

"Now, Wilbur. That ain't very nice. She's scared, just as you," Porter admonished.

Rather than respond, Wilbur looked at his phone as if he was expecting a different result from his last glance.

"Christ. Yeah, I ain't got much back home to lose, I guess. But still, it stings knowin' all my stuff is underwater. My guitar, my computer, my TV... Christ! My TV was actually a good 'un, you know? I went for it last Black Friday and got me one of them ones that curves? You know? I thought it'd be an eyesore, but cripes, it looks pretty damn good. Makes you feel like you're at the football games instead of jus' watchin' 'em."

Porter nodded, but he couldn't agree. One of the many doodads he'd eschewed was the television. His momma had called them "idiot boxes" and Porter figured she was on the money there. Besides, if there was a game he cared about, he could just listen to it on the radio. That's how he and his pals had always kept up with the playoffs back when he was young.

"That sounds like a nice setup, Wilbur," Josh said, relieved that the conversation had progressed away from Becky. "Real nice."

"Yeah. I don't wanna go back to a shitbox. But obviously, money will be tight after... all this," Wilbur groaned.

"What are folks gonna do about housin' after this?" Porter wondered. "My place is probably flattened by now. I know Colton Hick's lives even closer to the mountain than I do. Lenny should be fine. He's up in the hills. High up. But a lot of us folks—"

"Live in Poverty Gulch and around the base of the river," Wilbur finished Porter's statement with a nod. "Yup. Lots of homeless folks in this grocery store now."

"Jesus. I'm lucky," Josh whispered. "My house... it's up on the hills jus' outside of town. Wayfair Way."

"Sheee-yit. You rich?" Wilbur asked.

"No. I rent from an old lady out there with a guest house. Her son don't visit, and she needed company so, she gave me a real good deal. Nice little lodging, plus she cooks me dinner three times a week, so long as I tend her garden and keep her company when I'm not workin'."

"Where you work?"

"I'm in the lawn care industry. I wanna own my own grass cuttin' business someday, but right now I work fer Sam Whitacre."

"Shit. He hiring?"

"After this mess, I don't think there'll be many bushes worth prunin'," Porter tried not to laugh.

"Reckon yer right. Cripes. Wish I could call ol' lady Tawny. Let 'er know I'm okay. She's probably sick ta death with worry."

Porter knew that the old widow saw Josh as a surrogate son. Her own kid had left the city and never looked back, even as his ma got older and weaker. Josh had stepped in to help, looking only for lodging but finding himself a strange and meaningful friendship with Tawney Milton.

Porter felt very lucky to still be in touch with his own son, and even guiltier for doing things that would've pushed most kids away.

God, Carrey. If we make it through this, I'm giving you the biggest bear hug you ever did get in yer whole god-damn'ed life.

That was the exact moment when the mud hit the store.

While Kutty's was set on the top of a hill, it wasn't a very tall one. With the slushy water filling in the bowl beneath the store, the mud quickly filled the deposits and climbed up to the store's walls. Rocky hands punched through glass, and thick sludge slopped through the building and spilled over the aisles. The walls buckled, unable to hold back the concrete-hard wave.

In the back room, guarded by fortified walls, the strangers and acquaintances all fell together into a squirming pile of fear and worry. Porter and Josh hugged each other like they were relatives rather than buddies. They watched the door, hoping to god it wouldn't bend and break.

Water began to piss through the sides of the door's frame. The center of the door bulged, like the pressurized hull of a sinking ship.

Becky was screaming.

Lenny was shouting reassurances.

An old lady had a heart attack and died on the spot, her stiffening body held up by Colton Hicks, who couldn't help but wish he'd gone ahead and kept ahold of his swiped candy bar now that the world was ending—

The door fell in, and mud sluiced into the backroom.

The screams were cut short so dramatically it was like turning off a light.

Porter's mouth was instantly filled with mud, and he tasted its bitterness.

Oh, God. Oh, God. Oh, God. Oh, God—

Rain Won't Fall No More

Carrey McKinny stood outside his car and looked at the vacant lot where Kutty's had once been. His father's corpse had been found here two years ago, after a mudslide ran over the local grocery store and buried it.

His was the only corpse dredged up from the mud that day. The rest were found later, but Dad had climbed to the top, as if he wasn't so sure he'd be reaching heaven if he didn't put his butt in gear.

God.

I miss you, Dad.

Carrey had seen the body. It was laid out on the mortician's table, scrubbed but still stained with mud and bruises that would never heal. His face had been distorted, as if the mudslide had worn boxing gloves and went to town on him.

That yer father, son? He didn't have no blood or dental records we could find—"

"No. he didn't trust hospitals much, my dad."

"We just need you to confirm—"

"It's him. It's definitely him."

The doctors hadn't told him such, but Carrey knew from reading online that his father's organs had been filled with sludge. The mud had raped him, anally, orally, nasally, and even through his ears. It had crushed his organs and replaced them, filling him with it as if it so desperately wanted to wear the old man's body like a suit. He'd heard of a similar thing happening during a tornado.

A woman he'd once dated in high school told him she'd found the corpse of a farmer in her yard after a tornado had struck. The man's clothing had been ripped away, and the pink, foamy insulation from his decimated house had been stuffed into his mouth and gaping anus.

She'd cried describing that, and Carrey had been thankful he'd never seen such a thing. Maybe that hubris was what had brought the mud down on Dad—

No. Don't blame yourself. It was nobody's fault but God's.

He thought of the tornado that poor girl had survived. It was, in hindsight, even a miracle she'd lived to tell the tale. Those winds could also turn bits of straw into bullets, and they could rip a person to pieces before they even knew they'd been caught.

What's worse? Getting killed in a tornado or in a mudslide?

Either way... there ain't nuthin' lucky about it.

Carrey wanted to sigh, but he'd sighed too much as of late. His chest was beginning to burn with sighs.

"Carrey?" his wife, who he'd met after college, asked from the passenger seat. She'd rolled the window down and was sticking her head out.

"One sec, Andi," he returned, stifling a sob.

His car was packed, and his kids were arguing over a video game on his tablet. He had two kids, but in the years since his father had been killed by the mudslide, he struggled to think of Ernest and Patrick as *his* kids. They were simply Porter's grandbabies.

My old man could be an ornery son of a bitch, but you bring those kids out and his eyes would twinkle like stars and he'd start in on this silly voice you never once heard before... even when you yourself were a kid.

He was an old man, even when he was young.

Lived on the mountain, scraping by one cheap work, never needing or askin' fer much.

Talkin' like he didn't have no education even though you know he's read more books than eight Harvard scholars stacked together—

Christ, Carrey. You even sound like him. Not outside, no. You'll never speak like him, with that warbly drawl and those constant contractions. But you think that way. The way you speak in your head, where no one else can listen... that right thar's yer true voice, ain't it?

Porter McKinny hadn't been the only person to die when the mudslide hit. There'd been a memorial, filled with faces both familiar and strange. But none of them had really mattered to Carrey apart from his father's.

They'd moved in with Andi's folks for a while, and then they'd tried to return to Pottsville shortly thereafter. Carrey still had his position at Myers & Son's auto shop waiting for him, but the town was haunted by sour memories. Everyone walked around like a zombie, missing someone who'd been taken when the mountain gave up.

After two years and a few heavy conversations, it was decided that the McKinny's would move away from Pottsville in search of greener pastures.

"Back with my folks?" Andi offered. "I'm sure they'll take us."

"No," Carrey said, scratching his beard. Like his dad, Carrey was well built and tough. His eyes were dewy and his skin was tanned. He worked with his hands, so they were white with callouses. His wife was almost his opposite, with her twig-like body, waterfall length hair, and demure expression. She was so scrawny, carrying two babies at once had almost broken her back. "No. I'd feel bad takin' up with your folks again. I know they'd *say* it's no burden, but the way I and the kids eat... we'd send your momma into the hospital with exhaustion."

Andi laughed. It was true that their kids were growing animals, and they would eat the table if a plate wasn't set down fast enough.

"I'm jokin', but I'm also not. We've put your folks out enough. I think... we should find a small place to move that can be our home. Forever."

"I like the sound of that," Andi said. And he could see in her eyes it was the truth.

Their forever home was located just outside of Richmond, which was an hour's drive from Pottsville. The road looped through the mountains, so Andi had packed the car with water and Aspirin tablets in case the curves made anyone carsick.

"Now, boys," Andi had said after catching their attention during breakfast, "if either of you feels a tummy ache, don't be embarrassed to let me or your dad know, okay?"

Carrey's own stomach was cramped and hurting. Looking at the razed area where Kutty's had once sat had put a kink in his tubes, like a folded garden hose.

He hadn't planned on pulling the car over on the way out of Pottsville, but he had. And now, standing outside of his vehicle—one he'd repaired himself after finding it junked behind the auto shop where he'd worked since he was a teen—Carrey wished he'd gotten to say at least a few final words to his old man.

You were a good one, Pop.

Sure, we could get in spats, and we didn't always see eye-to-eye... but I ain't never known no one like ya. And I hope I can raise yer grandkids up to make ya proud.

A dot of cold rain landed on Carrey's head. He almost yelped.

Gingerly, he raised his hand ahead of him. Another spot of rain hit his palm, dead-center. The water wavered, then seemed to disperse like a colony of cockroaches exposed to light.

We've gotta haul ass if we wanna beat this rain, Carrey thought.

He turned and slipped back behind the wheel. Delicately, he wiped away a tear before it had a chance to dance down his cheek. His kids didn't notice their old man was crying, but Andi did. She reached over and laid a spidery hand against his knee, squeezing him reassuringly.

"You ready to go?" Andi asked after Carrey composed his breathing.

"Yeah," he said.

He pulled away from the dismal lot and wheeled toward the mountains. The road stitched through the wilderness, falling and rising with the hills. It was automatically rough riding, and he heard Ernest groan unhappily from the back.

"You okay, hun?"

"Yeah," the seven-year-old whimpered. "I'm good."

Carrey looked up at the sky. The clouds were starting to swirl, and there was even a gray tint to the sunlight. It looked like they were driving beneath an overlarge sponge, which rippled with lightning.

Carrey had been paying close attention to the weather. They'd warned that there would be light rain, but it wasn't supposed to be bad. Nothing like what had happened two years ago.

This is what we get for moving in the middle of spring.

April showers bring May flowers.

May flowers... the Mayflower...

Mean anything to you, Carrey? Don't mean nuthin' to me.

Huh.

God.

He sighed, and it was as if he'd lit a fire in his lungs. Wincing, Carrey focused on the road rather than the clouds. There was a nasty turn ahead, and he was half-confident that another driver would be screaming around the corner at just the wrong time.

They were hauling a trailer packed with their belongings with them. Rather than hire a moving company—which would only charge an arm and a leg for ungentle work—they'd borrowed the trailer from Andi's parents. Carrey didn't feel bad about this. He'd driven out by himself to pick the trailer up, and Andi's dad was planning to just hook it back up to his own truck when they came to visit for the Fourth of July.

While working with the trailer, Andi's dad has questioned Carrey about the new place.

"It's nice. Cheap, but nice."

"It ain't one of them studio apartments, huh?"

"No, sir. It's a duplex."

"So yer sharing the home with another family?"

"Kind of, but not really. The house is split right in two, but both sides are big enough to be their own places. You know as well as I do I'd like my own land, but the duplex... it's a good gig. And it could be a forever home if need be."

"And you already got a job lined up?"

"Interviewed at Pitts Auto. They just had one of their hardest workers catch an early retirement. He'd just about been crushed while working under a truck. Screwed up his ankle real bad."

"Christ! Hope you're more careful than that."

"I am. But they were looking for someone to take his spot and I swooped in just when they needed me. Was able to negotiate a pay raise right out the gate too, so I'll be makin' more than I did at Meyers. Even though I'm grateful for what Pa Meyer's has done for me and mine."

"Yeah. They must be good people," Andi's father muttered. "You doin' okay?"

"Better now. Pottsville was my home... but it's just not the same."

"I reckon yer right. Losin' someone like that... you know. Dad's always die 'fore their sons and daughters... but they shouldn't be *taken* from 'em. Maybe that's a blunt way of puttin' it, but shoot. Ain't no other way to be than blunt."

"I appreciate that. Honestly. I don't like tiptoes and don't expect anyone to walk on them around me."

"See. I knew you was the right man fer my daughter," the older man laughed, and Carrey had joined in.

And now, driving through the mountains, Carrey couldn't help but replay those words in his head.

Maybe that's a blunt way of puttin' it but, shoot. Ain't no other way to be than blunt.

Porter, being a tad eccentric and reclusive, hadn't met with Andi's folks without company. Now, in hindsight, Carrey wondered if his Pop and his father-in-law wouldn't have made best buds if given the chance.

Or not.

In death, an idealized version of Porter McKinny had been sculpted. But in real life, Carrey's old man could be combative, harsh, and obstinate. They'd have many arguments, often over trivial matters. Like cellphones, and child raising.

"I took a switch ta yer hind-side a time or two. And my folks did the same to me. Ain't neither of us grew up social rejects!" Porter had once snapped after watching Carrey calm Patrick down from a tantrum with reassuring words rather than a beating. "Yer generations just too soft, I'll tell ya. Too blasted soft!"

"Just because my style of parenting is different than yours, Dad, doesn't mean it's the wrong way."

"You think *I* raised *you* the wrong way?" Porter had spun, instantly ready for a verbal scuffle.

"No, Dad. But it's not *my w*ay, and you'll just have to grin and bear it in my house," Carrey had affirmed in a tone that meant "and that's that. And if you got any more to say on the matter, then you best say it to your friends at Packard's Bar and not here."

Well, no relationship was perfect. Being human meant that sometimes you butted heads with those you loved. Even the people in this car... he'd had arguments with his wife, shouting matches with his kids, and he'd even once or twice stared at his own reflection with a strong sense of self-loathing. No one was perfect, which made the stew of memories conflicting once a person passed, and especially when they passed all of a sudden.

Sometimes, Carrey thought of his dad and remembered all the petty disputes and fights. Other times, his memories were as idyllic and simple as the intro to *The Andy Griffith Show*.

Ol' Dad took me fishing loads of times. There was a little pond in the woods to the side of our house. Scummy little pond, but there were always fish in it. Even on slow days, we'd be sure to catch sumthin'. Even if it wasn't worth eatin', by God we'd catch it!

Another curve swept around the rocky outline of a towering mountain. Bracing himself, he took the curve slowly. He could hear his boys squirming and groaning in the backseat, already dampened with carsickness and ready for the whole ordeal to be over. They'd set the tablet aside, their video game forgotten.

Good. Those screens are heard on the eyes.

Maybe Dad had the right idea about... thingamajigs and doodads.

Feel like my eyes are burning. I spend too long looking at them things.

Sheee-yit. Didn't have nuthin' like 'em when I was a kid.

Didn't even own a TV!

Had me a little radio though, and even that was too distracting! I'd sit by that thing and listen to it so low Dad couldn't overhear it. Shut my eyes and listen to the games or the music. And it sounded tinny and distant then, but we didn't know no better. We thought, when we closed our eyes, that we was listening to a real-life orchestra in our bedroom. Performin' just fer me—

Then there was more blood. It sprayed and susurrated and blasted through the car, painting the windshield and dousing the screaming children in the backseat.

Another wave of mud slammed against the car, causing it to jaunt closer to the incline.

My wife is dead... my kids will die... so will I...

Numb with shock, Carrey tried to see everything that was happening all at once.

He saw his wife's body wilting as it was caked in more sludge.

He saw the backseat filling. The deluge was cramming itself into the car, just as it had crammed itself into Porter McKinny's body when he'd been trapped with it. He'd been stuffed like a turkey, his belly bulging with hardened mud. As if he'd swallowed wet concrete and waited for it to solidify.

He saw his kids scrambling to try to climb through the quick running mud, hoping to get to their dad. Because Dad always knew what to do. Dad knew everything about everything, and he'd figure a way to get them outta this mess. Yes, sir! That was Dad! Smartest man alive!

He didn't know what to do.

He didn't know what to say.

The kids both fell into his lap, and he clutched them close. They whined and whimpered, sobbing into him. He bore down on them, as if his arms could somehow protect them from the rising tide.

More mud pushed the car closer to the edge of the incline. The car was being lifted now. He could *feel* the wheels coming up from the road and riding on the surface of the slide.

Carrey looked out the windshield, which was almost blotted with grime.

He saw a crowd had gathered around the car.

Some were faces he recognized.

There was Dad's ol' pal, Josh Simpson. The poor widow he'd roomed with had killed herself after finding out he'd passed.

There was Lenny Bark, the manager at Kutty's. He'd always been so pleasant when the McKinny's came to shop, and he had a little bowl of wrapped candies he let the kids pick from.

There were also people Carrey had never met before, but he knew their names and character all the same.

There was Becky Rickson. She was supposed to graduate from college soon, and she'd been working double-shifts on top of her schoolwork just to pay rent and help with tuition. She knew her student loans were going to kill her, but, by God, she wanted so badly to be a doctor. Just like her old man.

And there was Wilbur Pryce. A man with many struggles and a lot of anger, but he'd been hoping that this would be his year to do things differently. He was looking for honest work, and he was hoping to kick his bad habits. He was even considering rehab, even though it frightened him an awful lot.

And there, beside him, was a man Carrey knew well.

It was his dad.

Porter McKinney.

He wasn't smiling or frowning. His face was set in the sort of scowl one expected of a "grumpy old man." But there was a twinkle in his eyes. Something that told Carrey that he wished things had turned out differently.

They had surrounded the car like sentinels at guard. But they weren't protecting Carrey and his kin. No. They were only guiding him into the inevitable, offering him something close to comfort.

It's got a taste of this, the mud does.

A taste of humanity.

It wants more.

It wants to collect—

Oh hell, I should tell my kids how much I love them before—

The mud swept the car over and tossed it down the hill.

JENNA'S SOLITUDE

MICHAEL J. MOORE

3

JENNA'S SOLITUDE

By Michael J. Moore

0. The Trauma.

Jenna's sprinting through the woods, barefoot, because after her right shoe slipped off, she used the tips of her toes to dislodge the left. The ground is damp with evening dew, and her socks were instantly saturated and soggy. They flapped with every step until they were finally left behind as well, and the bottoms of her feet are torn and likely bleeding now.

Though it's been a relatively clear Montana summer, the tree canopy is currently blocking any light from the moon or the stars which might have otherwise illuminated her path, so she knows it's inevitable she'll collide with a tree if she doesn't slow down. But if she does, something much worse awaits. Thankfully, the forest is thin, and she's thus far managed to avoid the inevitable.

Paul is so close she can hear him stomping over the twigs and thorns which have already dug into her soles. Her lungs don't burn yet, but she knows they soon will. Her body is mostly covered by red pajama-bottoms and a matching winter jacket, but as pine needles comb through her blond hair, jabbing into her face, she finds herself thinking, *Please don't let me die tonight.*

"Jenna!" His voice is hoarse and horrifyingly close. "Come on! What the—ugh! Jenna—just—would you stop running and talk to me?"

Jenna doesn't respond because oxygen is priceless and wasting it on words will only slow her down. Behind her, fabric rips; he curses. She imagines his white T-shirt catching on a sticker bush, and then the inevitable manifests in a red-hot explosion as her face, body, and foot smash into a solid, yet smooth bark. She knows there's pain, but doesn't register where because her fear of the immediate future is overshadowing.

Her first instinct is to hug the tree. It's thoughtless and pathetic, and once her disorientation has worn off, she hates herself for doing it. The bark is no bigger around than a basketball. It might be a maple, though she doesn't know much about trees. "Jenna! Jesus! Are you okay?"

"LEAVE ME ALONE!" she screams so loud her throat burns. Something flutters nearby, taking to the sky with slow whooshing swoops, and then the pain appears in her foot—where she suspects she's broken something—as a coppery taste fills her mouth. Without thinking, she reaches up and touches her gums, feeling warm blood slide between her thumb and index finger, and realizing a fraction of a second too late that she's just made a fatal mistake.

Still, she shoves off with both hands and maneuvers herself around the tree, stumbling to one knee and coming back up with a wet pajama leg. Twigs snap, and she can hear Paul's shallow breathing. However, it seems to have grown distant. So fueled by a spark of hope, Jenna bursts forth and her foot screams with pain, sending an electric jolt up her calf and causing her to topple over, one palm landing in the center of a fern. She scrambles to all fours, reaching under herself and feeling her second and third toes bent all the way back. When she touches them, they wiggle like a toddler's loose teeth.

"Jenna—" Now his voice is hovering above, so close it works its way into her ears and reverberates inside her skull. "Jenna, chill. Please, I'm not gonna—"

"AUGH!" She hops up onto her good foot, and her jacket is caught in something which prevents her from moving. It takes a fraction of a second for her to become aware that it's his hand. Screaming again, she turns and claws at his cheek, searching with her fingertips for his eyes and spotting something in his hand which might be a silver beer can, though it's difficult to tell in the dark.

She thinks, *It's not the machete. At least it's not the fucking machete.* And then, *you're sober, though. You son of a bitch, you're supposed to be sober.*

Her nails dig into soft skin, and she feels the one on her middle finger break as Paul grunts. He drops the can, wrapping his other hand in her coat as well, and shaking his face free. It's so close now she can feel his warm breath on the tip of her nose, and see his lips peel back to reveal his perfect white teeth.

"Stop it!" he growls. "Stop fighting! I said I'm not gonna hurt you!"

"Fuck you!" She thrusts the heel of her hand into his cheekbone. Then again. And again, but he's much larger than her and doesn't seem to even feel the blows. The muscles in his face tense, casting shadows in every crevice that makes Jenna think of a jack-o'-lantern just before she's lifted into the air. Not high—he has to press his torso into hers for leverage, and even then, it's clear he won't be able to hold the pose for long.

Jenna begins to slide out the bottom of her jacket, so she raises her arms and prepares her good foot to absorb her weight, but before she's freed, Paul sends her flying rapidly at the ground. She lands onto her back so hard the wind is knocked out of her. Then he's straddling her, and she's struggling to breathe. He presses down on her chest with one hand. She grips his wrist with both of hers. Warm tears are running down her face.

"Please, Paul! Please. I don't want to—I can't—I'm sorry!" She doesn't know what she's apologizing for. The words just spill out of her.

"I'm not gonna—" Paul grunts. Glances off to her side. He reaches for something, and returns with the can. "Stop making this more difficult than it has to be, Jenna! I'm not gonna kill you, damn it!"

He raises it to her face, and she sees now that it's not a beer after all, but rather an aerosol can. She's tempted to entertain the notion that he's about to spray paint her lips, but Jenna is a thirty-three-year-old woman, and even when she was a girl, she wasn't that naïve.

Don't breathe, she thinks. *Don't you dare breathe. You can't breathe it, or you're his. You have to take a breath and hold it until you can get him off of you.*

So between trembling lips, Jenna sucks in a gasping breath, and doesn't realize that it's too late until her lungs are overtaken by a freezing sensation that flows out from her torso and fills her entire body like she is a balloon made of skin. She becomes cognizant of the chemical taste and the sound of the plastic nozzle hissing from atop the can simultaneously.

And now she's coughing, thrusting her head to and fro as the gaseous assault continues. Paul is speaking. His voice is strangled yet soothing, and he's telling her not to be afraid because everything's gonna be okay. His eyes are so blue she thinks she can see them, even through the dark of the night, but she may be dreaming already.

Her heart beats to the rhythm of nearby chirping crickets, and as its beat slowly decelerates, so does their synchronized tune. She doesn't feel her grip lessen from Paul's slender, yet masculine wrist, but is distantly aware of her hands falling to her sides. Then she's sinking. The world is fading, and the dirt is pulling her into itself, and just before it all disappears, she thinks of her two-year-old son, who she'll never see again.

1. Denial.

JENNA GASPS LIKE SHE'S just emerged from being held under water, but not because she's out of breath. Rather, she's just awoken from a nightmare. Having no desire to return, she opens her eyes as wide as they'll go. It's bright where she is, but the light isn't that of the sun. It's ultraviolet. Before her lies a whitish-grey, grainy surface,which she instantly recognizes as cement. She's lying on it, and it feels like sandpaper pressed against the side of her face.

Her heart rate has once again accelerated and seems to be beating inside her ears. The air around her is lukewarm. Images of Paul and his machete flash in her head, and though it was nothing but a terrible dream, she wants to fly to her feet and run some more, because it was so realistic she's tempted to believe she's now in a hospital. But Jenna is laying on a concrete floor, so her mind works through a short sequence of thoughts that lead her to think, *You're still dreaming.*

This has happened before. She's woken from dreams, only to find herself in others. She hopes to all things sacred that she doesn't wind up back in the woods. Back with Paul, who her subconscious has chosen tonight to demonize. She's sure this is linked to newly discovered similarities between him and Wyatt's father. And though she's also sure he's not a bad guy, she has no desire to see him again. Not in dreams. Not ever.

Still, as she closes her eyes and attempts to expedite the process of moving from this place to wherever her sleeping mind will deposit her next, she can't help but think of the evening they met, nearly three weeks ago.

IT WAS A CANDLELIGHT meeting in an old VFW hall that smelled of mold, particularly in the corner where she sat. He was pretty for a man, but she didn't care about that because she had only been clean a few months and had never had a thing for pretty men. It was his first time in attendance that she was aware of, though it was now July and she, herself, had just begun going when her sponsor all but dragged her here one Saturday night in late May. His hair was a slightly lighter shade of blond than hers, but Jenna may not have paid him a second glance if the flickering light from the candles hadn't caused his blue eyes to almost glow like a lava lamp.

After the meeting, small groups congregated to socialize for a bit, before returning to the mundane lives about which they came here biweekly to complain. Jenna lingered alone by the coffeepots until he made his way over with a Styrofoam cup and asked her for a cigarette. Feigning disinterest, she informed him that she didn't smoke.

"Really? I thought everyone at these places smoked and drank coffee."

Holding up her own cup, she declared, "Guess you were only half-right."

"Well, actually, that depends on certain factors. I mean we'd have to establish nomenclature first, right? Like define what we mean by 'everyone in these places'. Then we'd need to collect data using a survey, and factor in who might be lying in order to know how many people drink coffee *and* smoke. It would probably all hang on some kind of averaging scheme."

When she asked if he was a mathematician, he laughed and said, "Actually, I don't even know if what I just said makes any sense."

"So you're a liar, then?" She giggled.

"Bullshitter, thank you very much. And as long as we're on the topic, I should probably confess that I don't smoke either. I just needed an excuse to come over here and talk to you."

At one point, she caught Val watching from a distance beneath a nest of curly black hair and attempted to use body language to assure her sponsor she wouldn't dream of deviating from AA recommendations and seeking intimacy before achieving the coveted year's sobriety.

But when they shook hands, his grip was somehow gentle and firm simultaneously, and it caused her to do a quick calculation in her head that ended on the number seven, because that's how many months remained. She told him how sobriety had carried her from Spokane, Washington, to what she'd hoped would be a fresh start in Montana, and he washed down what remained in his cup and asked if it had worked. Because he was a good listener, she told him he looked like a celebrity.

"Lemme guess," he chuckled, "Paul Walker?"

Laughing, she said, "Actually, I was thinking Barbie's boyfriend. But whatever you need to tell yourself, dude."

He was three years her junior, and though he had wanted to be a firefighter when he was young, he currently worked the night shift at Costco.

2. Anger.

JENNA ISN'T TRANSPORTED FROM one dream to another. Instead, she lies on the hard floor, staring at the backs of her eyelids until there's nothing left to do but reopen them and acknowledge reality. This isn't a dream. The cement appears darker than before, but it's likely a misperception, due to pupil dilation.

Placing her palm flat on the rigid surface, she props herself onto the opposite elbow, feels it press microscopic indentations into her skin. A few strands of yellow hair fall over her eyes, so she blows them from her face and follows the floor to a matching wall, which stands a few feet away. On either side, it connects to other walls. Jenna looks up and sees a ceiling identical to them and concludes that the door must be behind her.

If I'm not dreaming, she thinks, *then it was all real. Paul and his machete. What he did to Val and Chris. And now he has me locked in a basement somewhere. I need to get out of here. Now.*

But before attempting to climb to her feet, she recalls that one of them is broken. Assuming a sitting position with her legs flowing in front, she examines two pale, yet uninjured feet protruding from red pajama-bottoms.

"Don't panic," she whispers. "This is a good thing. Don't you dare freak out." She reaches forward, wiggling each toe with her fingertips. "How long have I been here?" *Who cares how long? Get up. You need to get up and get out before he comes back.* "Oh, Jesus." Her voice shakes because if she's been here long enough for her foot to have healed, and she's been unconscious this whole time, what has he been doing to her? She runs her hands over her torso, which is covered by the black T-shirt she wore under her jacket that terrible night.

Six to eight weeks, she thinks, because she's heard somewhere that's how long it takes for a broken bone to heal. This means she's been here at least a month and a half—probably longer, as there are no signs of physical trauma or disfigurement.

Images flood her brain of Paul, helping a comatose Jenna use the restroom in various ways—all of which make her nauseous. And what has she been eating? *How* has she been eating this entire time? She searches her arms and hands for puncture wounds where IVs may have been inserted, but they're as smooth as freshly blown glass.

And what about Wyatt?

The thought of her son sends an electric chill through her body that fills every inch of her, and causes her hair to grow rigid. She flies to her feet because, by now, Wyatt will surely have stood over an empty casket, or set flowers before a headstone engraved with her name. The State of Montana will have shipped him back to Washington. Back to everything from which she's fought to remove him.

And because this is unacceptable, she vows to herself that she will get out of this place, no matter what she has to do. She'll reclaim her son, and she'll move again, across the world, if that's what it takes to keep him safe. Her jaw tightens as her fear begins to dissipate, replaced by a determination that she's never known before.

Spinning on her bare heels, she feels them scrape against serrated cement, and then she beholds a grey wall, identical to the other three. A mirror image of the floor, and the ceiling as well, which means Jenna is in a concrete box that appears to be about ten feet by ten feet in every direction, and somehow has no door.

Gasping, she takes a step back. Then another. Clutching her stomach, she retreats until her cloth-covered buttocks touches a wall. She hunches over because she thinks she might vomit, and she's finding it hard to breathe.

The room begins to spin, and once it's finally stopped, she straightens back up and scans every wall once again.

"Where's the fucking light coming from?" Her voice shakes. There are no bulbs. No fixtures. Not even a hole through which the sun's rays can seep. So how is it so bright in this place? "Where's it coming from?" she repeats. "Paul? PAUL? PAUL! CAN YOU HEAR ME? PAUL, GET ME OUT OF HERE! PLEASE!"

And though she's aware her words are being wasted, along with precious oxygen, Jenna can't stop herself from screaming. She charges the opposite wall and punches and kicks until her hands and feet are bloody and throbbing and her throat feels as if she's just drank a cup full of lava.

PAUL WAS A BIT of an enigma, because though he was overly transparent with regards to his desire for her, he seldom opened up about anything else. All she knew was that he had been sober longer than her, and that at first, he wasn't crazy about her having a son. But when Wyatt climbed on him like he was jungle-gym, he seemed to warm up to the child.

Val said she was playing with fire, but Jenna assured her sponsor they were just friends. They would sit on the couch in her apartment and laugh for hours about trivial matters, until one afternoon during the second week, his hand slipped under her shirt, cupping her bare waist. She let him kiss her neck, but whispered in his ear, "You know I can't have sex with you, right?"

Paul smiled most of the time, and Jenna grew to find it disarming, so she laid her head on his chest that day, and told him what nobody in Missoula—save her sponsor—knew. "When I left Washington, it wasn't just for a fresh start. I mean, I guess I needed to get away from everything, but it was mostly Wyatt's dad. He was, uh—I mean, he wasn't so bad when I met him, but then we started using together and he totally changed. I guess drugs like meth and heroin do that to people, but he turned into like a completely different person."

"I put up with it when he would hit me. I mean, my mother has these beliefs about a woman's place in the world, and I guess it was kind of engrained in me early on. But then he started putting his hands on Wyatt, so I put his ass in jail, and reached out to the program for help. A girl back home put me in contact with Val, and she set me up with a job and a place over here before he was released. At first, my mother kept bugging me to let Wyatt see his dad. She would tell me how he was clean now, and I needed to come home and give him another chance—for my family, she would say."

"I would see him online, though—not that I was ever gonna take him back or anything, but I would check from time to time to see if maybe he at least deserved visitation—and he was never clean, dude. He was always the same old—well, his name isn't important. He was just—"

But before she could finish, Paul took her face in his hand and covered her lips with his. After that, they sat quietly until Wyatt came out of his room with a stuffed lion hanging at his side, and then Paul wrestled with him on the living room floor.

3. Bargaining.

JENNA SITS AGAINST THE wall that she once believed would have a door, with her forearms propped up on her knees. She may have been here for days, but it also could be weeks. It's always bright in her box, so there's no way of knowing. Sometimes she sleeps, but no matter how hard she tries to escape into dreams, they elude her.

She hasn't needed the restroom, nor run out of oxygen. At times, she experiences a phantom hunger, and these are the times she relishes, as they remind her what it's like to be human. To be alive, which she has begun to believe she is no longer. The first time she slept, she awoke to find her hands and feet healed, which only served to debunk her theory that she's been here for weeks.

Often she thinks, *I'm dead. I didn't survive that night in the woods with Paul. He killed me like he killed Val and Chris, and this is hell that I'm in because I was a junkie and a bad mom.*

But at least once a day, clinging to slivers of hope which she's sure will drive her mad eventually, she speaks to the walls.

"Please. If anyone can hear me, let me out of here. I'll do anything you want. Paul? If you can hear me, Paul, you don't have to do this. Wyatt loves you. We can be together. It doesn't have to be like this. Anybody. Anybody, please. I have a son. He's only two, and I'm all he has in this world."

It never echoes in Jenna's box.

PEOPLE STARTED GETTING SICK in the spring. At first, it was speculated it was a new variant of the last plague that had had the entire world in a state of impending Doomsday bedlam. Then, it was found to be something entirely different. Nothing more than a mutation of the common flu.

This time, the death count wasn't televised. The sickness wasn't politicized, and people simply went on with their lives.

FROM TIME TO TIME, Paul would look at her out the corner of his eye, and it brought to mind thoughts of Wyatt's father, but it never went any further. He might have been the meekest man she had ever known, and had she not been fresh out of an abusive relationship, she was sure this would have been a turnoff.

She'd made up her mind that she would sleep with him, and her sponsor knew it as well. So, when Paul invited her camping, Val and her husband, Chris, came along. Val's mother watched Wyatt, as she often did when they attended meetings, and two small tents were erected in a large clearing deep in the woods.

Paul had a campsite, which he said he'd inherited from his father. It was near a stream and secluded, but nobody could have known what he was going to do, so after dusk, they sat around a fire joking about how he looked like a Ken-doll.

Paul excused himself for a moment, and when he returned from his car, he appeared behind Chris with a black machete, baring his teeth. Chris's neck bone broke in half with one swing, but at first, he didn't topple out of his lawn chair. He sat convulsing and his head fell to the side and hung from layers of skin while air from his lungs hissed and gargled through his exposed windpipe.

Val shot up like she had been sitting on a spring, but when the weapon made impact, Jenna heard her collarbone snap. She shrieked and crumbled next to the fire, and Paul hacked away at her like he was chopping wood. At first Jenna froze, just watched from where she sat, her mouth agape. Then her sponsor fell limp, and Paul turned and gazed into her eyes. The fire reflected off his, causing them to glow the way they had nearly three weeks ago during the candlelight meeting at which they had first met.

Jenna's fell on the machete, which had dark-red streaks on its blade that looked like they had been finger painted there. Paul's chest heaved a few times, and then he opened his mouth to speak, but before he got a word out, Jenna flew to her feet and dashed into the woods.

4. Depression.

FINALLY, JENNA SUCCUMBS TO tears. She lies in the middle of the room curled up like a potato bug because she's lonely, and she's afraid, and the walls are not hollow. She's pounded on them in search of a *thud*, but the cement is thick and possibly buried deep beneath the dirt.

This place houses light that shouldn't exist and possesses healing qualities. It deflects hunger and dreams, but not sleep or waking thoughts. Jenna still isn't convinced she's not in hell, so she cries for what might be weeks, and though her tears never seem to run dry, neither do they puddle on the floor. Once they have seeped from her eyes and rolled down her face, they vanish like ghosts in the light. Jenna cries and she cries, and she thinks about Wyatt and wonders if he's thinking of her. She doesn't move from her spot on the concrete floor until eventually she's cried herself to sleep. Only then does she finally dream.

But this dream offers no escape, because though she's no longer in her box, she's now lying flat on her back. She attempts to move, and though she feels nothing restraining her wrists or ankles, she's somehow paralyzed and staring up into a yellow light. And even though it's the brightest light she's ever beheld, she can't seem to bring herself to squint.

It prevents her from perceiving anything else, yet it also fills her with hope because maybe this is the Ultimate Light, in which she was taught to believe when Val led her through her very first step. And maybe it's here to rescue her from eternal darkness.

Then it's obscured as a mirror is held over her face. Only it's not really a mirror, because though it's clear and reflective, it's moving about and shaped like a man or a woman. Its edges are impossibly smooth and it has no eyes, yet somehow it's gazing down at her.

In its reflection, somebody peers back who Jenna doesn't recognize, but who terrifies her nonetheless because she knows this person is her. Her pale head is shaved to the skin, and even her eyebrows are gone. A shiny silver rod runs through her from temple to temple, and all her limbs have been removed. Jenna is nothing but a head and a naked torso with bones sticking out, and only now, as she stares at herself, does she remember what happened after Paul caught her in the woods.

SHE AWOKE IN HIS car, curled up in the passenger seat, and she couldn't move, couldn't even feel the moisture she knew still clung to her clothing. All she saw was darkness and the light-blue seat her head lay on, but a song she recognized from Paul's playlist rang from the speaker and the car was in motion.

She attempted to speak, to beg him to let her go because Wyatt loved him, and this wasn't right. All that she managed, however, was an unintelligible groan. Then his voice appeared over the rumbling engine.

"Are you awake? Okay, that's okay. You're good, right? Don't worry, I'm not gonna hurt you. Sorry about your foot, and that I scared you. I'm not gonna spray you again. I know that was some nasty shit. Just try to relax, okay? I didn't want to have to hurt your friends. I'm not a murderer. But if I invited you here alone, would you have come?"

Then he was outside her door, pulling her into the night and carrying her like a bride, and though it was dark and she was limp in his arms, she could see they were still in the woods. Just before he set her in the dirt, she caught sight of a man in a white robe. He wore a turban and a pointed beard flowed down past his chest. Once he was out of her line of vision, he spoke slowly, in the raspy voice of a smoker, without the trace of an accent.

"What did you do to her?"

Paul said, "Excuse me?"

"Look at her. She's damaged. What did you do to her foot? And is she awake? Didn't you spray her properly?"

"She ran, man. And I lost the face thing from the spray can when I was chasing her. I mean, I don't know how easy you think this was, but I'm guessing there's a reason you didn't want to do it yourself."

"You understand that this is devaluing, right?"

"Devaluing? What exactly are you—"

"It means it brings down the value of the—"

"I know what devaluing means. How are a couple broken toes devaluing though?" "A couple? You're saying you broke more than one?"

"I didn't break anything, man! She did it to herself. What are they gonna do with her, anyway? Actually—never mind. What I really wanna know is: why the hell did they need her to be blond—and a girl?"

"Just consider yourself lucky they didn't want a blond boy," the man replied. "When they show up, go wait in your vehicle and I'll collect your payment. I'm assuming it will be slightly less than agreed upon based on the condition of the product."

Paul said, "No."

"No?" There was the hint of a smile in the other man's tone.

"That's what I said. No. We agreed on a price, and how do I know if I'll even be able to sell this gold? If it's from outer space, or wherever these things are from, what if it doesn't have the right elements?

"What are you going to do with the money anyway?" the man cleared his throat. "What do you think?"

"Enjoy it for less than a year?"

There was a pause, and then Paul said, "If they're really using this plague to exterminate us, what do they want with this chick, anyway? Why can't I talk to them myself?"

"Don't know," the man responded. "Do you really care? You don't speak their language anyway and they won't meet with anybody save me. Most importantly, are you armed?"

"What? What does that have to—"

"It's not a trick question. Are you armed?"

"No."

"Well, they are. So, would you really like to meet them? Give me that, please." Then the bearded man appeared in front of Jenna, gazing curiously into her eyes. He pointed the can at her mouth and sprayed until the world once again disappeared.

5. Acceptance.

THE REFLECTIVE CREATURE RAISES a hand, places a black mask over Jenna's face, and then she finds herself back in her box. All her limbs are intact, and the blond hair which her mother used to brush when she was young is back to where it belongs.

Jenna now knows where she is. Not the Jenna that's comatose, laid out on a metal operating table being mutilated and experimented on by alien creatures. That Jenna could be anywhere.

But her box is a place inside of her, and that's where she now resides. A lonely place in her mind, and one of which she'll never be freed until the other Jenna is used up and gone. And somehow, she now finds solace in this because it's not a prison after all, but rather a protective layer, suspending her in sleep, and secluding her from what's currently happening to her body.

FACE-MELTING DISASTER PORN

LUCAS MANGUM

4

FACE-MELTING DISASTER PORN

By Lucas Mangum

"Hell yeah, smell that sweet pyroclastic flow, bitches."

The woman had a gangly look, arms and legs that seemed too long in proportion with the rest of her body. Her hair was a mess of bleach blonde streaks and black roots of varying length. Lipstick the color of slaughterhouse walls was smeared across the bottom third of her face. Eye makeup applied too thickly stood out stark against her milky face and made her look like some trailer trash zombie. She was brandishing a silver revolver that looked like it belonged in the hand of a gorilla, not her meek palms with their chipped, glittery nail polish, but Naomi Wellington had little doubt this mean bitch knew how to use it just the same.

The sky over the California suburb where she'd taken Naomi's family was choked with ash and smoke. In the distance, the lava crawled at a glacial pace toward the abandoned single-family homes, an ominous wall the color of bruised blood oranges.

The woman had flagged them down a few miles off the Interstate. She'd been standing beside a sedan with steam flowing from under its hood in billowing corkscrews.

Naomi had wanted to keep moving. The whole area had been ordered to evacuate after a series of eruptions in the Long Valley Caldera. Naomi's family had been among the last to leave, and her anxiety was already nearing its summit, with every muscle in her body pulled taut like rubber bands between the fingers of mischievous children.

But Bear had insisted on pulling over. Said it was the right thing to do. Said it was a good example to set for their son, Walter, who was sitting in the back watching downloaded episodes of *Brainchild* on his iPad.

Bear was a good man, always putting others above himself and determined to teach their child to do the same. That was why Naomi had married him. And it was ultimately why she relented and allowed him to pull over to help the lady.

What an epic fuckup that had proven to be.

Now, this would-be damsel-in-distress had her revolver pointed at the base of little Walter's skull as they stood outside their car in front of a house with a sandy brick exterior and an unkempt lawn. The rest of the neighborhood was completely empty. She had thrown their cell phones and Walter's iPad out the back passenger window on the way over. No one was coming to help them.

"Now that we're here, are you going to tell us what this is about?" Bear said, ever the peacemaking pragmatist. "If it's about money..."

"Get your asses inside that there house," the gangly woman said, nodding toward its desert red door. "When we're inside, you'll have all the answers you want. Until then, keep your fucking mouth shut, or I make sure this snot-nosed maggot's mouth stays shut forever. Got me?"

Naomi stared daggers at the gangly woman. Her nails dug grooves into her palms as she made fists. She imagined digging out those stupid blue eyes and feeding them to the bitch. The smoky air made her own eyes stream, though, so she looked down and did her best to avert them from the ash-choked air. The sight of the revolver's muzzle less than an inch from the back of Walter's head made her jaw clench, but she began walking toward the house.

The gangly woman looked down the street and made a high-pitched whoop. "I never thought I'd get to see lava up close. How about you, boy?"

Walter didn't respond. He kept his eyes pointed at his feet as he shuffled toward the door. The lava had already claimed homes at the edge of the neighborhood, absorbing them like an infernal sponge.

Bear walked, too, but he couldn't stop looking around. He was completely at a loss at what to do. This wasn't a typical state for him. Usually, he could find solutions to seemingly complex problems, but he was out of his depth with this woman.

What could she possibly want? Naomi wondered.

She knew from listening to true crime shows that seeing a hostage-taker's face meant they had no intention of letting their captives go free. She and Bear—and maybe Walter too—would need to fight when they got the opportunity, but the time for that was not right now. They needed to bide their time and wait for their chance.

The gangly woman nudged Walter forward with the muzzle of the revolver. "Open the door," she barked.

Walter cast wary glances at his parents.

"Don't look at them! Do either of them have a gun pointed at the back of your head? No! So, you don't look to them for answers, you wait for directions from me. Got it?"

"Do what she says, sweet boy," Naomi said in a wavery voice.

The gangly woman cast Naomi a look of pure rage.

"Bitch, I don't need your help!"

Bear bristled. His jaws clenched and his eyes flared with abject hatred for this lady. The circumstances rendered his rage impotent, though. If he tried to take the woman now, she would most certainly put a bullet in Walter's head, so he only stood there trembling.

Walter wrapped his small fingers around the doorknob and turned it slowly.

The inside of the house was dark. Only silhouettes of furniture and fixtures could be seen in the dimness. A mismatched sofa and recliner. A floor lamp with a tilted shade. A coffee table littered with magazines and empty beer cans. A television on a cluttered stand. The whole place stunk like nicotine and rotted wood. It was hard to believe she could smell anything with how congested the outside conditions had made her. She wondered if the woman lived here and if she lived alone.

"What is this place?" Bear asked.

The woman gave Walter another shove with the muzzle of the revolver.

"Ow," the boy protested.

"We've done everything you asked," Bear said. "Want to give us some answers now?"

"Not everything," the woman said, menace radiating from her twisted features. "You and your wife get on that sofa."

Naomi and Bear exchanged glances. Her husband's darkened eyes made him look exhausted and scared. Naomi nodded once and took his hand. They went to the sofa together and sat down.

"What about our son?" Bear said.

With her free hand, the gangly woman petted the boy's hair. "He's a cute little guy, ain't he?" She snaked an arm around his shoulders, and he visibly cringed. "Hey, don't be shy." She faced Naomi and Bear, her expression stony and vacant of humanity. "I think I'm gonna let him sit on my lap."

She ushered the boy toward the recliner, then sat down, pulling him on top of her. She kept one arm around him and trained the weapon on the side of his face.

"He really is a sweetie pie," she said, rubbing her free hand across his chest. "I'd really hate to spoil these good looks, so you two best not try anything funny."

"Don't touch him like that," Naomi said.

"I'll touch him however I damn well please."

To show she meant it, she ran her fingers along the side of his face. The boy tensed, but otherwise remained still. He knew any attempt to run would mean a bullet to the head. He didn't even squirm when she moved her hand lower and suggestively squeezed his thigh.

"I'm gonna fucking kill you," Naomi breathed.

"Naomi," Bear said in an admonishing tone.

"What?"

"Don't make her mad."

The gangly woman guffawed. "You better listen to your hubby. He knows what he's talking about."

Naomi stared fiery daggers at the woman, but she didn't say another word of defiance. Sweat plastered her hair to the sides of her face. Her lungs felt like they were on fire. Though the possession of a gun trained on Walter meant that the woman held all the cards, she did stop rubbing the boy in that suggestive way. Naomi felt a new boldness that contradicted their frightening circumstances. This woman who had captured them *believed* Naomi's threat on some level.

All hope such a notion conjured quickly disappeared when it became apparent that they were not alone in this house. Someone was approaching from one of the dark, inner rooms with heavy footsteps. Naomi braced, but her mind reeled at the horrific possibilities. She envisioned a whole cadre of pistol-wielding, gangly women, ready to line up Naomi's family and execute them, firing squad-style. She pictured a leering rapist with missing teeth, a gangrenous cock, and the goal of raping Naomi and Walter while Bear helplessly watched.

She didn't expect a man she once thought she loved, but that's exactly who stepped from the shadows of the kitchen into the less dense darkness of the living room.

BACK WHEN THEY WERE dating, Eddie always used to tell Naomi that he had a deranged little sister. Naomi had never met the young lady in question, and sometimes the stories he told were so outlandish, she sometimes wondered if he was making them up. He used to regale her with tales of waking up to his sister using his morning erection to get herself off, of how he once caught her trying to stick needles into their pet hamster's eyes, and of how she wrote love letters to various men who were doing time for murder and rape—men she knew only by the crimes that made them celebrities to vile people like her.

Her name was Charlene, and she'd dropped off the face of the earth sometime before Eddie had met Naomi. Eddie sometimes used to say he thought she might be dead. Now the brother and sister were back in each other's lives, and Naomi's family was at their mercy.

Bear looked from Naomi's face to the face of the man who'd entered the living space. He caught on right away. "You know each other."

It wasn't a question.

"Well, shit, Nay," Eddie said. "You didn't tell your hubby bear about me? Fuck, I'd have thought I was worth more to you than that."

"Eddie, please," Naomi said. "My son."

"Eddie," Bear mouthed. He grimaced like he'd taken a shot of rotgut whiskey, then pressed his lips together so tight it looked as if the lower half of his face might fold in on itself. He balled his fists at his sides. Naomi could tell he would love nothing more than to use them. He wouldn't dare, though—not with Charlene pointing that handgun at the back of Walter's head.

Eddie had changed since she last saw him. His hair, once a nest of boyish blond curls, was now shaved on the sides and long in the back. A nasty scar split his face from his right temple to the corner of his mouth; it looked like a crack of lightning set against the pale sky of his cheek. Ugly, amateurish tattoos darkened what had once been arms without a single blemish. Skulls and snakes, knives and crosses were etched from his hands to his shoulders in black ink. Worst of all, he was missing teeth; they were the top front two, a trait which would've been cute on a little boy—a boy like Walter—but on Eddie, it made him look like some backwoods degenerate.

Outside, everything was ashed over and gray. It was like a fog bank had rolled through the streets, rendering the rest of the world invisible. It looked like something out of a dream, but Naomi would not allow herself to hope that simply waking up would grant them a way out. That only happened in fairy tales and amateur horror stories. They needed to find a *true* way out of here immediately.

She began scanning the room for anything to use as a weapon.

"Listen," Bear said. His voice sounded weak, ragged. It was a rare sound for him, and she hated hearing it. She opened her mouth to tell him to shut up, but he started speaking again. "I don't know what this is about, but you have to know this isn't the right way to go about it. Things didn't... work out... with you two, Eddie, and she has a family now. With me. What are you hoping to accomplish here?"

At this, Charlene began to chuckle. "'Accomplish,' he says. You fucking white-bred, red-blooded American men are all the fucking same. 'What are you hoping to accomplish here?'" She leered at him and cupped Walter's crotch with her free hand. The boy whimpered and tried to writhe free, but Charlene tightened her grip, making him squeal. "Pure fucking chaos and misery," she yelled over the boy's cries. "That's it. That's the goal."

Walter thrust the back of his head into Charlene's face. The sound of the impact would've been sickening under any other circumstance. It was both wet and crunchy, like an overripe grape stuffed with gravel.

When he pulled his head away, it revealed the mashed remains of her nose. Blood mixed with the smeared lipstick as it flowed across her philtrum, over her lips, and down her chin. He squirmed out of her grasp and spilled to his hands and knees. She flailed with her gun hand and squealed through the blood that gurgled in her throat.

"Charlene!" Eddie grumbled.

Rage flashed in her eyes, replacing the surprise and pain that had been there all too temporarily. Before she could retrain the gun on Walter, Bear launched himself off the sofa like a thick, human-shaped rocket. When he collided with her, the recliner tilted backwards with both of them in it and hit the floor with a resounding crash.

Naomi cried out and reached for her son. Eddie reached for her. She was jerked to her feet and spun to face her assailant. She opened her mouth to scream in protest and grief, but a closed fist met her cry, turning her world dark and silent.

Then...

THE LAVA PUSHED AGAINST the glass of the living room windows. It was like time had frozen. Eddie stood over the fallen Naomi. Walter was on his hands and knees, his mouth open and eyes streaming. Bear was mounted atop Charlene, with his teeth bared and a fist reared back—he was the sort of man who would never hit a lady, but this was a woman who had threatened his family and groped his six-year-old son; if any woman had it coming, it was her—yet he did not strike.

It was a freeze-frame on a fucked-up movie, the sort of exploitative disaster piece that would do more than either get a 100% on Rotten Tomatoes or be forgotten within weeks. It was a scene from the sort of text that would divide critics into camps, each one striving to be more rabid than the opposing side in its fervor. They would decry its sleaziness and grime. They would praise its unflinching cruelty. Some would call its creator an edgelord while others would call her a provocateur. People would search for meaning among all the blood and fire, while others would dismiss any inherent genius—intended or accidental—and scream into the digital void about how it triggered them and how the filmmaker should be behind bars.

Not one person from any of these potential camps would feel the heat felt by the players in this scene, because this was no moment from a film. This was real life, and shit had just gotten a lot hotter for everyone in the nondescript suburban house that lay in the middle of an evacuated neighborhood.

The heat made the glass shatter. Tendrils of blackened orange sludge spilled inside, melting the paint from the wall at its edge. The arrival of the lava snapped Naomi awake.

When Eddie saw that her eyes blazed the same fiery orange of the invading substance, he took two stumbling steps backwards. He looked to Charlene for guidance, but she was still trying to squirm free under Bear's weight. Bear had decided not to coldcock her, but he wasn't about to let her up, either.

The only other person in the room to see the new life that burned in Naomi was her boy. Walter had stopped sobbing. He watched his mother rise, first to a sitting position and then to her feet. Her hands were open, with the palms facing her attacker.

Eddie's right eye twitched, and his bottom lip trembled. For an instant, there was a glimpse of the man he was before Charlene had found him again. In that instant, his face possessed the softness and vulnerability, but also the rugged worldliness that Naomi had found so attractive all those years ago.

But that Naomi was no longer here.

This Naomi had magma in her veins.

When she screamed, the heat expelled by her lungs was near-nuclear. It wafted against Eddie's face like white-hot fire on the wind, and his skin began to melt like candle wax. Only, that wasn't quite right: candle wax tended to be a solid color, while his rapidly liquefying face was a kaleidoscope consisting of red, yellow, white, and varying shades of all three, an ice cream sundae of blood, fat, and flesh spilled on the pavement on a sweltering day. He hardly had a chance to scream himself before his tongue melted, drowning his molars in liquefied muscle and filling his throat until he could only emit a burbling sound like someone gargling a milkshake.

Eddie collapsed to the floor, now a soupy mockery of his former self. Even the threads he wore had burned away, now mere flecks of ash in the human puddle. Only the bones remained solid, but they wouldn't for long.

Naomi scanned the others in the room. Walter watched her expectantly. He started to get off his knees but stayed there. He repeated this action again and again. His clothes were soaked through with sweat, and he was shivering despite the intense heat in the room.

"It's okay, baby boy," she said in a voice that wasn't the voice he knew but was soothing, nonetheless.

He stopped trying to get up and remained on his knees. He wanted to run and hug her, but he knew it was a bad idea. He also wanted to get up and leave, but he needed to know what happened next.

Bear had dismounted from Charlene and now stared at his wife like he no longer knew who she was; that was because he didn't. Though she'd never been some meekly domestic caricature of a housewife, she'd also never been able to melt someone's face simply by screaming at them. This was Naomi, as he'd never seen her, as no one had seen her. His mouth simply hung open, while his eyes were unblinking. His face was streaked with sweat and ashes. She terrified him, even though he was not the object of her fury. He had also, strangely, never found her more beautiful than he did now.

Charlene was now sitting up. Her face was a bloody, ashen mess. The whole lower half glistened with crimson, the upper half with mascara and sweat. Flecks of volcanic ash peppered the grotesque mask like freckles gone gray with disease. The gun was within reach, but she wasn't going for it. She was too stunned. She, too, could only stare at the woman whose family she'd made the mistake of kidnapping.

Naomi met her mortified gaze with eyes that blazed, not just with her own fury, but with the fury of the earth itself—the same fury that caused lava to flow through the streets and smoke to smother the skies.

"It ain't my fault!" Charlene yelled through a fit of hacking coughs. She spat out a wad of phlegm and wiped the redness from her lips and chin. "I had a bad childhood. You're a woman like me—you understand. It ain't my fault!"

Naomi's only response was to let out another scream of extreme heat, one that liquefied the gangly woman's desperate excuses and pleas for mercy. Under exhalation of fiery breath, Charlene's face morphed from a bloody mess still recognizable as human to something like melted roadkill. Blood, mucus, and ocular goo melded with melting flesh and tangled hair. The gooey substance that slopped from her skull looked like curdled milk mixed with splashes of food coloring.

While Charlene melted in her smoldering clothes, Bear gathered Walter in his arms and helped the boy to his feet. They both watched Naomi in terrified awe. Walter's lip was trembling.

"Come with us," Bear said.

But that's not how this movie ends, and she told him this by simply giving him a look, so with tears in his eyes, Bear nodded and hauled Walter toward the door as the loveseat burned in the spreading pool of lava. At the door, Walter cast a final look at his mother, mouthing her title but not her name. She raised her hand to say goodbye, then closed her eyes.

She did not burn; she ascended. Bursting through the roof, she was an angel of death, a vessel for the earth's fiery vengeance. In the smoke-filled sky, she reopened her eyes and saw she wasn't alone. As Bear and Walter reentered the car, prepared to escape the nightmares of the day, she saw she was joined by others imbued with the earth's rage: fire-eyed angels with face-melting screams just like hers, ready to use them to destroy those who meant them and the planet harm.

FAMILY PLANNING

CAITLIN MARCEAU

5

FAMILY PLANNING

By Caitlin Marceau

Gianna leans against a tree, trying to catch her breath as the smoke gets thicker, the air impossibly hot as the fire grows and spreads around her. Her feet are cut from running through the woods without shoes, her skin blistered and burnt from the flames that bite at her heels. She used to know this trail like the back of her hand but now—thanks to the chaos of the animals fleeing for their lives, the panic she can taste at the back of her throat, and the heavy smoke and ash that blackens out the sun—she has no idea where she is or where she's headed.

She looks around, trying to spot the road, but it's hopeless; she can hardly make out her hand in front of her face.

As the roar of the wildfire gets louder, the crackling and sizzling of leaves as patches of underbrush burst into flame too close for comfort, she knows it's time to run again. The muscles in her legs scream from the effort of keeping her balanced as she moves down the mountain, her swollen ankles sore and tender, and her lower back tight from the effort, but she pushes herself forward.

She needs to get to safety.

For her and the baby's sake.

"ARE YOU SURE YOU didn't want us to pick anything up?" Gianna asks into the phone, her eyes glued to the trees outside the window, their leaves turning crimson and ochre thanks to the changing weather.

"Positive," Evelyn says on the other end. "It's just going to be the four of us. And if we *do* end up needing anything, then I'm sure one of the guys will be happy to go get it for us."

"It's a three-hour drive from the cabin to town. I'd rather make sure we have everything we need *before* we get there."

"I told you; we do. It's *fine*. Seriously, just get your ass up here."

"Alright, alright. We'll see you soon," she says, rolling her eyes.

"Awesome. Bye!"

"Later!"

Gianna smiles to herself as she hangs up the phone. She reaches for her purse on the floor of the passenger's side but sighs and quickly gives up when her round belly is too much in the way for her to get it. Instead, she slips her phone into the compartment on the door and hopes that anyone who needs her will call Wyatt instead.

"She's already there?" he asks.

"Yeah, she and *the doctor*," she says, over enunciating the words and laughing to herself as she turns to look at her husband.

His eyes are glued to the road ahead, and he runs a hand through his thick dark hair, brushing a curl out of his way. His sunglasses are clipped onto the collar of his dark green sweater, and she smiles at how put together he looks now that his grease-stained coveralls and steel-toe boots have been swapped out for clean jeans and running shoes.

"Why does she keep calling him that again?"

"At first, it's because she couldn't remember his name. Now, I think it's to make him sound important," she admits.

"It doesn't make him sound important. It makes him sound like a professional Doctor Who cosplayer."

Gianna laughs, picturing her uptight friend painting herself blue like the Tardis and attending weekend conventions instead of overpriced day spas.

"Somehow, I doubt Evelyn even knows what that is."

She turns her attention back to the trees outside the window. Although autumn is her favourite season, she's grateful that her child won't be born until early winter. As much as she's looking forward to dressing her baby up as a pumpkin and buying cute clothes for them for the fall, she's happy that she doesn't have to worry about finding a sitter for the baby while she celebrates Halloween at one of Evelyn's legendary parties—or misses it entirely to stay home with Wyatt and the baby. She's even more relieved that she doesn't have to go on a road-trip with a screaming infant to visit her parents in Kingston for Thanksgiving.

"I'm excited for this weekend," she says, smiling to herself. "It'll be nice to have a final hurrah with everyone before the baby comes. I mean, not that we won't be able to do stuff like this when we have a kid, it's just... well, you know what I mean."

"Mhmm," he says.

She turns to look at him, sad but not surprised to find him frowning instead of sharing in her joy.

"What's wrong?" she asks.

"Nothing."

"You sure? Because you don't look like nothing's wrong."

"I've just got a lot on my mind."

"You're thinking about the baby again." Gianna doesn't phrase it like a question because it's not one.

She knows Wyatt isn't as excited to be a dad as she is to be a mom, much like he wasn't as excited to be a husband as she was a wife. Unlike his proposal, which came after years of her asking for a ring and his friends pressuring him to give her one, her pregnancy was an unexpected surprise after a good night and a bad IUD. She'd been happy to find out she was expecting, but Wyatt had been upset by the news and worried about how her pregnancy would impact his future.

Although he seemed to come around eventually, there were moments that Gianna could swear she still felt his resentment about starting a family so soon after getting married.

"I'm just thinking about the future," he says with a shrug.

"Did you want to talk about it?"

He turns to look at her and grins. "It's fine. Don't worry about it."

Wyatt goes back to looking at the road and Gianna tries to enjoy the drive, trying not to think about how his smile doesn't reach his eyes.

GIANNA COUGHS AS SHE sinks down on all fours, trying to breathe in what little air there is next to the ground. Her lungs ache from breathing in hot ash and thick smoke as she runs for safety. She crawls forward, her hands grabbing at dead leaves and sharp branches as she pushes herself onward. Soon, her hands find patches of grass and she moves even faster as the grass turns into rough gravel, the forest giving way to the small road she knows will lead her back to town.

She picks herself up off of the ground and pushes herself to run again, the rocks sharp and hot against the burnt and blistered soles of her feet. She debates running through the grass that lines the small road, knowing it would be easier on her body, but worries that she'll accidentally veer off course and find herself back in the woods. As painful as it is, she knows it's better to continue forward this way.

As Gianna moves for all she's worth, she's grateful she continued running after she found out she was pregnant. She'd been worried that being with child meant being *without* the gym, but her doctor had encouraged her to continue training and keeping up with her five-mile mornings (albeit at a gentler pace the further along she got). Although her chances of escaping this wildfire are slim, she knows they could be even slimmer.

As she continues moving through the blackness of the smoke, she realizes there's a light in the distance. Her heart begins hammering even faster as she worries that the fire has spread ahead of her, cutting off her only path of escape. She debates turning around and trying to find another way out of the woods, but she can feel the heat getting ever closer—ever hotter—behind her and so she forces herself forward towards the unknown.

Slowly, the light begins to change shape, and she realizes that it's not a fire far in the distance but two dim tail lights only a few feet ahead. She lets out a wail of relief when she finally makes out the license plate on the back of Evelyn's stationary car, waving her hands over her head in the hopes that her friend will see her in the rearview mirror.

As Gianna approaches the passenger side, Evelyn throws the door open and stares at her with wild eyes as she takes in the extent of her friend's injuries.

"Get in!" she screams.

Gianna is quick to oblige. She throws herself into the car, slamming the door closed behind her as Evelyn takes off down the road.

"What are you doing here?" Gianna asks, her voice hoarse.

"I wanted to make sure you and Wyatt got away from the cabin, but when I didn't see your car following mine, I got worried. I've been waiting here, calling your phone, for like twenty minutes."

"Thank you," Gianna manages, between gasps for air. "Thank you, thank you, thank you."

"What happened?" Evelyn asks, quickly glancing at her friend as she navigates the narrow road. Although the drive up the mountain was an easy one in the daylight, now that the sky is back and soot sticks to the car, the high beams are hardly able to illuminate more than a couple of feet ahead of the vehicle let alone where the road ends and the steep hillside begins.

"He tried to kill me," Gianna says, her throat raw and burning. The skin on her chest, along with most of her left arm, is tight and blistered from where she'd been thrown in the fire. She closes her eyes and lets out a shaky breath as she remembers the attack.

"What? Who?"

"Wyatt."

Evelyn stares at her in disbelief before remembering to look back out the window. There's a loud bang as the car hits an animal trying to escape the blaze—*A racoon?* Gianna wonders—and her friend grimaces to herself, her foot still firmly on the gas.

"Wyatt?"

"Yes! He tried to fucking kill me!"

"Fuck. FUCK!" Evelyn shouts in a panic. "Is he still at the cabin?"

Before she gets a chance to answer the question, the back of Evelyn's car is rammed hard from behind. Gianna protectively wraps her hands around her stomach and closes her eyes as the car spins off of the road, down the hill, and into the trees.

"YOU GUYS!" GIANNA SCREAMS excitedly, tearing up. "You shouldn't have!"

She stands at the entrance of the cabin and looks around, shocked at both the number of people who've shown up for her surprise baby shower and the stunning decorations that cover the inside of the small house. Evelyn smiles and runs up to Gianna, giving her a big hug. It's hard for the two of them to wrap their arms around each other and they laugh as Gianna's stomach gets in the way.

"As if *I* wasn't going to make a big deal over *your* pregnancy!" Evelyn says, clicking her tongue against the back of her teeth in disapproval. "I make a big deal about *everything*!"

The two women laugh and make their way further into the cabin as family, friends, and close colleagues welcome and congratulate Gianna with each step. She smiles and laughs, grateful to be surrounded by so many loved ones, and turns to say something to Wyatt only to discover he's not with her. She scans the room for him and spots him by the front door, his arms crossed over his chest and a frown on his face. After greeting everyone hello, Gianna and Evelyn make their way back to Wyatt.

"Sweetie, come say hi to everyone!"

"You said it was going to be a quiet weekend," he hisses to Evelyn, ignoring his wife's request.

"No, *you* said you wanted a quiet weekend. *I* said we needed to throw a party."

"It's fine," Gianna says, trying to cheer her partner up. "It's going to be fun getting to see everyone and getting to—"

"That's because I didn't want *this*," he gestures to Gianna's stomach and the decorations around the room, "shoved down my throat all fucking weekend. I just wanted to get away and have two days—*two fucking days*—where I could pretend things were normal and fine and the way they're supposed to be."

The tips of Gianna's ears are suddenly hot, and she's sure her face is red with embarrassment. Although Wyatt was keeping his voice low, she knows that people nearby can hear him complaining about both the shower and her pregnancy. She rests a hand on her stomach, as if trying to keep the baby from hearing anything else, and she fights to keep a smile on her face.

"Wow, way to be a complete piece of sh—" Evelyn starts.

"Not here," Gianna interrupts, voice shaking. "*Please*, not right now."

Wyatt's head snaps in her direction, like he's only just noticing his wife is there, and plasters a fake grin on his face. "Of course. Sorry, I was just... surprised by the unexpected attention."

"Yeah, and we all know how you are with *surprises*," Evelyn says through her teeth, her words dripping with sarcasm and disdain. She turns to her best friend and wraps an arm around her shoulder, leading her towards the kitchen and away from Wyatt.

"So, where's the hot doctor you're dating?" Gianna asks, trying to change the conversation and feeling ashamed of Wyatt's behaviour.

"He got called into work, but he should be coming up tomorrow," she says. "But enough about disappointing men. Come check out the cake I made you."

GIANNA BLINKS HER EYES open slowly, trying to make sense of the world around her as she comes to. The trees look like they've been bathed in orange light, the golden leaves glowing softly on their dark branches. She turns her head and squints, trying to understand why she feels like she can see the air—thick and grey—swirling around her. She coughs, wincing in pain. Her chest is sore and bruised, her ribs feeling too tight around her lungs, her shoulder hurting from where the seatbelt bit into it.

The windshield ahead of her is smashed to pieces and the metal of the hood is wrapped around the thick trunk of a maple tree. Her face feels bruised and sore, and she realizes it's from where she was hit by the airbag during the accident.

Beside her, Evelyn moans in pain and mutters to herself in confusion, trying to undo her seatbelt. Her eyes are wide and glassy, and she coughs from the heavy smoke that grows heavier by the second.

"What the fuck happened?" Evelyn asks. "Did a deer jump out or...?"

"I think someone hit us."

"Fuck!"

"Are you hurt?"

"Fuck fuck fuck!" she shouts again, voice thick with pain and panic.

"Evelyn, focus. Are you hurt?"

"No, I don't think so. You?"

"Just sore, thank God."

Gianna unbuckles her seatbelt and grabs the door handle, trying to push it open. The panel is warped and wedged in the frame. She grunts loudly as she pushes against the passenger side window with her sore shoulder.

Eventually it gives way, metal scraping loudly on metal as she frees herself from the car.

She falls onto the ground, choking on the air, and looks around for the other car. Although she can't make out the shape of the vehicle or any signs that the driver's alive, she spots a set of flickering headlights not far from them in the trees.

"Hey," Gianna calls to the other car. "Are you okay?"

She starts making her way towards the vehicle but stops when she hears Evelyn struggling behind her.

"I'm stuck."

Gianna turns back and heads over to the open passenger side door. "What?"

"I'm stuck," she says again, desperately pulling at her seatbelt. "I can't get out."

Gianna peers into the backseat to see if there's anything she can use to help her friend, but it's hard for her to see in the darkness. She yanks the door open, glad this one hasn't been crushed shut, and feels around the backseat for something useful.

"Can you open the trunk?" Evelyn asks, taking the keys out of the ignition and holding them behind her seat for Gianna to take, jingling them so her friend can find them easily. "All the cake stuff is in there, including the knife and server set that I brought from the bakery."

Gianna wiggles herself out of the backseat, annoyed at how long it takes her to do anything thanks to the size of her belly. She grabs onto the doorframe and pulls herself out of the car, her back screaming in protest as she stands up. She makes her way to the back and feels along it for the keyhole, frowning as she discovers that the trunk is too warped and dented to open.

She waddles back around and crawls inside, her fingers searching for the middle seat. Once she finds the leather tab she's looking for, she pulls the seat down to reveal a small opening to the trunk.

"What should I be looking for?"

"Everything should be in a small Tupperware."

Gianna presses herself against the small gap in the bench and reaches a hand through, feeling around for the plastic container. She winces, the skin across her chest tight and painful. She finds the lid with her fingers and pulls it towards her excitedly, before realizing that it popped off of the bin during the crash.

"Fuck," she mutters to herself, feeling around blindly.

"What?"

"The container spilled open," she says, her fingers grazing against smooth metal. She grabs at the utensil and pulls it out of the trunk, disappointed when it turns out to be the cake server and not the knife. She pushes herself hard against the seat, jamming her arm in as far as it will go. She feels around faster, trying not to notice how the soft orange glow around them is getting brighter by the second. Eventually, her hands find the hilt of the knife and she pulls it out of the trunk.

"Got it!"

"Fuck yes! Pass it!"

Gianna takes hold of the blade and is trying to shove the handle into Evelyn's palm when someone grabs her by the legs. She's dragged roughly out of the car, the knife spilling out from between her fingers and onto the floor before she can process what's happening to her. Her stomach hits the hard lip of the rocker panel on the way out and she gasps in pain, covering her face just in time to prevent the same panel from smashing into her mouth and nose. She kicks her legs behind her wildly, trying to dislodge whoever's taken hold of her, and they let go of her as she kicks them.

"Gianna!" Evelyn shouts, desperately trying to reach the knife on the floor behind her from her spot in the driver's seat. "What's going on?"

Gianna rolls onto her side and uses her upper body strength to push herself up, knowing that the size of her stomach and the extra weight of the baby will make sitting up from a supine position practically impossible. As she's sitting up onto her knees, something collides with her back, and she falls forward onto her stomach. The wind knocked out of her. Another blow connects hard with her body, this time the kick lands against her ribs, and she gasps from the pain as she gets into the fetal position.

"Gianna!" her friend shouts again, unable to see what's happening to her.

Her attacker swings his leg to kick her again, but this time she grabs onto him when he swings it. It collides painfully hard with her face—she tries not to think about the wet crunch her bottom lip makes as her teeth are forced through it by the heavy blow, or how the taste of old pennies fills her mouth—as she clutches his leg, holding on for dear life. While he's caught off guard by Gianna and struggles to keep his footing, she jerks sharply to the right and forces him off balance. He falls to the ground, and she uses the opportunity to try getting to her feet once more.

She pushes herself onto her knees and is in the process of standing up when he throws himself back onto his feet and charges at her. She wraps her arms protectively around her stomach as her attacker grabs a fistful of her hair and rips her head violently back, trying to force her onto the ground. She catches a glimpse of his face in the light of the fire.

Wyatt.

Instinctively, she grabs onto his hand and tries to pry it loose from her long caramel locks. She grabs at him, scratching and pinching his skin, desperately trying to bend his fingers backwards so he'll be forced to let go.

"Wyatt, please," she starts, desperate to get through to him, "I know you don't—"

Before she can finish her sentence, he lets go of her hair and kicks her hard in the stomach.

"OH, NO, WE *REALLY* don't have to do this," Gianna laughs, pulling the sparkler away from Evelyn. "We won't know our kid's gender until later, so—"

"So then it's a good thing this is a time-honoured tradition meant to placate your boomer parents by announcing whether your kid is going to be born with a peen or not," Evelyn jokes, keeping her voice low enough so that only Gianna can hear her.

"I just find gender reveal parties so fucking stupid."

"Because they are, but your mom was insistent and bought the sparklers, so—"

"You *can* just tell her no."

Evelyn looks at her, aghast. "I've known your mother since you and I were in kindergarten together, and never once in my life have I told her no. I'm not about to start now. Besides, she terrifies me, so you're doing this."

Evelyn motions for Wyatt to join her and Gianna at the front of the crowd outside the cabin. He subtly shakes his head, but with all eyes on him, he's forced to relent and join the women. Evelyn stuffs a sparkler in his hand and then motions for him to touch the tip of his to the tip of Gianna's. Once they're in position, Evelyn lights the sparklers at the same time with the end of her lighter.

For a moment, nothing happens. Then, both sparklers erupt into bright white light that slowly changes to dark pink.

"It's a girl!" Gianna's mom screams.

The crowd erupts into cheers and excited shouts, the women of Gianna's family gathering around her to tell her how much of a blessing it is to have a baby girl. She smiles and looks over at Wyatt, eager to see his reaction to the news, but his face is hidden from view as her male relatives surround him and wish him 'better luck next time.'

"I can't *wait*," her mom says excitedly. "I'm going to spoil this kid rotten."

"I know you will, Mom," she laughs.

Gianna opens her mouth to say something, but a loud voice in the distance interrupts her.

"What the hell are you thinking?"

"I didn't mean to!"

The group around her gets quiet as the voices near Wyatt get louder.

"Does someone have any sand?"

"Does anyone know where the extinguisher is?"

Before she can ask what's wrong, people start shouting.

"Someone call 9-1-1! There's a fire!"

GIANNA THROWS UP FROM the force of the kick, her stomach hurting in ways she didn't think it could. She screams in panic at the thought of him hurting her child again and she wraps her arms around herself once more.

"Wyatt!" she screams, trying to crawl out of his range. "Wyatt, stop!"

As she drags herself away through the underbrush, clawing at the ground, she finds a large rock. Seeing her husband get closer, she picks up and whips it at Wyatt. It hits him hard in the face and there's a loud snap of bone breaking and cartilage bending as the stone violently forces his nose to the left. He shouts, cupping his hands to his face from the pain.

"You bitch!" he shrieks, charging towards her.

Gianna kicks at him, putting as much force as she can behind it from her spot on the ground. He's not paying attention to what she's doing as he gets closer—he's too distracted by the pain—and her foot connects with his ankle. He shouts as he falls forward on top of her, his face streaked with blood and soot, his breath hot on her skin as he looms over her. He tries to get his hands around her throat, but Gianna grabs at another rock and hits him with it, this time striking him hard on the side of the head. He blinks at her, as if suddenly confused, and she hits him again, cutting through skin and exposing part of his skull. This time, his eyes roll back in his head, and he slumps down on top of her, unconscious.

Wyatt is heavy, and she struggles to move his limp body off of hers, the pressure on her chest unbearable. She eventually gets him off of her and onto the ground, before lying back and trying to catch her breath. Her stomach is on fire, the muscle cramping and contracting, and even before she finds her thighs slick with blood, she knows something is wrong.

Gianna tries to push herself up, hoping to get a view of the damage Wyatt's caused, when a tremor of agony passes through her. She screams, nails digging into the ground, as she forces herself to breathe through the contraction.

"Gianna?" Evelyn shouts again. "I'm coming! I'm almost through the seatbelt!"

She wants to answer her friend but can't as her body seizes up. She tries not to think about how much heavier the smoke is getting, how hot the air is on her back, and how bright the forest is as the wave of pain ends and a new one begins.

GIANNA TRIES NOT TO panic as the people around her begin running to their cars, the air hot and clouded with smoke as the fire spreads. As Evelyn leads her away from the cabin, she can't help but look back at it over her shoulder. The building crackles and burns, black smoke billowing up into the sky as the log building and the surrounding trees burn to ash. Gianna stumbles over the gravel, her high heels getting caught as she walks, and she's grateful to have her friend by her side.

Evelyn leads Gianna to her car and is opening the passenger side door for her when Wyatt shoves it closed.

"What the fuck? We need to go!" Evelyn shouts at him. "Get in!"

"My wife is coming with *me*," he says, eyes wide and his nostrils flaring. "You worry about yourself."

Evelyn shoots Gianna a look and opens her mouth to argue with Wyatt when her friend cuts her off.

"It's fine. Go, we'll meet up with you in town," Gianna tells her as Wyatt grabs her hard by the arm and pulls her away.

Evelyn gives her friend a worried look before getting in her car, starting the engine, and beginning her descent down the mountain as the trees continue to catch fire around her.

Gianna stumbles as Wyatt drags her over the gravel.

"Careful, I'm going to fall," she says, worried about twisting an ankle or hurting the baby. "I can't walk fast in these shoes."

"So why are you even wearing them?" he snaps, letting go of her as she approaches the passenger's side of their car. "You knew we were coming out here!"

"What the fuck does it matter? We need to go! Did you see what started it?" she asks, grabbing the car handle.

"The sparkler. It was still hot when I dropped it on the ground. I didn't think it would—"

She tries to open the door, but it's locked.

"Babe, open the door, we need to go!" she says, the air around her dangerously hot.

"It wasn't supposed to happen like this," he says from behind her.

"It was an accident. We'll figure it out. But we need to go!" she says, pulling at the handle desperately.

"I just... I told you I wasn't ready to be a dad."

"Wyatt, we'll figure it out, but we *need to go*," she says, the air thick with smoke. She coughs and pulls the collar of her dress up over her nose and mouth. She knows it won't do much, but she tells herself that it has to be better than breathing in ash.

"I wanted this weekend to be special. I wanted you to feel good, to enjoy yourself, to enjoy nature one more time. And then..." he looks at her with a frown, "you'd slip."

"What?"

"You'd slip. It would be quick and painless and over in an instant. And I'd be free from this fucking nightmare," he says, eyes widening in anger as he points to her. "I told you I wasn't ready. I told you I didn't want this. Fuck, I didn't even want to get *married* and now you're having *my* baby? I just... I can't. It's too much."

Wyatt approaches Gianna and grabs her by the shoulders. He looks down at her for what feels like a long time before pulling her close to his chest, hugging her tight.

"Wyatt, let go of me," she says, suddenly afraid of him.

"It's okay. I can still make this work. It's going to be okay."

Before Gianna can understand what he means, Wyatt begins pulling her towards the burning cabin. The air around her is getting hotter, and she feels like she's going to suffocate against his chest in the thick air. She struggles, beating her hands against his back and kicking his shins, her high heels flying off as he drags her over the gravel.

"It's okay. It's okay," he says.

Gianna isn't sure if he's talking to her or himself.

The flames are too hot and too close, and Gianna can't help the scream that escapes her mouth as he lets go of her and shoves her hard towards the fire. She trips over herself and falls to the side. She braces herself with her left hand as she crashes to the ground, screaming as the fire burns her arm and begins spreading across her cardigan. She pushes herself away from the flames, panicking as the front of her sweater is still ablaze. She pulls the cardigan off and throws it to the ground, brushing and beating her hands against her skin and dress as she makes sure the rest of her clothing isn't aflame.

It's not.

Wyatt grabs her and begins pushing her back towards the fire.

"It's fine!" he yells. "It's going to be fine! Just get the fuck—"

Gianna claws at him, her fingers finding the cold metal of the car keys in his jacket pocket as she fights back. She stabs him through the back of his hand with the key and he screams in surprise, letting go of her. She pulls the car key out of his skin before throwing it towards the cabin.

"Those are mine!" he shouts.

As Wyatt chases after his keys in the smoke, Gianna heads to woods, running for her life.

GIANNA SCREAMS AGAIN, EVERYTHING she learnt from her doula already forgotten, as pain rakes her body. Once the contraction passes, she looks at Evelyn.

"We need to get it out."

"What? What are you—"

"I'm not dilated," Gianna says, "but the baby's coming, anyway."

"You're hardly in your third trimester. It's too early for her to—"

"Evelyn, *listen*. Something is *wrong*. Wyatt, he..." she shakes her head, trying not to panic as she feels a fresh wave coming, her muscles beginning to contract. "We need to get the baby out *now*."

Evelyn stares at her, confused, the roar of the fire thunderous and getting louder. "How? You said it yourself, you're not—"

Gianna screams and gasps for air as the contraction crests and slowly ebbs.

"Get the knife."

"You can't be fucking serious. I'm not—"

"Get it!" she screams.

Evelyn hesitates, but the encroaching fire must be close enough that the fear of the blaze outweighs Gianna's insane demand, and so she runs to the car and gets the cake knife. She holds it out for her friend to take, but Gianna shakes her head.

"I need you to do it."

"Are you out of your fucking mind?" she shouts. "I'm not cutting you open. There's no way!"

On the ground next to her, Wyatt groans and grumbles. Although he's unconscious, Gianna knows it won't be long until he's awake again. She may have hit him hard with the rock, but she doubts it was hard enough to keep him down.

"Evelyn, we're running out of time."

Gianna looks over her shoulder, already knowing what she'll see.

The fire is growing fast and spreading, engulfing everything she sees in flames. The air is sweltering and burns the back of her throat and deep inside her lungs with each breath she takes. Her skin is hot and blistering and she knows that it won't be long until the very clothing on her back bursts into flame from the heat that's engulfing them.

She looks back at her friend, sweat rolling down the side of her face and cutting trails through the ash that sticks to her skin, and smiles.

"Just pretend like you're cutting through one of those weird hyper-realistic cakes."

The two of them laugh at the joke, but the moment is cut short as Wyatt moves and mumbles under his breath as Gianna chokes back a scream as another contraction hits. Evelyn holds the knife, her hands shaking, and helps Gianna pull her dress up to expose her stomach. Both women are pale and breathing hard.

"Ready?"

Evelyn smiles at her friend and lines the tip of the knife with the top of Gianna's stomach. "Shouldn't I be the one asking you that?"

Before Gianna can answer, Evelyn pushes the blade through her friend's skin. The woman gasps at the pain and tries not to faint as Evelyn drags it down her chest, trying to be careful without being too slow. She screams as she looks down, a trail of crimson staining her skin as the knife cuts through it. Once Evelyn gets to her pelvis, she puts the knife on the ground and tries parting Gianna's flesh. Although the woman bleeds, her skin doesn't open, and she realizes that she didn't go deep enough.

Another contraction rips through Gianna, and Evelyn picks the knife back up, finding the hilt in the dirt. As her friend shrieks, she pushes the knife in even deeper and drags the blade back through the wound. This time, Gianna's skin splits, her blood oozing out in thick streams. Once her torso is open, Evelyn reaches inside, moving her bladder and intestines out of the way as she searches for the baby. She eventually finds Gianna's uterus, the wall still intact, and Evelyn pierces it open with the knife, careful not to stab the baby.

Gianna gasps as Evelyn pulls the child out from inside of her, making sure to wipe as much fluid and viscera away from its small face as possible. The baby is still and for a moment, both women worry that it's dead. But soon, the infant is wailing and pounding its tiny fists in the air, and Gianna begins sobbing with relief as Evelyn hands her child over to her.

"You—you need to get her out of here," Gianna says, her lips cracking and bleeding from the heat.

Evelyn stares at her wide-eyed.

"I need to close you up first," she says, pointing to the car. "We can use clothes as a compress and then maybe if I tie the seatbelt around you, we can secure—"

On the ground next to Gianna, Wyatt begins to wake up. He feels his head, moaning to himself as his fingers find torn skin and exposed bone.

"You fucking bitch," he mutters, voice weak.

"Go," Gianna whispers, kissing the top of her baby's head. She looks at her friend and smiles, the ground underneath her slick with her blood.

Evelyn wants to argue but knows there's no point. The fire is only a few meters away and quickly burning a path towards them. The air is impossibly hot, and she knows the baby—born almost a half a trimester early—won't survive these conditions if she sticks around much longer. Gianna passes her the baby, the flames roaring behind her, and smiles.

"Make sure they give her my last name," she says, voice hoarse.

Evelyn nods, holding the infant close to her chest. She says something, but Gianna doesn't hear it; she's too distracted by Wyatt trying to sit up next to her.

"Go!" she screams.

Evelyn doesn't argue as she runs towards safety for all she's worth.

"It wasn't supposed to happen this way," Wyatt says to himself, watching as the fire gets closer. He sits up and tries to stand, falling forward onto all fours as he sways. He looks at Gianna and frowns. "It's your fault! This is all your fucking fault! You b—"

Gianna grabs the knife. She's worried that the handle is going to slip out from between her fingers, but she manages to keep a hold on it as she swings it down into Wyatt's back.

"Bitch," she finishes for him. "I know."

He screams in pain, and she musters the strength to pull the knife out and bring it back down on him a second time, this time at the base of his neck. She lifts the blade up a third time, but she's losing strength fast and it falls from her fingers, bouncing off the back of Wyatt's head and onto the ground.

Gianna watches as Wyatt twitches in the dirt, choking on his blood as the fire gets closer. Her skin begins to redden and blister, the flames close enough that she should be in agony, but she's not. As she watches her husband writhe and scream as he begins to burn, she wonders if it's the shock or the blood loss that keeps her from feeling any pain.

She shrugs to herself and laughs, her eyes getting heavy as her dress begins to smoke.

"I told you," she says, knowing Evelyn can't hear her but pretending she can, "gender reveal parties are fucking stupid."

MECHANICAL ANIMALS

TIM MEYER

6

MECHANICAL ANIMALS

By Tim Meyer

We were two hours into our son's eighth birthday party when the Nor'easter unexpectedly started dumping inches and inches of snow around town. Things quickly went from, *Oh hey, it's snowing* to, *Oh hey, maybe we should consider wrapping things up and heading home before the roads get too bad.* We never accomplished the latter. Mostly because when things got bad, we couldn't see five inches in front of us. A complete whiteout.

But that wasn't the only thing wrong with the outside world.

That shape in the parking lot...whatever it was...

It wouldn't let us leave.

In 1995, if your kid was having a birthday bash with their friends, it was happening at Porky Penguin's Pizza Palace. Leo's party was already my second trip there that year, and it was only March. Once Cody (Leo's best friend) had his party there back in January, there was no convincing Leo to have it anywhere else. And I *tried.* The kid wouldn't budge, just *had* to have his party there or he would "die." Karina and I gave in, and it wasn't long before Leo was calling us "cool" parents once again.

Everything was going great that afternoon—honestly the place wasn't too bad once you settled in and got past the bright flashing lights, the goofiness of it all. They had a beer bar for adults. The pizza was decent as far as chain restaurants go (if not too doughy) and they had a great selection of arcade games that catered to the thirty-five-year-old me. Totally brought me back to more than a decade earlier (the best part of having kids, really, getting to be a kid all over again, sort of). I got to play *Asteroids* and air hockey with the other dads while Karina chatted and gossiped with the attending mothers. Aside from the incessant screaming and occasional infant crying, the only annoying aspect was the animatronic characters that occupied the concert stage, their intermittent conversations and sing-a-longs in the most nasally, cartoonish voices imaginable. I tried to keep away from them—animatronics freak me out on the premise alone—but every time their performances were initiated, their amplified voices boomed through the loudspeakers, so the only way to avoid them was by hiding in the bathroom or going outside. There were only so many times a guy could pee or get some fresh air, and those songs came on every twenty minutes or so.

The titular penguin was by far the most annoying—but the red-lipsticked alligator, the fedora-wearing polar bear, the blue scarfed and eye-glass-sporting turtle, and the mohawked wooly mammoth in a trench coat all vied for that crown with each dumb song lyric, dad joke (before that was a thing), and dialogue that had to have been written by preschoolers.

This was some kind of hell for the right person, I suppose.

I was kicking Earl Chestin's (Cody's father) ass in air hockey when people started to migrate toward the glass windows that fronted the place. Porkys was in a strip mall sandwiched between a homemade soap boutique and a sports card and collectibles shop. The parking lot was kind of full, but I assumed most of the cars belonged to Porky's patrons.

"What's going on?" I asked Earl, whose attention was lost amongst the wandering crowd. Our game was stuck on 5-2, yours truly two quick scores away from victory.

"Dunno. Storming outside, it looks like."

I saw the white stuff falling. "Just snow," I said with a shrug.

People were acting like it never snowed in Bricktown.

Earl squinted at the window, seemingly concerned. A few seconds later, his attention turned back to the game, but his heart wasn't in it, and I scored the last two goals easily. He didn't even seem to care, which sucked a lot of fun out of the W. Earl was much bigger than me and played fullback in high school, whereas I was too skinny and scrawny to hold his jockstrap. I should have been relishing the victory—instead, I found myself migrating toward the windows like everyone else.

We watched the snow dump on us. The first flurries had stuck to the ground, and within a matter of five minutes, we couldn't see blacktop. A few patrons collected members of their families and went for the door, but by that time, the whiteout had already begun, and we couldn't even see the cars anymore—just a white haze that seemed to shroud the entire town.

Karina came up behind me, wrapped her arms around my waist. In my ear, she whispered, "101.5 says the storm is supposed to pass in a few hours—five to eight inches."

"Wow," I said. "How'd we not expect this kind of snow?"

"I checked the forecast in the paper—said flurries were possible, but not this."

I didn't think much of it—even if we got a quick eight inches, my '89 Blazer would get us home. Plus, the town had always been good about plowing.

I wasn't worried. But Karina looked nervous. She chewed her thumb like she had always done when the anxiety kicked in.

"Let's not worry about it," I suggested. "Look at the kids." I nod over to Leo and the other boys, the group taking turns on the basketball arcade game, each trying to beat the last person's high score, laughing as they shuffle in and out of line between rounds. "They're not worried."

"You're right," she said. "It's just a passing storm. No need to worry."

"Exactly."

Just a passing storm.

I wish that had been true.

FOUR HOURS INTO THE whiteout and the storm showed no signs of slowing down. The wind picked up, howling above us, rattling the windows, making every old bone inside the plaza crick and creak. At this point, most of the grown-ups had grown nervous enough to voice their concerns. The radio wasn't coming through anymore, so we had no updates on the storm. The televisions stationed around Porky's hadn't been set up for cable—the VCR just looped an hour-long featurette staring Porky and his animal pals.

We were at the mercy of the Nor'easter. Whenever it let up, we would leave.

But it was starting to feel like we might be stuck here—for a while, anyway. The snow had accumulated so much that people were beginning to whisper the word "blizzard." Each gust of wind threatened the power, causing the lights to blink. A few more families decided it was best to leave now before things got even worse—but it was already worse. Some of us tried to convince them to stay, but they bundled up and headed outside, the white glow outside swallowing them up as they disappeared into the parking lot. I will always wonder what happened to them or if they made it home alive.

I'm guessing not, considering what was out there, roaming the white haze that had taken over.

I was trying to keep my mind off things, lose myself in a game of *Pac-Man*, when Karina came over, rubbing her knuckles and biting her lower lip. Her thumbs were raw, nibbled bloody.

"What's up?" I asked, already knowing the answer—*um, perhaps you haven't noticed the goddamn Nor'easter?*

"Everyone's getting really nervous. Telephone lines are down. Last person to get an outside line said the governor declared a state of emergency."

"Okay?"

"Okay?" she said, pinching her brows together. "How come you're not freaking out about this?"

"Look, it's just snow. It has to stop sometime."

"And what if it doesn't? For a whole day? Or longer? We could be trapped here."

I glanced around, eyeing the walls filled with pictures of hot, steamy pizza, slices being lifted from the pan, taking stretchy strings of cheese along for the ride. "There are worse places to be trapped in."

She shoved me playfully. "Knock it off. I'm serious. What are we going to do?"

I studied the other folks—most of them were still watching the storm from the windows.

"Let's not panic," I told her. "The kids see us worry. They'll start getting scared. Let's just have fun until—"

Something crinkled overhead—like God was popping bubble wrap. It obviously wasn't fireworks, so my first thought was some crazy thunder. But it didn't let up, and when I heard more coming from the front of the building, I knew exactly what it was.

Hail. Huge, baseball-sized ice rocks from the sound of it. Pelting the roof of the strip mall, the overhang out front, the street, the parking lot—the goddamn cars. Through the gusts of hellacious winds we could hear our windshields cracking and breaking as fists of ice pummeled them. We gazed helplessly into that white abyss, listening to metal dinking and denting, glass splitting from the force of the falling glacial rocks. For a few minutes we stood there looking at each other like one of us had some clue as to when it would all end. But it was clear we knew nothing about this storm.

We were forced to listen to the destruction.

Karina moved from the window first. I followed her to the opposite side of the restaurant, back near the glass cabinets that showcased cheap plastic toys you could purchase with tickets won at the arcade. Karina had her hands over her face when I walked up behind her.

"Hey," I said, rubbing her shoulders, the way she liked.

She spun to me and buried her face in my shoulder. "This is awful."

I massaged her back while she cried into my shirt—the fabric got wet pretty quickly. "It's okay, we're fine."

"We're not fine," she said, pulling back. Some of her makeup was running. I pecked her forehead near the hairline, pulled her close again. "We're stuck here."

"We're not stuck here," I said, sounding confident—but then I corrected myself. "I mean, at the moment we are, but not, like, forever." I continued comforting her, hoping it was helping to calm her down. "All storms end eventually."

She let go of me, wiped her tears on her sleeve, then composed herself. You're right. I'm being silly."

"I shook my head. Nah. It sounds scary out there—and the Blazer...Trust me. I'm crying on the inside."

She smirked, and I felt better.

I nodded over at the kids, who were taking turns playing whack-a-skunk, bashing the black-and-white mechanical mammal back into one of its hidey holes. I didn't even notice Cody was missing from the pack until I turned back to Karina and saw him standing near the stage, looking up at Porky. I couldn't tell, but I think he was whispering something.

"We should check on the birthday boy," I said.

Karina nodded softly. "Yeah, good idea."

We strolled over to Leo, watched him take his turn on the game—he gave the skunk a pretty good whooping, earning himself about two dozen tickets when it was over. The other kids dispersed after the round ended, when they noticed us approaching, and moved over to the table hockey game.

While we had Leo alone, we explained to him the situation. Not that he wasn't already aware, but we were truthful about the predicament, told him we might not be going home right after the party, that we were kind of stuck at the moment.

"Cool!"

"Yeah, not cool, actually—it's actually hailing outside. It's causing a lot of damage to people's property. Not cool at all."

"Oh," he said, sounding disappointed.

"And I know being stuck inside an arcade sounds like fun, but your mom and I are pretty nervous."

"Why?"

"Well...because we don't know how long it's going to last, I guess. Plus, sounds like the hail has broken some car windows and one of them might be ours."

"That sucks."

"Hey," Karina said, flicking his shoulder lightly. "You know I hate that word."

"Sorry, Mom," he said, hanging his head.

I was about to bring up our next biggest threat, but right on cue the power flickered. It was like the universe could read my mind.

"And there's that," I said.

"What?" Leo asked.

"The power. Storms like this can bring down power lines. We hope it passes before it comes to that, but there's a possibility we lose power."

"Is that bad?"

"I mean—goodbye video games."

He glanced around the place, slumping his shoulders. "Bummer."

"Hopefully, it ends before that happens."

In that moment, something changed. It was the mood of the room. And though it was seconds before the shouting began, I felt it. Everything being altered. Like it was a real, material thing. Something to witness and behold.

Karina was the first to hear them arguing. Low voices, some of them whispering like they didn't want to be heard, another voice rising like it wanted the whole town to listen to every word.

"You're not listening, man!" said the shouter. It was Earl—Cody's dad—and he was wagging a finger in Chris Melbourne's face while simultaneously pointing at the animatronic penguin with his other hand. "It was talking!"

"Of course it was talking!" Chris said, trying to keep his voice low, careful not to escalate things. He was clearly frustrated though. "That's what they do—they *talk*."

Earl grabbed the sides of his silver Yankees cap, his cheeks swelling with shades of rose red. "You're. Not. LISTENING."

Karina glanced at me, and I shrugged. "Don't you think you should go over there? I mean...the kids." She nodded to the small line of children—some of them from our party, some of them random patrons—looking on at the arguing adults. A few other responsible grownups and one teenaged staff member wedged their way between the opposing parties.

Karina continued to stare, hard, at me. I threw my hands up in surrender, then moseyed over to the gathering. Earl was still gripping his ball cap, baring his teeth.

"What's going on, Earl?" I asked as the other adults continued to sort through the story, gathering the details from Chris.

"Oh, Ralph," he said, shaking his head as he separated himself from the group. Everyone was too busy chatting with Chris to see us stray from the pack. He nodded for me to follow, then led me around the other side of the stage, opposite from where the animatronics were facing the restaurant. "Something weird is going on."

"Weird? I mean, besides the Nor'easter that came out of nowhere? That kind of weird?"

He swallowed. Nodded. "Weirder than that." He glanced back over at the group. "None of them believe. But I caught Cody talking to them."

I squinted at Earl, trying to follow along. "Talking to who?"

His eyes slowly shifted to the stage, the mechanical animals. Porky the Penguin in particular. "He talked to *that*."

"The fuckin' penguin?"

Gravely, he nodded.

"So what? Kids talk—"

"No, no, no. He was talking to it. Having a conversation with it."

"Kids play make-believe sometimes, Earl. So what?"

"So, I heard it talk back."

I rolled my eyes. "Look, these things are programmed to—"

"Not like that, dammit!" He rubbed his forehead like I was giving him a headache. "It didn't talk like it normally does during the skits, with its cartoony actor voice or sing-alongs. It was different, okay? A *real* voice."

"Oh, okay," I said, not wanting to instigate him. He was really working himself up over this. I wasn't sure what changed since our game of *Asteroids* and air hockey, but something broke him. He wasn't acting like the Earl I knew.

Maybe it's the storm, I thought, but then knew how silly that was—sure, being trapped inside a place might have some psychological effect on the human brain, but not after a few hours. And we weren't trapped either. The Nor'easter would pass like they all do, and we would leave. This was a temporary inconvenience.

Nothing more.

But Earl was acting all stir-crazy from the get-go.

"Okay," I said again, humoring him. "What did he say? The penguin, that is."

Earl's eyes went all lost-like. Like his gaze just wandered from him, got tripped up in some vacuum inside his mind. I had to snap my fingers in front of his eyes and pose the question again.

This time he just said "um" a few times before giving an actual answer. "It said one of us has to die. Or we all will."

THINGS SETTLED DOWN AFTER that. Everyone went to their separate corners, sticking in groups with the people they came here with. The workers clustered together in employee-only zones. Earl stuck by himself, mostly slumped in a chair farthest from the stage. Farthest from the talking robots. His kids hung out near the stage, a little too much for my own liking. Every now and then they would glance up at Porky, like they were waiting for a response. It didn't sit right with me, but who was I to police other people's children? Soon after, more kids gathered near the stage, all of them collecting as if they were waiting for the next number to come on, to hear the animals play their instruments and sing their happy, uplifting songs.

Karina gave me that *you-need-to-talk-some-goddamn-sense-into-him* look again, nodding at Earl. But what was I going to do? Earl was clearly going through some stuff at the moment, and I doubted much of it had to do with the unexpected Nor'easter. But I was his friend—probably his best friend currently present—and I had to do something.

"Earl," I said, approaching him with my arms folded across my chest. "Listen, we need to talk. Whatever you're going through, buddy, I need you to put it off until we get out of here. People are starting to worry."

He didn't face me, but said, "You should be worried. We should all be worried."

"Damn it, Earl. Why are you doing this? Huh? People are scared, and the power could go out any minute. We have no idea how long we're stuck here, and you—"

"Ssh," he said, holding up his finger and tuning his ear to the stage. "You hear them?"

I wanted to punch him. Maybe that would have knocked some sense into him. Or the nonsense out of him.

"Do you hear what they're saying?" He looked like he wanted to cry, the dimmed lights in the auditorium casting a glassy reflection. "Do you hear what they want from us?"

I told him I didn't, asked him again to snap out of it for his children's sake.

"Don't you understand?" He faced me now, and there was a hideous laughter bubbling up from his throat. "This is the end, friend. This is the end, and they..." His eyes fixed on the stage. "They are angels. Come to save us."

"That's dumb and you know it."

"Look at them," he said, nodding at the mechanical animals. Porky the Penguin was facing us, his frozen grin sporting perfect white teeth. His sailor's cap was pushed back on his head, giving him a decent stretch of forehead between his buggy cartoon eyes and black plastic hairpiece. His Hawaiian shirt was unbuttoned, showing off his fuzzy white tummy. He reminded me of Kurt Russell in *Captain Ron*, only if Kurt Russell were a penguin instead.

"What about him?" I asked, tired of this game. Nothing was getting through to him and now he was talking about *the end* and fucking *angels*.

All because of a little winter weather.

"Listen," he said, cupping a hand around his ear.

I humored him and listened. There was nothing at first, just the background whispering from the groups of people trying to console each other and figure out the best next steps. I tuned them out, concentrated on Porky's bright orange beak, the eyebrows that would jump up and down when the intermittent performances would kick on. I listened and...

It was like the penguin staring at me.

Into me.

And it was like those eyes were real. Like they had a soul behind them—something human. Or maybe not human. But surely something alive and cognitively active, something that could process the information and...

Speak?

I listened like Earl told me, truly listened.

Then I heard it: *Choose one to die, and the rest will live.*

The voice was almost mechanical itself, like the way you might think a cognitive robot might speak just after learning a human language. Slow and practiced, wanting to get every word right. Rough, unrefined articulation.

My blood froze and invisible spiders shimmied down my spine. I wanted to believe I didn't hear that or Earl arranged for this to happen—maybe he was in cahoots with another adult (or kid), and someone was hiding under the stage, waiting to pop out and say, *Gotcha, loser!* But that didn't happen. And I knew. I knew the voice was coming from the penguin, inside of it.

I turned to Earl, feeling sick to my stomach.

His face lit up; eyes bugged. "You heard it..." It wasn't a question because he knew the truth; my face gave everything away. He stood up like he meant to shake my hand and congratulate me. "You fucking heard it. The angel."

"I...I..." I couldn't even fucking lie, pretend I didn't.

"We have to convince them, the others."

Just then, the stage lit up, and the speakers blared out the next number. I must have jumped five feet out of my skin. The cartoon characters came alive, strumming and beating on their musical instruments, the penguin singing lyrics about being your best friend no matter what—it had this funky hip-hop vibe that I normally would have found refreshing in less stressful environments.

The beat of the song pounded in my ears, but my heartbeat louder and ten times faster than the Turtle's kick drum.

Porky sung:

Gather 'round, my pizza friends
And listen to this funky beat
The music is loud and fresh
And the food here is all-you-can-eat!

The lyrics, however, we're laughably childish. I started to calm down from what I thought I heard earlier, the penguin talking to me, telling me we had to choose one to live or the rest will die, but then the second verse kicked in, and everything I thought I knew had strayed from the course.

Gather 'round, my favorite pals
And listen to your best friend Porky!
Look to the friend next to you
And remove his eye with that there forky!

The music continued to play as every adult in the room exchanged confused glances, most of them filled with concern, *did I just hear that?* eyes that swept the room. But we heard it—we all heard it, and there was no ignoring it this time.

Earl had been on to something.

Not thirty seconds later, someone let out a scream. We all whipped our heads toward the sound, saw a mom yanking some boy up from the ground. When I got closer, I saw the boy she was tearing away from the scene, holding a fork in his hand, some object skewered at the end of it. Glancing down at the floor, I saw another kid (not from our party) lying on the ground with a hand over his left eye. Blood was squirting through the cracks between his fingers. He screamed until his voice cracked and gave out.

The mom, with the help of three other parents, pried the fork from the boy's hand. She screeched in horror as her son's eyeball stared back at her, jellied, sinewy strands dangling down, touching her hand. A crowd surrounded the boy, flocked around the mother, who almost passed out and had to be helped to the ground.

It was madness.

But Porky and his friends kept playing their instruments, singing their songs. Laughing.

I stared at the penguin, and the penguin stared back, the intelligence behind its plastic gaze drilling tunnels of ice into the center of my chest.

Choose one to die, and the rest will live.

THE POWER WENT OUT about forty minutes after the eye forking. The kid who'd done the deed sat catatonically in the corner of the pizza parlor, planted on a stool in front of the old-timey soda counter. He hadn't answered a single question since the event. No reason given. But we all knew what happened, even though most of us did not want to believe it. Some of the adults flat-out refused.

The boy who was now missing an eye rested far away from his attacker, holding an icepack over the damage. They'd gotten the bleeding to stop, and the kid was told his eye was likely gone forever given the situation, but the boy didn't seem to care. None of the kids did. They were all different after the attack, somehow changed by the tune the cartoon band had played. If I didn't know any better, I'd say they were all under a spell.

Some of the other adults and I were discussing what to do next when Earl took the stage. I was so nervous about what he'd say that my stomach felt like a rattled cage of butterflies.

"Excuse me!" he said, holding up his hands. He started clapping when the conversations wouldn't die out. The louder he clapped, the more the talking began to taper off. When the whispers expired and silence fell over the room, Earl continued. "I don't like what I'm about to say, but we're all smart enough to know what really happened earlier. And some of you have heard them by now—what these things want from us. What the storm wants from us. What God wants from us." Groans made their rounds around the room. A few called for Earl to exit the stage and stop scaring the children, but the children didn't look scared. Even Leo looked like he was in a trance, and there was no snapping him out of it—Karina had tried. "I know, I know—I don't want to believe it either." He spun and faced the animatronics for just a second before spinning back and facing the crowd of eager listeners. "But there's something profound happening here. Something I believe to be...beautiful." With his eyes heavy with regret, he licked his lips. "The devil is out there, in the storm. And we have no choice but to give the angels what they want. They're giving us a chance to survive, and we must give them what they desire."

"What do they want exactly?" one of the adults spoke up.

Earl looked pained by the answer. "It wants one of us to die, so the rest can live. A...a child." Those who hadn't already heard the penguin's demands recoiled in shock, wrapping protective arms around their kids. "I know—it's crazy. But after hearing that song, the lyrics, and then witnessing what happened after...if we don't pick one of them to die...then we all die. In the most violent, brutalizing ways imaginable."

"Why a child?" someone asked; I could tell they had been crying from the sound of their voice.

"Because..." Earl closed his hands together as if reciting a prayer. "It's God's will—and the angels demand it. And we have witnessed what will happen if we do not comply. That boy's eye was only the beginning."

"Power's out," some genius spoke up. "How is that thing gonna talk without any juice?"

Earl bit his lip. "Something tells me the angels don't need electricity."

"Bullshit! This is all bullshit!" someone else shouted—but Earl's supporters (and he had many at this point) shut down the man's negativity in a few seconds, barking over him and threatening him with violence.

Once everyone was settled, Earl continued. "It sounds insane. I know—trust me. But people—this is our new reality, and we must face it. We must pick a child to die. So, the rest can live. So, *we* can live."

Everyone started talking at once, arguing, shouting over each other—I'm not sure how Earl expected this to go, but it played out much how I anticipated. Just...chaos.

"Why don't you choose your own child?" someone called toward the stage.

Earl only lowered his gaze. Then waved his hands in the air, asking everyone to hush. No one listened. They continued to speak over each other. Some of the parents almost came to blows, standing nose-to-nose with each other, arms cocked and fists ready to fly.

"SILENCE!" Earl shouted, and that quieted everyone. "If no one is willing to sacrifice their own kin—and God, who could blame them—then we must run a lottery."

The idea brought on more backlash, and the room devolved into an anarchist's wet dream once again.

But then the lights came back on, bringing every conversation to a halt. It wasn't the electricity coming back—the lights above us remained out—but the stage lights. They were bright. Too bright. Like someone cranked up the luminance beyond what the bulbs could handle. But the brightness held, and I had to shield my eyes from the burning brightness. The animatronics came to life. Porky the Penguin laughed, then counted down from three, leading the band into the next ditty. He sang an upbeat polka song, complete with an accordion solo after the second verse, and I think the lyrics had something to do with going on an adventure with your parents. But the last verse came, and we all listened intently, every face in the room looking like we were gazing upon the ghosts of our dead relatives.

So come on kids, let's go outside and get some sun!

I sure haven't seen a day that's nicer
Grab your mother by her hair
And scalp that bitch with this pizza slicer!

Right on cue, Chase Speedman, one of Leo's best school friends, snatched a pizza cutter off a nearby table, marched over to his mother, jumped up, grabbed her long curly hair, and began running the tool across her scalp, splitting open her flesh. Scarlet dribbled down her face in thick rivulets.

The nearby parents rushed toward Chase, tackling him to the ground, but not before the kid really opened his mother up, deepening and widening the gash. He began growling and foaming at the mouth, and after a few seconds of fighting and failing to break free, the kid went comatose in the other parents' arms.

Two hours later, a girl in pigtails stabbed her father in the crotch with a steak knife because the penguin *(angel)* sang about it.

Two hours after that, a boy in a Ninja Turtles shirt hacked off his mother's ear with a meat cleaver because the penguin *(angel)* demanded it.

After that, a whole group of kids tackled one of the adults to the ground and began chewing his face down to the bone like it was a fucking zombie movie—because the fucking penguin *(angel)* said the flesh and blood would taste like pizza (the too doughy kind).

We tried to kill the animatronics after the second incident. Some dad in a leather jacket, who reminded me of Rob Halford, stormed the stage and started punching the trademarked characters in their metal heads, but his fists of fury did absolutely nothing—about twelve haymakers later, the man's heart exploded—like, literally exploded, as if it was detonated by a pack of C4—through his chest, splattering the stage and characters with gore and meaty shrapnel. Someone else took a *break-in-case-of-fire* hatchet to the wooly mammoth-looking character, but the second the ax end connected with the metallic animal's shell, both of the man's arms broke off near the elbows, blood-soaked bones shooting through his skin and all. One mother, a smoker, got the genius idea to set the fuckers on fire (without giving it much thought), doused the penguin in cheap beer from the bar, struck a match and dropped it on the penguin's Hawaiian shirt. The flames didn't take to the material—instead, the mom herself went up in flames, and we weren't able to put her out until it was too late, until after she was barbequed, extra crispy.

Needless to say, we didn't try killing them after that.

Instead, we decided to make our choice.

Earl led the lottery—we took all of our kids' names, wrote them down on napkins, threw them into a plastic pitcher used to serve beer and soda, and handed them to Earl, who stood on stage, eagerly waiting to pull one name and end this.

That was when I saw *it.*

The thing outside.

It looked like a person but clearly wasn't. Taller than your tallest human. Maybe eight, nine feet tall. And thicker—wider. Thin extensions grew out of its back, like extra arms or legs, almost antennae-like, and they were blowing around in the storm, whipping wildly in the winds. The whiteout only revealed a dim silhouette, so I couldn't tell for sure. When I nudged Karina to look at the window, the whiteout only got worse, and the figure got lost in the big white blur of it all.

I couldn't prove it, but whatever that thing was, it had to be responsible for all of this. It had to be controlling the animatronics somehow.

And, in turn, controlling us.

It was then I also realized the Nor'easter wasn't just a Nor'easter. The snow wasn't just snow. And the hellacious winds and hail were not acts of a tumultuous environment. It was something else—*alien,* I guess—and whether it had come from above or between, I would never know.

Maybe it came from below. Earl's *devil.*

"Leo Briggs," Earl said, snapping me out of these dark thoughts. I turned my head to the stage.

There was a delay in processing what just happened. It took several seconds to adjust, to understand what had just transpired, to figure out why every head in the place was slowly rotating toward us—our close friends first, followed by strangers whose names we would never know.

"No," Karina said in a whisper. She was breathing fast, too fast, and it wasn't long before she started to hyperventilate. She wobbled, and I caught her before she fell back, helped her over to a nearby table. "NO!" she screamed out once she was sitting.

Someone brought her water, and she knocked the plastic cup with the cutesy penguin face right out of their hand. Karina screamed, sobbed, and thrashed around while I tried to corral her. After Earl jumped down from the stage and came ambling over, she told him to go fuck himself with the hatchet he was holding. He just gawked at her with tears in his eyes, struggling like everyone else to find the right words—but there were no *right* words for this. There were no words at all.

To me, he said, "Shit, I'm sorry, Ralph."

"You can't do this," I told him, shaking my head. No one would look me in the eyes—except for Earl. He at least could do that.

I fought the mob when they took Leo from us, ripped his lethargic body out of our hands. Punched, scratched, kicked—nothing worked. Even if I had five other adults on my side helping me, we could not stop the mob from doing what needed to be done.

I screamed when they brought him up on stage. Bent him down before Earl. When Earl raised the hatchet.

I couldn't watch what came next. I covered my ears and let out a long, continuous, siren-like squeal. Not a sound any human should make. My heart felt like someone had dropped it into a blender, cranked the fucking thing up to warp speed. Karina buried her head in my chest and screamed into me—*through* me.

When it was over, after they cleaned up the mess on stage so we wouldn't have to see his remains, the sun came out. The crowd migrated toward the window. Slowly, the whiteout faded, the sunshine exterminating every frosty, floating particle.

Earl clapped a hand on my back as he made his way to the door with his son and daughter. He didn't speak—didn't need to. His fingers were still sticky with Leo's blood.

Everyone left Porky's like nothing happened. There was no damage to our cars in the lot. The roads were clear. A few inches covered the grass but that was it. It wasn't even that cold for early March, in what was promised to be a long winter. Pants and t-shirt weather, no jacket necessary.

We drove home and didn't speak. The closer to home we got, the less of what we experienced inside the Pizza Palace could be remembered. When I pulled the Blazer into the driveway, it was like the whole day never happened. As if we went out for brunch at Mario's, not to Porky's for our only kid's birthday bash.

Kid?

We had one of those, didn't we?

We thought we did. But when we got inside the house, when I went to his room, I found an office. A desk. A chair. A computer. A mountain of paperwork I needed to tackle before Monday morning.

No posters of professional wrestlers or Power Rangers.

Just work stuff.

Karina went through our medical records—there was no birth certificate. Our family photos hanging on the den wall just depicted us.

We didn't talk about him after that. From that day forward, we pretended like Leo never existed—because technically...he never had.

Although, whenever it snows, however softly, I can still hear those mechanical animals humming their tunes.

PRIME

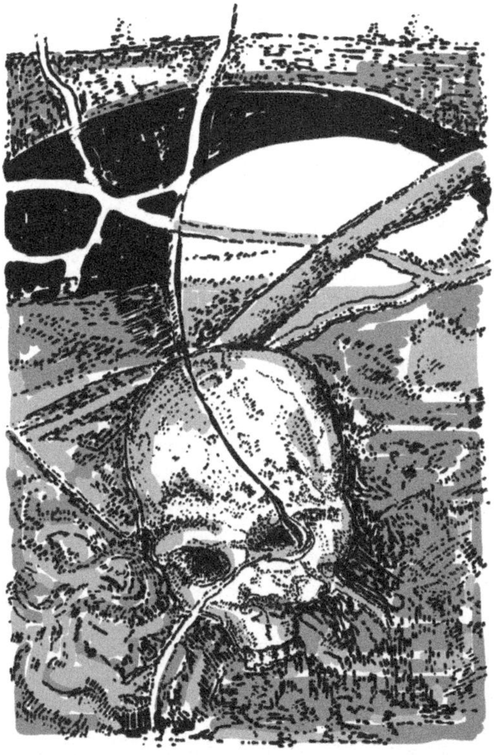

ANDRE DUZA

7

PRIME

By Andre Duza

You had to have been living on Mars to not have heard the warnings. An unprecedented global convergence of natural phenomenon was forecasted to unleash one big gang-bang of potentially extinction-level destruction on this planet of ours. The News media did their fear-mongering, and the public did their panic-dance. Terrified citizens crowded stores, stocking up on weapons, canned goods, and, of course, toilet paper. People fighting in the aisles. A few shootings. The contrarians balked and stood defiant. They were the first ones to go.

Hurricanes bum-rushed coastal regions and left entire cities flooded. New York City. New Orleans. Miami. Honolulu. London. Venice. Amsterdam. Tokyo. Bangkok. Mumbai. Floodwaters soaked through layers of sediment and rock, loosening fault lines under massive stress and instigating a chain-reaction of seismic activity across the globe. Multi-vortex tornados greeted folks escaping inland.

Millions dead. Millions.

Residual weather conditions played cleanup on the survivors of "Mother Nature's opening salvo of payback against humanity."

What was left of the News-media ran casualty reports, survivor stories, and shots of correspondents standing amidst ruins of popular landmarks, canoeing down small-town main streets with first responders, and in hip-deep water, fighting to keep from being blown around like rag dolls. Expert panels relayed grim statistics and survival advice. A colorful cadre of left-over pundits crawled out of the woodwork to point fingers at Republicans, at Democrats, at minorities, at the LGBTQ community, at big business, at humanity.

I only know all this because of Delilah (I call her Dee), who immediately took a shine to me when I was brought into the fold last month, a lost soul searching for purpose. Sometimes she lets me use her phone to listen to music or to watch old 80s films. Mostly, I read and watch the News apps on her home-screen. Aside from father and a select few elders, access to the outside world is restricted in our family. Cell phones, tablets, laptops, and other forms of communication/entertainment are prohibited.

By the time the mainstream news trickles down to the rest of the family, it has been filtered through father's very... shall-we-say... narrow viewpoint. It's even worse for us newbies. They keep us isolated as part of the initiation process. But Delilah is father's sister-in-law. Around here she's considered royalty. So, the rules are different for her. If you haven't guessed, our family is a bit... eccentric.

More on that later.

The media warnings shifted to a new threat, this time from the ensemble of long dormant volcanos that had been belching to life and portending to projectile-vomit hot magma, ash, and a tight-knit cluster of noxious gases that would block out the sun for months and render the air toxic. Could be any day now. Mauna Loa. Tamu Koba. Kilimanjaro. Sangay. Mount Etna. Mount Shasta. Mount St. Helens. Just to name a few.

Then it all went dark. Nationwide blackout. They're saying it might even be worldwide.

"Once you go black." Richter joked. He's one of the newbies, like me.

"Except for us, of course," I shot back. We were running on generators, so we still had power.

In our family, it was known as the Forever Night; a time when light was supposed to come from darkness. Blah. Blah. Blah. It was one of the main tenets of our family's religion. There's a special mass planned and everything.

IT HAD RAINED FOR three days straight before father decided it was time to leave Citadel Prime. Formerly the Douglass Cooper School for Boys, the place had been the family's home for thirty years. Supposedly, it was haunted by two students who had died at the former school. Or so I've heard.

Consisting of two main buildings that formerly housed the elementary/middle schools (Hub #1), and high school (Hub #2), surrounded by four, three-story dormitories that looked like your average apartment building, the Citadel, as we called it, had survived two tornados, a suspicious fire, and an FBI raid five years ago. Maybe you've heard about that one. The media loved to gloat about how the government busted Elias Prime, the patriarch of the Mid-West branch of the Family Prime.

Yep. *That* Family Prime. Or maybe you're more familiar with "the FPC" (Family Prime Cult), as the mainstream media has branded us. We're worldwide, ya know.

The Feds buried Elias so deep within the penal system that it made finding him next to impossible, and then came word that he had died in custody; killed during an incident with a fellow inmate. The details were vague, and the Feds refused to turn over his body; said it went missing. Imagine that.

With the O.G. out of the picture, his oldest son, Julian, took over. Father Julian was similarly charismatic, but a hothead, who was known to make rash decisions. Some people felt that that attitude was what the family needed. Others preferred Elias' more measured approach.

Julian made extensive fortifications to the compound after the raid. I was in Hub #2, with the other newbies. There were five of us, altogether, all in our early-to-mid-twenties, attractive, from similar backgrounds of dysfunction, equally lost, and looking for purpose. I'm closest to Richter, who's the most normal of the bunch. The rest are Ryder, aka stone-faced Ryder, Nora, and Marco. Together, we looked like the second-string talent of a modeling agency. Clearly, Family Prime had a type.

They kept us separate from the other family members in Hub #1. Full disclosure... Hub #2 had a few shortcomings. I guess they had run into trouble acquiring materials to complete the renovations once the government started pressuring vendors not to work with the FPC.

Those shortcomings allowed the relentless, Hokuto Shin Ken barrage of raindrops the size of small fists to punch its way through the shoddy roofing. One leak turned into several, and soon we were dodging minefields of buckets just to get from one room to the next. We scrambled to relocate the perishables from the flooded basement. We repeated the process when the flooding reached the first floor, and again, when it swelled to ankle deep.

The wind howled like some phantom hybrid of every scary thing you've ever imagined might lurk in the night and hurled large objects at the sides of the buildings. It sounded like those same phantom hybrids trying to breach our safe space. If you're wondering how we maintained our composure through all of this, let's just say... at the time, they were all drinking the Kool Aid. I say "they" because, by that point, I was only taking sips.

We were assured that the windows wouldn't give, and that the Forever Night Mass would go on as planned. Each window was protected by a cage of lattice and a pair of steel shutters that closed over them. So, you'll understand everyone's surprise when they suddenly decided that it was time to abandon Citadel Prime... in the middle of the night.

If you know anything about the Mid-West branch of the FPC, then you're aware that our numbers are in the hundreds. Three-hundred-twenty-five, to be exact. Yet only sixty-five of us made the trip to higher ground, stuffed into a fortified greyhound bus, driven by a low-key rage-aholic named Enrique Prime, whose idea of finding safe passage was to barrel through recently abandoned automobiles peppered along flooded I-80—some of them probably not so abandoned.

The interior of the bus was divided into two sections; the larger front, which contained traditional seating (where the elders and the rest of the family sat), and a small lounge-area, in the back, separated by a door that they kept locked from the outside. That's where the newbies sat.

An elder by the name of Daniel Prime used to run a company called Core Vigilance that constructed bunkers for doomsday preppers. In fact, it was Daniel's company that handled the fortifications for the Citadel, and who retrofitted the greyhound to look like a huge, black, phallic battering ram on wheels. Three years ago, Core Vigilance had been contracted to construct several bunkers for the residents of an upscale condo community in the Pocono Mountains.

The residents had failed to pay the final balance—some issue with in-fighting over politics—so the access codes were never handed over upon completion, and the place sat dormant. According to Daniel, the bunker was impenetrable without the codes, which he had saved in a folder in his phone. So, that's where we were headed.

The elders told us that the two hundred and sixty folks we left behind would be rewarded tenfold for their sacrifice. Any questions were deflected.

And when that didn't stop the questions from coming, they were met with a reprimand.

Father Julian or one of the elders would occasionally engage us over the intercom, to boost morale or to quell any assumed anxiety over the tumultuous ride with sing-a-longs; perennials like "You are my Sunshine," and deep cuts from Father Julian's own songwriting catalogue. He had a short-lived career as a commercial jingle writer/artist. But you probably already knew that.

We were so terrified by the wind shoulder-checking the bus to a near horizontal listing, the creaking hull as the vehicle's immense weight shifted and the wheels threatened to leave the ground on one side, then the other, the crash of the reinforced front bumper ramming its way through obstacles, the jarring thump/bounce as the wheels rolled over... whatever they rolled over, the click, clack, bang of foreign objects pelting the outer shell, and the rain punching down with impunity, that we sounded like a chorus of painfully shy zombies.

Fear and weakness are frowned upon in the Family Prime, so we put on brave faces and fake smiles whenever one of them came back to check on us.

When we ran out of songs, Father Julian placated us with the usual playlist of sermons. The one about the family being superior beings on earth—hence the surname Prime. The one about the persecution of our family members. The one about The Forever Night.

The night was pitch-black, and the view through the heavily tinted, reinforced glass was mostly obscured by endless sheets of water flowing downward. Every now-and-then, the wind and the lightning worked in concert to provide a peek-a-boo glimpse of the wholesale destruction, and the bodies that floated by all mangled and bloated. Sometimes the lightning-flashes were numerous and exploding in rapid-fire succession, giving the continuous loop of devastation a strobe-light effect that might have looked cool in a movie.

Eventually, the gridlock of vacated vehicles, miscellaneous large objects, and bodies floating in the road became unpassable. We ventured off-road, through partially submerged neighborhoods, punching down walls of lesser structures on our improvised reroute. In the back, we bounced around like popcorn kernels under high heat.

We found ourselves stuck in a ditch about a mile outside a shitty little turnpike-town called Harmarville, PA. After several unsuccessful attempts to dislodge the stuck front end, the decision was made to take temporary shelter in the Best Western motel just over the blackened horizon.

We made the trip on foot. The rain was unrelenting, making quick work of our umbrellas (and we had the expensive kind) as we waded precariously through water that was chest deep at times, weighted down and chilled to the bone by soaking wet clothing that clung like a soggy, second skin. The elders fashioned floatation devices out a pair of wooden picnic tables to transport the waterproof trunk-boxes full of supplies, weapons, and food that we brought with us.

We had the entire Best Western, Harmarville, to ourselves. The first floor was flooded, hip-deep. We were spread throughout the second. They put the newbies in Room 205. We used collapsible solar lamps, meant for camping, to light the rooms. Those things are pretty-darn-bright. You could see where the previous occupants of Room 205 had obviously left in a hurry. I heard them say that the other rooms were the same.

The main elders were in Room 206. That would be Father Julian, Mother Saphron (Father Julian's wife), Uncles Daniel, and Enrique, Delilah, and a rotating crew of family security, each of whom were elders themselves. The room was connected by a thin wooden door that stayed locked from their side.

They were discussing something heavy in there. Every once-in-a-while, I could hear their raised voices over the rain, the wind that occasionally caused the large window at the front of the room to rattle, and the random thunderclaps.

Marco and Ryder dealt with their anxiety by burying their faces in the family's scriptures. We were each given a pocket-sized pamphlet that we were to keep on us "AT ALL TIMES!!!"

Part of the initiation process.

Richter and Nora sat Indian style on the bed, quietly blowing smoke up each other's asses about how great the Forever Night will be. They used words like "glorious," and "magnificent," that you generally don't find in the vocabulary of your average twenty-something.

I'm not saying I don't believe, but I'm a curious son-of-a-gun. I need answers.

I sat near the window, feigning interest in my scripture book so as not to attract the attention of Jack Six Prime, sitting in the corner concealed by shadows, from the chest up, repeatedly shuffling a deck of cards in his lap. That was his thing. Jack Six is one of the elders, and part of the family's security detail. He was put in here to watch over us.

Jack dressed like a cowboy biker, and he had a face that you could never quite put a finger on, as it was usually concealed in the shadow of the brim of a cowboy hat. He had an almost supernatural knack for finding shadows and living in them, no matter where he might be, and doing so in a way that seemed organic and not forced. It was the strangest thing.

I could vaguely hear voices coming from outside the window. Family security, standing on the balcony that wraps around the entire second floor of the motel, making small-talk and calling out time checks.

"1:32 am!"

"2:20 am!"

"3:15 am!"

I was curious as to why they were so concerned with the time. And then, sometime after 3:15 am, I heard one of them say that it was raining people.

You heard me right. People!

They fell from the sky as if poured from a giant bucket. I didn't see it, as we were instructed to stay away from the windows (for safety reasons, of course), but we could hear the perplexed play-by-play from the security officers on the balcony, the hurried feet, and the vocalizations of surprise, confusion, and dismay as family members scrambled out of their rooms to have a look-see.

And then, about thirty seconds later... the bodies started hitting the ground. It sounded like giant, cupped hands slapping shallow water, followed instantaneously by a damp thud that you could feel in your bones. One after the other. For minutes, it seemed. It had the same effect as explosions or gunfire in that it made you shrink from it and cover your ears. When it was over, the wind, the rain, and the random thunder were like a welcome reprieve.

Afterward, more family members came out onto the balcony discuss what had happened. I was close enough to the window that I could hear them talking. Some of them were claiming to have seen... something moving through the dark clouds above the raining bodies; giant, winged silhouettes exposed by aggressive lightning flashes. To some, they were angels. To others, military aircraft.

Then it got quiet.

AFTER A WHILE, JACK Six got up and walked over to the window. Somehow, the shadows followed.

Don't ask.

He fingered the ugly window-dressing aside and looked out. I was sitting close enough that I could lean forward and steal a glance or two. So, I did.

The lightning revealed the aftermath of the sky-fall floating in the waist-deep water that flooded the three connecting parking lots between The Best Western, The Marijuana dispensary next door, and the Sheetz convenience store about two hundred feet away; bodies broken and twisted into impossible poses like crushed insects on a windshield. More bodies floated prone and supine... and somewhere in-between. A few of them were in pieces. An arm here. A leg there. A torso. Blood. Lots of blood, even as the rain actively washed it away.

Delilah came in through the connecting door and startled the shit outta me. It was nice to see that she startled Jack Six, too. She flashed that warm smile of hers and gave us all a helping of "All is well," while side-eying me that it really wasn't. At least, that's how I interpreted the look.

Afterward, she had a brief, whisper-chat with Jack Six, and then left the room. I was hoping for another side-eyed dialogue, or maybe even a few words from her, but she seemed to be in a hurry.

After almost twenty minutes of eerie silence (save for the rain, the wind, the random thunderclaps), a muffled voice from outside the window goes, "What are they doing now?"

Jack Six got up again, went over to the window, and fingered aside the ugly window-dressing. The shadows followed. I leaned forward and stole a few more glances.

This time, there were two men in hoodies standing on the wraparound balcony. An equidistant awning mostly protected them from the rain. Machine guns strapped to their backs. Hoods up. The one on the left held a pair of military-grade binoculars to his eyes as he looked out into the layered curtains of rain. That was Dax. The other one looked like Freeman. They're two of the family's security detail and the owners of the voices we'd been hearing outside the window.

I saw a woman's head and shoulders leaning out of the doorway of 206. That would be Mother Saphron. It was her voice I heard just now.

"Still lying there," Dax replied while looking through the binoculars.

He's talking about the bodies. When the lightning flashed, I could see them floating in the parking lot in front of the motel.

"They appear to be wearing some kind of tactical gear," Dax said. "Like a black-and-grey wetsuit with protective padding on the chest and back."

Mother Saphron nodded and started to slip back into the room.

"One more thing," Dax added. He lowered the binoculars, half-turned toward her, and said with a degree of surprise. "They're alive. All of them. And their injuries have healed."

Jack Six cleared his throat. I looked up and saw him glaring down at me. I mean, I couldn't actually see his face, but I could feel his eyes on me. I guess I had stolen too many glances.

I leaned away from the window and raised my hands in a surrender-pose.

Jack maintained the stare for a solid minute before returning to his chair and leaning back into the shadowed corner of the room. He slid a deck of cards from his pocket and began to shuffle them in his lap.

Whew!

I had seen enough to back up Dax's assertion that the bodies had somehow healed and were floating fully intact in the parking lot. I could hear the elders discussing it in 206. Raised voices. Concern in father's voice. The others could hear it, too. I think I can speak for all of us when I say that we were unnerved. None of us had ever heard him sound like that. In fact, the Kool Aid would have you believe that he was above emotions like concern or fear. But remember, I was only sipping.

The conversation next door eventually died down. A light knock at the connecting door came sometime later. Delilah walked in. She had her head pointed downward, like she was trying to hide her face. That's not like her.

"Everybody okay?" she asked.

"What's happening? Is this the Forever Night?" Nora sheepishly asked.

Richter jumped down her throat. "Of course it is, you idiot!"

Dee stiffened, pointed her face directly at Richter. Her back was to me, but I'm guessing she was shooting daggers... or is it lasers? Richter reacted as if he'd seen his own ghost's ghost, his smart-assed scorn thwarted, just like that.

Afterward, Dee turned to Jack Six and said, "You're wanted in the other room."

Jack left. The shadows followed.

Dee waited for him to close the door, and then she looked up, and I gasped.

Her eyes were a piercing yellow-red. When she said to Nora—and the rest of us, "You're all in danger," I saw that she had a set of inch-long, curved fangs in place of canine teeth.

"What the fuck?!" I thought aloud.

The others have already seen this and are still cycling through varying degrees of shock.

"Relax. I'm not here to hurt you," she said. "I'm not one of them."

"One of... *them*?" I dared ask. Apparently, I was the only one who could find the words to convey what we were all thinking.

"Vampires," she replied as matter-of-factly, as if the big reveal had been that they were plumbers or used car salesmen. And then, as if to address the looks on our faces, she added, "Think about it. All that talk about superior beings existing alongside humanity. Living in the shadows. Traveling around at night. The Forever Night?"

"Wait. What's happening here?!" Richter coughed out as if he was still in denial and attempting to salvage the shiny, happy initiation fantasy.

"The Forever Night is real; a time of prolonged darkness when all the families will come together to take their place as the superior species. It's been part of their belief system for centuries. You-all are not here to be initiated into the Family Prime."

"What?!" Marco cried out. "But Father Julian said—"

"Father Julian lied!" She said, cutting him off. "Did you hear any of what I just said?! They've all been lying to you."

"Then why are we here?" I asked, even though I kinda already knew the answer, by that point."

Dee took a long breath, and then said, "You were all hand-picked to be sacrificed during the Forever Night Mass."

Shock across the board. Nora literally fainted. Richter cried. Marco started to spiral-rant under his breath. Stone-face Ryder remained stone-faced.

"Keep your voices down," Dee scolded.

"Those people outside in the parking lot are soldiers, created by the United States Government, from Elias Prime's blood. They've been sent here to take down Julian and the rest of the FPC, by any means necessary. A similar team has already taken out the compound. Julian was tipped off that they were coming. That's why we left in a hurry."

"Father Elias is alive?" Richter queried.

"Barely. He's strapped to a table, in a lab, where he's been since we took him into custody five years ago. Elias is an original, born into the bloodline centuries ago. Aside from Julian, the rest of the family were all born human. My sister included. I thought I could save her, but—" Dee took a moment to bury her emotions.

"Look. The bottom line is that those soldiers out there are stronger, and faster than the rest of the family, and trained for combat, and they've been engineered to tolerate sunlight. Things are going to get ugly soon, and I don't want you-all getting caught up in it. So, I need you to move into the bathroom, and—"

"They're getting up! I repeat, they're getting up!" Dax yelled from the balcony.

Commotion in Room 206. Dee hurried over to the window, shoved the window dressing aside, and looked out. I came up behind her and peeked over her shoulder.

Outside the window, complete darkness bespeckled with dozens of tiny, glowing lights. A lightning strike lays it all out. Down in the flooded parking lot, a squadron of soldiers, 50-to-60 deep, stood at attention in the waist-deep water, their eyes glowing yellow-red, and laser-focused on the motel façade. Seconds later, darkness returned and swallowed up the particulars, save for the floating cluster of yellow-red eyes slicing through the pitch-black veil of night.

In the distance, maybe 100-feet-back, an ambush of man-made floodlights. Large baritone engines roared to life. Based on the sound and the formation of the lights, I'd say they were military vehicles lined up side-by-side. A minute later, a voice came over a megaphone.

"Julian Prime. This is Lieutenant Colonel Charles Roxborough of the United States Marines. I'm here to inform you that the Forever Night has been... *cancelled*. There will be no celebration. No span of rule as the *superior species*."

The Lieutenant Colonel spoke in a belittling tone with an underlying sense of glee, as if hassling vampires gave him an erection.

"The family members that you left back in Ohio... are all *DEAD*! Your extended family in the north, south, and the west... are *DEAD*! You and your people in that motel are all that remains. This is the end of the line for the FPC. As such, you have two options. Either you surrender peacefully, or I will instruct these men and women you see standing before you to take you, and every last blood-sucking, walking-virus in there with you down with extreme prejudice. You have until 6:52 to decide."

"Why 6:52?" I asked.

"Sunrise." Dee replied.

Suddenly, the time checks all made sense.

"What time is it now?" I asked.

She checked her watch. "6:17."

I heard the front door to Room 206 swing open. "I don't think so!" Father Julian yelled back at the Lieutenant Colonel. "Maybe you haven't done your homework on us, but at sunrise, your men are dead."

The Lieutenant Colonel chuckled into the megaphone, and then replied, "No. It's *you* who hasn't done your homework, Mr. Prime. We've solved that problem. With your father's help, of course. These soldiers will be just fine. Will *you* and your people be, though?"

"My father?! He's alive?!" Julian muttered quizzically to himself before addressing the Lieutenant Colonel. "My father would never help you!"

"He had no choice."

Father Julian slammed the door. Raised voices from 206. Father Julian was the loudest.

Dee turned around and shoved me backward. "All of you into the bathroom!" And when we hesitated, she yelled, "NOW!"

We scrambled into the bathroom.

"Close the door behind you," she instructed. "You can get out through the window in there."

"And go where?!" I asked.

She hesitated, and then said, "Would you rather stay here?"

I WAS STANDING IN the bathroom doorway when the connecting door between rooms flew open and in stormed Father Julian looking all vamped out in yellow-eyes and fangs. Even in this ghastly state, he radiated an undeniable charisma and a palpable magnetism that made it difficult to take your eyes off him.

"Fucking BITCH!" he growled at Dee in a voice that was a few octaves deeper than normal.

Mother Saphron had her arms wrapped around his torso, trying to hold him back. "No! Please?!" she pleaded, her eyes, teeth, and voice similarly affected.

Dee backed away as Father Julian stomped toward her. The next thing you know, she's pinned to the wall by Jack Six, who came out of nowhere. I catch a glimpse of his face when he leans into and then quickly backs out of the light. It was... awful; nearly skeletal, with bulging eyeballs and a skeletal smile with long, curved fangs for canines. There was healthy skin from the neck down and up around the sides of his face. The border between bone and healthy skin looked singed and melted away. Crazy to think how that might have happened.

"No! Leave her alone!" Mother Saphron screamed.

Father Julian shoved her away, walked up to Dee, and got in her face. She attempted to struggle to no avail, and then she put on a defiant face and met his glare with one of her own.

Father Julian smirked at Dee's defiance. He wrapped a clawed hand around her throat and then forced her head back, exposing the underside of her chin. He leaned in close and sniffed her about the neck and head. Dee groaned and resisted as he forced her mouth open, reached inside with the other hand, and pinched one of her curved fangs between his index finger and thumb. He gave it a tug. The teeth came out easily.

"Of course!" he said, holding the fake set of fangs up for everyone to see. "Who are you with?"

Dee ignored him.

I didn't think it was possible for Father Julian to look even more pissed than he already was, but...

"Please don't hurt her!" Mother Saphron said.

"Shut up, Saphron!" Father Julian replied. "She chose her side. *WE* are your family now!"

And then he turned back to Dee and appeared to study her face. He used two fingers to force her right eye open.

Dee maintained her defiance as he held the index finger of his other hand at a hover, directly in front of her eye. But I could see the fear rising to the surface.

Father Julian moved his finger closer to her eye, the clawed tip aimed squarely at the white of her eyeball.

"The FBI!" Dee blurted out at the last second. "I'm with the FBI!"

"Too late," Father Julian replied, and then he thrust his index finger deep into her right eye.

Dee screamed and thrashes and my heart plummeted into my stomach. My legs grew weak from the sound of her anguish.

"No! Stop it!" Mother Saphron cried out and charged Father Julian to stop him.

I'd never seen someone move so fast. She was like a blur, as was Daniel Prime, who intercepted her before she could reach him, and held her in a bear-hug, kicking and screaming.

His finger deep into Dee's eye-socket, Father Julian twisted and pulled, using his thumb to assist, and eventually he snatched Dee's eye from the socket. Dee's screaming and thrashing subsided once the eye was removed. She passed out from shock, but Jack Six shook her awake. This happened a second and a third time as Father Julian inspected the eyeball. He impaled the back of it onto his clawed index fingernail, and pinched a yellow-red, colored contact lens from her iris with the other hand.

Mother Saphron's screams turned to crying. She fell limp in Daniel's arms, but he didn't let go of her.

"Cute," Father Julian said, as flicked the contact lens away, and looked at Dee with utter disdain. "What I wanna know is why I didn't smell you? I can usually smell a human a mile away."

"Pheromones. From your father," said Enrique Prime, who was standing just inside the connecting door. Several more elders were huddled together, in 206, peering in through the connecting doorway. "Has to be. I didn't smell her either."

"I smelled the bitch," Jack Six said in a voice that sounded as awful as his face looked. "I thought you all was just waitin' for the right time to spring on her."

Father Julian rolled his eyes and then turned his attention back to Dee, who was somewhere between drunken consciousness and complete catatonia. He leaned in close to her and whispered in her ear. I couldn't hear what he said, but I'm guessing, by the way her one good eye rolled over to me, as I stood in the bathroom doorway, that it was about us newbies.

Dee started to mouth something at me when Father Julian lunged forward and ripped out her throat with his teeth. Her face went into a full shock-mask.

Jack Six let go of her and she slid down the wall, choking and gasping for air.

Mother Saphron screamed, "Nooo!" and struggled in Daniel's grasp. He released her, and she ran over, knelt next to her sister's slumped corpse, and cradled her in her arms, weeping.

Father Julian looked over at me, chewing on a mouthful of torn-away muscle and skin, and dangling esophageal tissue, his entire face covered in fresh blood. Dee's blood. He swallowed the last bits of her throat and then smiled at me.

I nearly passed out.

"It's 6:32," Enrique whined. We don't have time for this."

Father Julian paused. He used his sleeve to wipe the blood from his face, and then he looked around as if searching the air for an idea. His face lit up. He turned and looked right at me, standing in the bathroom doorway, and the other newbies crowded into the bathroom behind me.

"We'll use *them* as hostages."

I slammed the bathroom door shut just as he started walking toward us. I yelled for the others to "Help me!" as I held onto the doorknob with both hands, pulling against it with all my weight in anticipation of Father Julian's strength.

Richter ran over and grabbed hold, his hands on top of mine. I started to thank him when the door was yanked open like we weren't even holding onto it.

Father Julian was on the other side, holding the knob in one hand, yellow-red eyes swirling with hate and bearing down on us. We were able to plant our feet at the last minute and stop the door from completing its swing.

We pulled with all our weight and the knob slipped out of Father Julian's hand. We nearly fell when the door slammed shut, but we managed to stay on our feet. That one attempt was like a workout, and we were both breathing heavily. We waited for a second attempt. Marco ran over and grabbed hold on top of Richter's hands. And then, stoned-faced Ryder grabbed hold on top of Marco's. Nora was cowering in the corner, too scared to move.

We waited and waited, but instead of trying to open the door again, Father Julian simply punched through it. He pulled his arm back and took a large chunk of the door with it. Moving in a blur, he continued punching through and snatching chunks away until it was futile for us to continue holding onto the doorknob.

We backed away as he wrapped his clawed fingers around the doorframe and snatched what remained of the door completely from the hinges. Chunks of wood everywhere. I scrambled away, reached blindly for anything that I could use as a weapon, until there was nowhere left to go.

The others screamed as Father Julian thrust himself forward and lifted me off the ground by my shoulders. He leaned in close to my face. I squeezed my eyes shut and turned my head away from his hot breath. I've never smelled anything so foul.

"I'm gonna make an example outta you!" He groaned.

I panicked and blubbered something like an apology, and then I realized that I was holding something in my right hand. It was a piece of wood from the door. And it had a jagged edge. I waited for an opportunity, an unguarded moment. Thankfully, one came when Father Julian turned to the others and threatened, "When this is over, I'm gonna make an example outta all of you!"

I seized the opportunity and thrust the jagged piece of wood upward toward the left side of his chest. To my surprise, it went in... deep. I got a quick image in my head of a hot knife cutting through butter, and for a millisecond, I wondered if wood had a similar effect on vampire skin. That's how easily the jagged piece of wood pierced his chest.

Father Julian dropped me and let out a high-pitched shriek. He stumbled backward and then began to flail and thrash around the tiny bathroom, in a blur, banging into walls like a shrieking, fleshy pinball. We hid in the corners, curling into upright, fetal balls as he flailed and thrashed past and occasionally into us. For a second, he grabbed hold of me and clawed and scratched, before letting go and flailing and thrashing in a different direction.

He stopped suddenly and stood there in the bathroom doorway; a look of terror frozen on his face. Tears streamed from his eyes. He took a few clumsy steps back and collapsed to his knees. He looked at the elders standing over him, staring in shock. Daniel. Enrique. Jack Six. And Mother Saphron, who had sprung to her feet during Father Julian's flailing thrash-dance.

"But we're the superior species." He whimpered like a disappointed brat. And then he face-planted. Dead.

His body began to smoke. Flames kicked up and raged for a good 30 seconds, and then, without warning, what was left of Father Julian Prime imploded into nothingness.

Afterward, the elders looked up simultaneously, and suddenly I was the center of attention. Their dismay morphed into rage, and they made their feelings known with a chorus of angry hissing. Flashing snarls and bearing claws, they sunk into aggressive poses, and—The window in the front of Room 205 exploded inward. Within seconds, the room was awash in sunlight and Government Issue vampires. The elders scrambled for the dark spots, their bodies catching a brief sizzle wherever the sunlight touched.

One soldier grabbed Daniel and pulled him into the sunlight. He shrieked and thrashed as his body sizzled and then burst into multi-colored flames before finally imploding.

Another soldier grabbed Mother Saphron and yanked her into the sunlight to a similar, but much more explosive, effect. Another one grabbed Enrique, who appeared to cook from the inside out to the sunlight's touch. Rather than imploding, he left a shriveled, charred corpse.

Jack Six was the only one who seemed to give the soldiers any trouble as he slipped in and out of the remaining shadows, eluding their attempts to grab him, until there were too many, and he, too, was pulled into the sunlight. His death was the most spectacular, like a whirlwind of small explosions that ended in a shower of glitter-like flecks of... vampire?

We ran to the bathroom window and climbed out one-by-one. It was a tight squeeze, but we all made it out onto the rear balcony. We had grown so accustomed to living at night that the daylight hurt our eyes. It took a few moments to adjust. A terrible ruckus rang out from every room on the second floor as the siege on the Family Prime continued. We could hear it over the wind, and the rain that was still punching down like small fists, and the occasional thunderclaps.

"Everybody okay?" I asked.

"I'm good." Richter said.

"Me, too," Marco said.

"I think so," said stone-faced Ryder.

It took a while to reach Nora, who was still reeling from the events inside Room 205, but she eventually nodded.

And then, out of nowhere, a fanged G-Man landed on the balcony railing and crouched over us like a predatory raptor trying to decipher whether-or-not these helpless looking things cowering before him were edible.

Nora screamed.

I slapped my hand over her mouth, and then I turned to the soldier and attempted to appeal to his humanity.

"We're not your enemy," I said in the most gentle, non-threatening voice I could muster. "We're the good guys. Those assholes were gonna kill us."

"They were gonna sacrifice us!" Richter added, like he was actively trying to wrap his head around what that meant exactly.

The soldier glares quizzically, his vampiric visage shifting from aggression to confusion to at-peace, and back again, as if his humanity waged an inner war with his new, primal urges.

"Oh shit," I said when, after a few moments, his expression suddenly shifted sinister.

His eyes filled with wanting as he glared down at us. His lips curled back. He tightened his grip around the railing and crouched lower. His body adopted a forward lean, as if he was about to lunge, when suddenly, a shrieking figure appeared, or was thrown, in the bathroom window above us.

It was Dax. His skin sizzled as soon as the sunlight hit him, and he ducked back inside.

The fanged G-Man hissed at the commotion and then leapt over us and into the bathroom window.

"Go! Go! Go!" I yelled, and we ran like our lives depended on it.

We heard them tussling inside the bathroom as we ran for the stairs and down to the flooded rear parking lot. We keep running through the hip deep water; the motel growing smaller and smaller in the distance. It was raining so hard that it was difficult to keep your eyes open. The stinging water alerted me to all my scrapes and bruises, and I was starting to realize how cold it was outside. Funny how adrenaline circumvents that shit. I looked down at my left forearm.

"Looks like a bite-mark. Shit!"

Must've happened when I was struggling with Father Julian.

I quickly hid my forearm so the others couldn't see the bite. That's gonna be a problem.

SPECIAL SNOWFLAKES

BRIDGETT NELSON

8

SPECIAL SNOWFLAKES

By Bridgett Nelson

Prologue

Snow wasn't meant to cause sickness.

Humidity hung heavily in the summer air, water vapor swirling through the atmosphere as, in the distance, a seasonal thunderstorm threatened. Local weather forecasters had predicted a sunny, but scorching hot, Independence Day, and that's exactly what the townsfolk of Jasmine Hills, West Virginia, had experienced...so far.

The sun glinted off tiny droplets of moisture floating through the clouds, creating mini rainbows only birds could see, and continued to do so until its vibrant rays were hidden behind rapidly forming, ominously gray clouds. Thick clouds that hung low and filled the sky with a bleak, desolate visage.

Snow wasn't meant to cause body disfigurement.

The temperature plummeted. Birds, unable to regulate their bodies quickly enough to adapt, lost all reactivity in their wings and plummeted to the earth. Their terrified chirps echoed throughout the sky.

Atmospheric water droplets froze, forming tiny ice crystals. As they made their circuitous paths to the ground, the vapor around them turned to ice and attached to each of the crystals, creating the six identical arms of a snowflake.

Snow wasn't meant to kill.

No. Snow wasn't meant to kill. But these icy flakes were unique. Secreted deep within their cores, microscopic visitors hitched a ride. Microscopic visitors about to make a *brutal* mockery of America's holiday—good ol' Independence Day.

July 4th - Noon

"Is it winter yet?" Shasta asked, a clownish grin on her face as she spread out a red, white, and blue blanket beneath the shade of a tall oak tree. "The heat, I can deal with, but this humidity is kicking my ass."

Theo grabbed a piece of ice from the portable cooler he'd had strapped to his back and placed it against her sunburned neck. She jumped from the intensity of the cold, but soon purred like a cat as he rubbed the rapidly melting ice over her heated skin. "Better?" he asked.

"Better." She gave him a quick kiss. "Thanks, babe."

"This hike is more than I bargained for," Lainey said, fanning herself with her hand. "I thought running around the hospital every day at work kept me in shape, but I was clearly delusional." She plopped down on the blanket, gulping the muggy air into her lungs.

Jillian handed her a bottle of cold water. "Here, babe. Hydrate." Lainey removed the lid and took several long pulls. She drank so quickly, water escaped and dribbled down her chin. Jillian laughed and took a seat beside her. Lainey's free hand made its way to her thigh.

"I just don't understand why we had to leave at nine o'clock this morning. What kind of bullshit is that?" Jack asked. "It's not going to take us a whole day to get to the top of the mountain. Everybody knows West Virginia's mountains are more like giant hills, anyway."

"Quit acting like you don't get it, Yaeger," Theo responded good-naturedly. "I've explained multiple times that we wanted to start while it was still cool, stop for lunch and a nice rest, and reach the summit before dusk. We need time to pitch the tents, start a fire, and have dinner before the fireworks show."

Jack cracked open a beer and mumbled under his breath.

"Who wants food?" Shasta asked, holding up the turkey and Swiss sandwiches she'd made the previous night. Everyone took one, along with an apple and a Gatorade.

"Did you really buy red, white, and blue varieties of Gatorade?" Lainey said, looking at each of their bottles with a delighted grin.

"I sure did!" Shasta said happily. "Independence Day is my favorite holiday."

"She's not kidding. She usually makes me go to some patriotic place with her on the 4th...the Liberty Bell, Washington D.C., Mount Rushmore." Theo said, a trace of amusement in his voice. "This year I convinced her to stay home and go on a hike with all you fine people."

"I bet you're regretting that now!" Jillian laughed and glanced at her phone. "My weather app is showing that the humidity today is nearly ninety percent. My phone won't stop alerting me of heat warnings. I think we need to take the rest of this hike very, very slowly. I may be a doc, but my specialty is babies...not heat stroke." She slapped a mosquito on her arm. "Does anyone have insect repellent spray? I'm being eaten alive."

Lainey dug into her backpack and pulled out a spray bottle. "Here, babe." She sternly looked at the rest of their group as Jillian misted her skin with the insectifuge. "And I may be a nurse, but I'm on vacation...so no medical emergencies. Y'all hear me?"

"I know this part sucks, but once we reach the summit, I bet we'll have a nice breeze. We can relax, have some delicious hot dogs and S'mores, and enjoy the Jasmine Hills fireworks display," Shasta said enthusiastically as she gathered the empty bottles and apple cores.

"Well, I don't know about the rest of you, but I'm still hungover from last night. If this is our so-called rest time, I'm going to take advantage," Jack said, leaning against a tree and pulling the brim of his cap over his face.

Looking vaguely guilty, Lainey said, "I'm not going to lie, this heat has sucked away my energy. I'm pretty depleted. I wouldn't mind a brief nap, either."

A short time later, with Shasta's phone set to alert them in forty-five minutes, they had sprawled across the blanket, eyes closed, bodies in repose.

None of them noticed the subtle changes taking place in the sky.

"Seen any good movies lately?" Shasta asked, trying to distract them from the treacherous climb. She was grateful for her hiking poles...the ground was rocky and difficult to navigate.

"I never have time. I'm always at the hospital," Jillian said, huffing.

Lainey rubbed Jillian's back. "That's not true, love. We streamed that great romantic comedy the other night, though I'm blanking on the name."

"I'd completely forgotten about that. Guess I was more focused on the memories we made afterward."

Lainey blushed. "Jilly!"

"How much farther?" Jack piped up as he wiped a layer of sweat from his forehead.

They took a brief break to let Shasta study the map. "If we're where I think we are, about two miles." The shiver that wracked her body went unnoticed. "And all of it is a pretty steep incline, unfortunately."

"I've gotta say, I'll be glad to get there," Theo said, his face red with exertion. "This hike has been a damn ball-buster. Way tougher than I expected."

Shasta immediately felt guilty. She knew he was carrying a large portion of their camping supplies.

Theo looked at the sky as the light filtering between the tree's branches dimmed. "Is it supposed to rain?" The question was directed at Shasta, but everyone pulled out their phones to check the local forecast.

"Not according to my app," Jack replied.

"Same," Lainey chimed in.

Shasta stared at the gnarly pewter strips of sky she could see. It looked foreboding. "I think the apps may be wrong. Those clouds look scary." She paused. "And have any of you noticed the temperature dropping? I'm not even sweating now."

"Now that you mention it, yeah." Jillian said. "It's definitely more comfortable than it was when we stopped for lunch."

"I think we need to pick up our pace. I don't like what I'm seeing." After one last worried glance at the sky, Shasta started back up the slope, her pace urgent. Exhausted, the others reluctantly followed. She wasn't usually such a worry-wart about the weather, but they were miles from town and not terribly close to the summit. She didn't want to be stuck on such a treacherous incline in the middle of a furious summer thunderstorm.

The light dimmed further. As the breeze caused the sweat on their skin to evaporate and their core body temperatures to cool, the shivering began.

"WHAT THE FUCK?" LAINEY said, her body covered in gooseflesh. "A couple hours ago, I thought my brain was going to boil inside my skull and ooze out my ears from this heat. Now I'm more concerned about icicles forming in my nostrils." She turned to Jillian. "Baby, please don't let me end up like Jack Nicholson's character in the final scene of *The Shining*. That's *so* not a good look."

"I hear ya, and of course I won't, my sweets. I'll make sure to keep you nice and warm." Jillian waggled her eyebrows and winked, then rubbed her hands over her bare arms. "I've gotta say, this is an extreme turnaround, even for West Virginia weather."

"Uh, guys?" Jack's voice sounded small, unsure.

Shasta turned and saw he was some distance behind them. "Come on, Jack, catch up! We need to get where we're going and set up camp!" She peered anxiously at the churning, low-hung ashen clouds and added, "We're gonna need those tents up...and fast."

Theo heard and reassuringly took her hand inside his.

"No, seriously, guys. Stop for a minute, and tell me what you see." He turned in a circle, staring wide-eyed at the forest around him. "I know I had a few beers at lunch, but there's no way I'm that drunk."

They paused impatiently.

"Holy shit," Theo whispered a few seconds later.

"You're seeing it, right?" Josh asked, his excitement building. "It's fucking flurrying in July!"

"Okay, clearly it's the end of the world," Jillian said, her tone sarcastic. "How do we know this isn't just ash from a fire? Everybody knows how irresponsible people are with fireworks around here."

"Oh, come on, Jilly. You know that's a bullshit theory. It's freezing! Of course it's snowing!" Lainey wandered the trail, head thrown back with childlike glee, catching snowflakes on her tongue.

Shasta's gut was screaming at her—something was very, very wrong. "Look, we need to go. *Now!* I can see none of you are taking this seriously, but it's snowing, the temperature is dropping as we speak, and we're in tank tops and shorts in the middle of nowhere. We're going to need shelter if this continues...desperately." She herded them together and forced them to continue on the pathway.

"She's right, guys. Let's hustle," Theo said.

"Do you honestly think we're going to get a blizzard in *July*?" Lainey snorted. "It's much more likely that a cold front moved through, caused some weird anomaly in the atmosphere and, within the hour, the sun will be shining again. But sure, let's kill ourselves getting to the summit lickety-split."

Long minutes passed as they trudged toward the peak. What had started as light flurries became threatening whiteout conditions. Jillian cleared her throat and, lips quivering from the cold, said, "Lanes, I think you owe Shasta and Theo an apology." The words were clumsy and slow as her blue-tinted lips struggled to form them. Snow fell heavily to the ground, accumulating rapidly around their boot-clad feet.

"I just *cannot* believe this shit. What the fuck is even happening? I mean, I must be sleeping off a bender somewhere right now, because this can't possibly be real," Jack said.

"I hear you, bro. It's like something out of a movie...like *The Day After Tomorrow* or some shit. My brain is refusing to process any of it," Theo responded. "But you *are* awake, Yaeger, so don't puss out on us."

"Yeah, well, fuck that," Jack said.

They'd instinctively huddled closer together to share body heat during the climb, but the situation had gone from startling and exhilarating to dire and life-threatening in a matter of minutes.

"How worried do we need to be about hypothermia, Jillian?" Shasta asked.

"Very," Jillian responded grimly. "We're all exhibiting early symptoms already."

"Shit."

Fear set in and with it, steadfast resolve. "Pick up the pace, everyone! Get those muscles moving and that blood circulating! Come on, you can do it!" Shasta stumbled over a rock but kept going. "We need to take shelter immediately or face the consequences. Now MOVE!"

Everyone but Lainey began awkwardly jogging up the hill. Glancing back at her, Jillian said, "Lanes?"

"I don't feel so good." She spoke in a mumble, head down.

"I know. It's your body temperature dropping. You need to move so your muscles can contract and create body heat." She grabbed her by the arm, but Lainey shrugged her off. When Jillian saw her face, she flinched, then called out, "Hold up, please! Lainey is sick!"

"Holy shit, what happened to her?" Jack asked, nonplussed.

"I have no idea," Jillian said.

Bright crimson blood dribbled down Lainey's chin. Her skin was pale and waxy, glowing with a sheen of sweat despite the frigid temperature. Her eyes were bloodshot, and pustule-like blisters had formed in clusters on her normally beautiful skin.

"Did you bite your tongue, sweetie?" Jillian asked. It seemed like a ridiculous question, since *of course* it wasn't as simple as her biting her tongue, but she couldn't understand what she was seeing.

"I don't feel so good," Lainey repeated, ignoring the question. Her words were slurred. Without warning, she spewed purple vomit across the freshly fallen snow—a mixture of fresh blood and blue Gatorade.

"Can somebody help me, please?" Jillian asked, urgency in her voice. "She needs medical attention that I can't give her on this incline! We need to get her up the mountain quickly, but she can't do it on her own."

Without pause, Theo jogged toward them. Minutes later, the entire group was heading back up the mountain, Lainey held securely between Jillian and Theo.

"We're getting close! Another three-quarters of a mile to go, and then we can warm up in our tent and sleeping bags!" Shasta shouted above the howling wind, trying to boost their morale.

The midnight-like darkness of the foreboding sky couldn't hide the rapid accumulation of the stark white snow, which now reached their shins. Hiking through a foot of blinding snow on the side of a mountain, while inappropriately dressed for the climate, was the scariest thing Shasta had ever experienced. Instead, she focused on the goal of taking off her soppy wet clothes and snuggling naked with Theo in their sleeping bag. "Is everyone okay?"

"I'm freezing my balls off, but I'm okay!" Jack answered.

"I've been better, but I'm hanging in there," Theo said, his exhaustion evident in his voice.

"Lainey and I are fine, aren't we, my love?" Jillian looked at her and saw clot-like clumps of blood hanging from her mouth. "Honey, we're almost there, okay?"

Lainey rolled her head toward Jillian, her neck seemingly without muscle control. Her maniacal grin showed a mouthful of clenched, gore-encrusted teeth.

Jillian recoiled.

"You're gonna be just fine, aren't ya, Lanes?" Theo's smile was warm and reassuring, though Jillian could see the worry in his eyes.

Lainey's head rolled bonelessly toward Theo. If he was taken aback by her appearance, he hid it well. She aggressively sniffed the air—a wolf hunting its prey. "You smell good." Her words ran together—one long mass of syllables—and her ability to swallow seemed impaired. She kept dry-heaving, as though something were stimulating her gag reflex, and she was drooling worse than the St. Bernard Shasta's family once had.

"Uh, Theo..." Jillian began, but he shook his head and motioned for her to stay quiet. He grinned at Lainey. "Well, I put deodorant on this morning, but after all the sweating I did earlier, I doubt there is much of it left."

The two of them were basically carrying Lainey at this point. Her feet dragged behind her along the surface of the snow, creating thick, parallel divots from the friction of her clunky hiking boots. Shasta could tell they were bone-weary, dealing with the incline, the ice, the snow that now reached their knees, and Lainey's dead weight, in addition to the gear strapped to their bodies.

"That's not what I meant," Lainey said with a crazed cackle, blood-tinged saliva spraying from her mouth in slimy strings. She sniffed the air again. "I'm talking about your blood. *Give me your blood, Theo.*"

She tore free from Jillian's grip and lunged at Theo's neck. There was a wet, tearing sound, followed by obscene sucking, and then an unidentifiable gurgling.

Shasta screamed, running toward them but tripping and falling on her ass. Jillian grabbed Lainey's shoulders and pulled. A loud popping sound echoed through the subzero air, as Lainey's mouth detached from a perfectly round two-inch puncture hole in Theo's neck.

They fell against a snowdrift, their bodies sinking into the wet fluff. Jillian's arms wrapped around Lainey's chest as she fought to escape. "Stop it, Lainey! Just stop it, for fuck's sake!"

Theo crumpled to the ground, his life's blood gushing from his neck with each pump of his weakening heart.

Her skin red from frostbite, her ankle and butt smarting from the fall, Shasta crawled to him. She pulled off the handkerchief she'd been using as a headband and pressed it against the spurting wound. Then she cradled his head against her belly and stroked his wet hair. "Theo, can you hear me, baby? It's going to be okay. You'll see. I'll get you all bandaged up once we're in the tent." Her voice quavered as she fought not to cry. "Yep, gonna fix you right up, sweetie. And then we'll snuggle like we always do, because you know my happiest place in the world is inside your arms."

Theo coughed up blood, looked her in the eye, and said, "Tuhg! Tuhg!"

"I...I don't understand." She knew he was trying to tell her something—something important—but she had no idea what.

"Tuhg! Tuhg!" He was getting more and more agitated.

"Okay, I get it now," she lied, trying to ease his distress. "I'll take care of it. I promise."

Shasta felt him relax and chose to ignore how his beautiful brown eyes now stared sightlessly into the starless sky; how there were no reflexive blinks when the snowflakes landed on their surface. Instead, she continued murmuring words of love and undying affection to his rapidly cooling body.

"Will somebody help me?" Jillian screamed. "I'm losing my grip on her. Do something, goddammit!"

Hearing Jillian through the fog of her grief, Shasta knew what she needed to do. She gently placed Theo's head against the snow-covered ground and forced her stiffening body upright. Trudging through the blizzard, she grabbed her hiking pole and made her way toward them.

Jillian was struggling, using what little strength she had left to control the thrashing, slobbering, blood-sucking monster sprawled across her torso. Her arms and legs were wrapped tightly around Lainey, but Shasta could tell how fatigued her body was. She was barely holding on.

"Yaeger," Shasta yelled, "get my other hiking pole, and get the hell down here." She heard his footsteps breaking through the icy surface of the fallen snow, and then felt him beside her, his cold skin pressed against hers. "Have the pole ready. When I tell Jillian to let her go, she's probably going to attack...be prepared if you don't want a hole in your neck, too." She stifled a sob.

"Yeah, fine. Let's just do it already."

Shasta looked at Lainey. "Why would you do that to Theo? He loved you and was just trying to help. Why would you...bite him?" She struggled to say the words.

Lainey stopped flailing and a close-mouthed smile stretched across her face. "It wasn't me."

Her speech sounded a lot like Shasta's when her tongue had swollen after she got it pierced—bloated and somehow...slushy.

"Of course it was! We all saw you. Don't play games with me!"

"I'm telling you, it wasn't me!" With that, she opened her mouth.

At first, Shasta saw nothing but a dark, gaping maw...until a cream-colored, crab-like appendage protruded from the darkness and rested on Lainey's lower lip. It was quickly followed by two beady black eyes, what appeared to be a shell, and multiple pairs of legs flailing around.

Shasta screamed. How did that hellish monstrosity get inside Lainey's mouth? She screamed some more.

"What *the hell* is that?" Jack shouted, stepping away and pulling Shasta with him. "You're seeing this, right? Jesus Christ, has the entire world gone insane? What the absolute living fuck is going on?"

Lainey laughed...a laugh which showcased nothing but a deep well of insanity.

"What? What is it?" Jillian's voice was panicked, unable to see the monstrosity from her angle.

The louse—Shasta didn't have a better name for it—looked like a ghastly prehistoric nightmare. Even worse, Lainey kept pulling it into her mouth, then sticking it back out again, moving it up and down lasciviously in an obscene, hellish mockery of licking. Shasta couldn't see any sign of Lainey's own tongue...which led her to believe the crustacean-like creature had *become* her tongue.

Her body shuddered in revulsion.

"Get your pole ready, Jack," she whispered. They didn't have time for this. Already her movements were clumsy and becoming more so by the minute. Her fingers were numb, her skin alarmingly hard like a mannequin's. She didn't want to think about possible amputations in her future, but she likely wouldn't have to. Hypothermia would kill her first.

"Jillian, let her go," Shasta demanded, her voice firm and unyielding.

"I can't." Jillian choked back sobs. "I know what you're going to do to her."

"Once you see why, you'll be thankful. Lainey isn't Lainey anymore. Now please..." Shasta's voice cut off as tears trailed down her cheeks, "just do it."

Seeing the steadfast reassurance on her face, Jillian ever-so-slowly relinquished the last embrace she and Lainey would ever share. As soon as the bond loosened, Lainey tore away from Jillian with an alienesque screech and charged toward Shasta and Jack like a bull at a red cape.

For Shasta, time seemed to decelerate. She saw Lainey sprinting toward her, but the movements seemed lackadaisical...unhurried. She noticed Lainey's blistered skin sloughing off as she ran—stinking wet, putrescent chunks that plopped into the snow and disappeared beneath the surface, creating geysers of malodorous lavender steam.

She saw the isopod peeking from between Lainey's lips, both pairs of its antennae quivering in anticipation of fresh blood.

Lainey's eyes were blind, hardened and cracked like ice cubes, her once blue irises now a lifeless, silver. Crystalline stalks protruded from her tear ducts, crawling across the bridge of her nose and tangling together.

Shasta was no longer sure *what* was most abhorrent—her face was vile from top to bottom.

In what felt like slow-motion, she brought her hiking pole up, the metal spike pointed toward Lainey. She felt the pressure as Lainey's body pushed against it, the slickness as it slid through skin and fat, the jerks and lurches as it impaled organs and viscera, and the abrupt halt as the stake penetrated her spine. Lainey hung there, skewered, her appearance in death somehow far worse. Shasta let the pole, and Lainey's body, drop to the ground.

Jillian sat in the snow, head in hands, weeping piteously. Shasta empathized, but wasn't regretful. The past few moments had forever altered the course of both their lives. She went to Jillian and held out her hand. Jillian looked up, her eyes laden with tears, and took it.

As she stood, Jack uttered a loud string of curses. They turned to see Lainey's 'tongue' crawling free of her mouth. Its lined carapace had overlapping segments that gleamed in the dim light. Its fan-like tail left a series of equidistant depressions in the snow. Fourteen jointed legs— seven on either side—carried it surprisingly quickly across the hiking trail, skittering toward the surrounding woods.

Jack chased after it, slamming the hiking pole through its back. It screamed—a high-pitched squeal that went on and on—as its legs writhed, failing to find purchase. He brought his hiking boot down hard on its head, and the haunting shriek ceased.

"What's happening?" Jillian asked quietly. She looked lost. Forlorn.

"I don't know, but we need to move. We need shelter, or we're going to die." Deciding to leave her poles behind—the idea of pulling them out of those bodies was more than she could handle—Shasta took one final look at Theo and continued her journey to the summit.

She'd mourn later. Now she just needed to survive.

"GODDAMMIT!" SHASTA SWORE AS they reached the summit.

Hypothermia had obviously had an effect on their mental faculties—they were lethargic and not thinking clearly.

The gear Theo and Lainey were hauling had been left with their bodies...including the larger tents.

"It's fine," Jack said. "The three of us can squeeze into my one-man tent. The closer contact will help us keep warm. It will work, Shasta. We'll be okay. You'll see."

The snow had not stopped. It was now level with their hips.

As Jack went about setting up the tent, Shasta used her binoculars to see if she could discern what was happening far below in town.

What she saw made her violently ill—fires, smoke, flashing lights—even mutilated corpses lying on the snow-covered streets.

"It's bad," she told the others. "There are burning buildings and dead people, and..."

She couldn't continue. Jack pulled her into his arms. He was shorter and scrawnier than Theo, but at that moment, his embrace was exactly what she needed.

"Thanks," she said.

"Anything for Theo's girl," he said, his voice choked up. He went back to finish with the tent.

Shasta could no longer feel her legs, but kept jogging in place, trying to keep her blood pumping and heart oxygenated. Jillian stared blankly at Jack while he worked, but made no offer to help. Shasta suspected she was deeply in shock.

Once the tent was ready, they got Jillian inside, crawled in after her, and zipped the flaps closed.

"Okay, I know it's awkward," Jack said, "but we need to get these wet clothes off."

Only the sound of rustling clothes could be heard as they struggled to maneuver in the tight space. There was no embarrassment; they were simply doing what needed to be done. Then they unzipped their sleeping bags to use as blankets and wrapped them around their bodies.

"When I've warmed up a little," Jack said, his teeth chattering, "I'll see if I can find some dry wood and try to start a fire."

"Do you think it will even stay lit?" Shasta asked. "The wind gales are non-stop, and it's pouring snow."

"Dunno. But it's better to try than not."

"Yeah," she conceded. "You're right."

Nobody spoke for several minutes, the only sound the whistling of the wind through the trees.

Shasta was nearly asleep when Jillian whispered, "We need to drink."

"What?" Jack said. "Speak up."

She cleared her throat and repeated, "We need to drink. Dehydration decreases circulation, which will make us even colder. After all the sweating we did earlier, we're undoubtedly dry. I mean, I haven't even peed since early this morning. We just..." She sighed. "We *need* to drink."

Shasta reached behind her. "No problem. We still have ...." Her body stilled, and a bitter laugh escaped. "Theo had the drinks." When nobody reacted, she clarified. "Theo *still* has the drinks."

"Well, shit." Jack sounded resigned. "What the hell are we gonna do?" Then his voice brightened. "What's wrong with us? The cold has really fucked with our brains. We have plenty to drink. We're surrounded by snow!" He pulled a couple of collapsible camping cups out of his bag, unzipped the tent flaps just enough to put his hand through, filled one cup, and then the other. "I only have the two. Sorry."

"You two go ahead," Shasta said. "I can wait." Though she knew Jillian was undoubtedly correct, her nearly frozen body rebelled against the idea of eating cold snow. It sounded about as appealing as doing a polar plunge.

Since there was no chance of the snow melting on its own, they simply tilted their heads back and let the flakes fall into their open mouths.

Jack grimaced. "Jesus, it tastes like soured milk."

Jillian nodded, but kept going.

Shasta yawned. "Guys, I'll hydrate after a nap." She curled into a small ball, her sleeping bag wrapped tightly around her body.

The climb, the heat followed quickly by the intense cold, the shock, and the profound emotional loss had taken their toll. She couldn't keep her eyes open. By the time Jack and Jillian finished their cups of snow, Shasta was asleep.

IT WAS DARK WHEN she awoke, her body trembling in the cold. Pulling her phone out of the side pocket of her backpack and turning it on, she was surprised to see it still worked. Wasn't technology supposed to go haywire during the apocalypse? It was six o'clock p.m. She'd slept a couple hours, yet her body was screaming for more. The skin that had been exposed to the elements during the snowstorm tingled and burned, and her mouth was dry and chalky.

Rolling over, she tapped on Jack's sleeping bag. "Jack," she whispered. "Hey, Jack? Can you get me a cup full of snow?"

He didn't respond. She patted as much of the blanket as she could, but felt nothing.

Using the flashlight on her phone, she illuminated the tiny tent. Neither Jillian nor Jack was inside. Anxiety flooded her body like a tsunami.

Something was wrong.

Her wet clothes were now coated in ice, so she grabbed a fresh t-shirt and shorts from her bag, along with a clean pair of socks. It was the last of the clothes she had with her, and though she hated to use them already, she couldn't risk getting her sleeping bag wet. It was her only source of warmth. She had no other shoes with her, so she reluctantly pulled the heavy, wet hiking boots back on. Getting ready to leave the relative comfort of the tent, she thought longingly of the parka hanging in her coat closet at home, her favorite sweatpants, and the fuzzy pink slippers she loved so much.

Taking a deep breath and bracing herself against the cold, she unzipped the tent and stepped outside.

The air stole her breath. Snowflakes pelted painfully against her skin. It was hard to even open her eyes, but when she did, the first thing she noticed was a large rock with a flat top.Sitting atop it, in the shape of a teepee, were some branches and leaves. Jack had clearly been working to get a fire started for them, but where was he?

The second thing she saw was bright red blood splashed across the stark white snow. Two sets of footprints led off into a heavy copse of trees.

She did not want to follow those tracks, but there really wasn't a choice. She knew in her gut her friends were in deep, deep shit.

God, I feel so sick...

After sleeping for about an hour and thawing out his frigid body, Jack had crept from the tent, making sure not to wake the ladies, and began gathering supplies for a fire.

He didn't believe there was a chance in hell it would stay lit in this fucked up weather, but they were operating in survival-mode, and he had to try. He didn't want search and rescuers to one day find their frozen corpses and laugh at their stupidity.

"Why do you think they didn't start a fire, Fred?"

"Cuz they're dumbass millennials, that's why, Judd."

Nope. Jack wasn't going to let that happen. He'd likely fail, but, given the circumstances, that was okay. The conditions were not ideal.

Finding dry wood was nearly impossible, but he managed to gather a few pieces, along with a rock to use as a platform. He remembered from watching *Survivor* that the logs should be arranged in a teepee formation, with the kindling stuffed loosely into the crevices.

As he worked, he felt something land on the back of his hand. Something viscous and warm.

Blood.

But where had it come from?

Jack looked up, but saw only foreboding clouds. He ran his hands over his face and then stared at his bloody palms. *Wait...I'm the one bleeding?*

That was when the nausea hit...and the pain. His mouth throbbed with achy soreness, his vision became blurry, and his skin felt like it was on fire. When he puked, it was mostly blood, with some liver-like chunks...and a few smaller versions of the louse that had come out of Lainey.

Well, that's just fucking great.

Had Lainey been contagious? Had that *thing* he'd killed somehow contaminated him? Why did his tongue feel so weird? And his eyes?

Something caught his attention, and he sniffed the air. His eyes landed on a white-tailed deer. It looked like a doe. Suddenly, all he could think about was how thoroughly delicious her blood would taste.

He gave chase.

JILLIAN HAD HEARD JACK leave the tent, but she pretended to be asleep.

She had no desire to make conversation, especially with Jack. She'd never really cared for him, but he was Theo's best friend, and she adored Shasta and Theo. She and Shasta had grown up together in these West Virginia hills, and she knew they'd always have a special bond.

But right now, all she wanted to think about was—all she *could* think about—was Lainey. Lainey in her nursing scrubs, Lainey watching scary movies and hiding her face in a pillow, Lainey standing in the kitchen wearing the apron Jillian had bought her, which read, 'Whatever happens, we ARE eating it.'

She wasn't able to process that Lainey had killed Theo; that her body had harbored that disgusting creature—which, to Jillian, had looked like a super-sized pill bug; that Lainey was gone...forever.

Tears ran down her flushed cheeks and puddled on the nylon floor of the tent, along with the blood dripping from her mouth.

Losing Lainey wasn't fair! Jillian had dedicated her life to creating happy families, making sure every baby she delivered was as healthy as possible. So why had *her* family been destroyed?

Desperately needing some fresh air, she didn't even try to be quiet as she exited the tent. She was focused entirely on getting outside and sucking the cold, icy air into her struggling lungs.

Sickness thundered through her body in one booming crash. Her legs weakened and were no longer able to support her weight, so she fell on her bottom into the snow and thought longingly of death.

She wasn't cold.

She didn't even *feel* the cold.

That was probably bad.

As she sat there, her body resting on several feet of snow, she spat out her withered, shrunken tongue. A moment later, she could no longer see. Not that it mattered. She'd have no trouble navigating, despite her blindness...her new friend could help.

She felt the louse tug on the root of her tongue—all that was left of it—as it edged its shrimp-like body between her lips. Its antennae twitched spasmodically as it evaluated their surroundings.

A picture formed in Jillian's mind, and she knew what she needed to do. Without a second's pause, she dashed across the ground to the tree line straight ahead, not once considering that she was entirely nude...in a blizzard.

THE DOE'S BODY SPASMED one last time as Jack's tongue penetrated the puncture hole in her neck—the louse thrusting viciously in an orgy of bloodlust.

Although Jack couldn't see, he sure could feel. He stroked his cock aggressively as his awesome new tongue fucked the deer. When he ejaculated, his creamy white cum held hundreds of tiny, translucent isopods.

Sweet, sweet babies.

He grinned around his porn-star tongue as a strip of flesh on his leg peeled away and fell off.

BLOOD. OH GOD, YES! Blood.

Jillian stopped running. Although her eyes no longer functioned, her new friend's antennae's sensory perception told her exactly what was happening.

As I expected, Jack is a pervert.

Her friend also detected the deer was nearly bloodless, so Jillian attacked something even better...Jack.

Shasta moved cautiously through the trees, her phone's flashlight her only illumination. She stopped frequently and listened, hoping to hear her friends' voices. She could already feel the effects of the cold and knew she'd need to get back to the tent shortly.

A scream tore through the forest and cut off just as abruptly. It sounded close.

It sounded like Jack.

Weaving through the maze-like thicket, trying to avoid impaling herself on any branches, Shasta made her way in the direction of the scream.

She found him quickly. And though she'd like to say the scene shocked her, it was exactly what she was expecting. Well, except for the deer. She wasn't prepared for the poor deer.

Jillian, naked and unashamed, was on her knees, her body hovering over Jack's, the parasitic tongue sucking up his lifeblood.

Despite knowing he was already dead—hell, his parasitic tongue was literally crawling up Jillian's back—Shasta screamed, "Get off him, Jillian! What would Lainey say?"

Jillian's parasite popped back into her mouth, but not before Shasta saw its pink and bloated body...a tick ready to pop. Jillian turned toward her, gore coating her smiling lips.

"I think she'd say..." she slurred, "...yum!" Throwing her head back, she laughed insanely. "And I also think," Jillian added, "she'd be cheering me on as I do the same thing to *you*!"

With surprising speed and agility, Jillian bounded upright and charged straight at Shasta. Defenseless, Shasta did the only thing she could...she turned and fled. Her phone slipped out of her hand, but it was nearly dead anyway, so she left it and kept moving.

As she ran, she prayed she wouldn't trip or plow into a tree and knock herself unconscious. Her breaths came in short, panicked gasps and her frozen joints wouldn't stop popping.

She could hear Jillian behind her, but at a distance, so Shasta stopped briefly, hid behind a tree, and attempted to catch her breath. The cold air was so dry, she felt as though she weren't getting enough oxygen. Resting her hands on her knees, she focused on deep breathing.

A stream of light filtered through the thick clouds—whether sunlight or moonlight, Shasta wasn't sure—but it offered enough illumination for her to realize she was standing on the precipice of a cliff.

A very high cliff.

If she hadn't stopped running when she did, she would have plowed right over the edge and plunged to her death.

Jesus fucking Christ.

"I smell you!" Jillian called out in a singsong voice. She was close again. Too close.

Shasta had only one option. Checking the branches attached to the tree to find a sturdy one, she gripped it with her hands and waited.

Jillian crashed through the copse of trees, the louse sitting on her lower lip, and ran straight at Shasta. Her blind eyes gleamed with madness.

She never slowed down.

Not when Shasta warned her she was going to die.

Not even when she was a few feet away from the final attack.

Jillian grabbed at her, but missed, as Shasta swung herself over the void, praying fervently the branch would hold her weight...and that her frozen fingers wouldn't give out. Jillian flew over the edge, seeming to hang mid-air for far too long, the parasite evident between her lips. Then she plummeted, giggling hysterically all the way down. A loud cracking sound from far below let Shasta know Jillian would no longer be a problem.

But seriously, that was creepy as fuck.

Shasta worked her way down the branch, hand over hand, until she was close enough to wrap her legs around the trunk. Then she dropped to the ground and cried.

The tears continued for far too long, but she couldn't stop. She cried for Jasmine Hills and its residents. She cried for Jillian and Lainey, who'd been blissfully happy during the six months of their marriage. She cried for Jack, whose three-year-old daughter would grow up without a daddy.

But mostly, she cried for the love of her life...and the baby they'd made together. She affectionately rubbed her belly.

Theo hadn't known.

She'd planned to tell him during the fireworks show, which, on a normal 4th of July, would be happening at that very moment. The tears came harder.

Shasta heard a chittering sound and looked up. An adorable little squirrel was making its way down the tree, its cheeks bulging with nuts or seeds...Shasta couldn't tell which.

As it got closer, she recognized the blind eyes, and the segmented legs protruding from its mouth. Horrified, she ran back to the tent.

Epilogue

A DAY PASSED.

A second.

Then a third.

Shasta had been sipping from a bottle of water she'd found buried beneath her supplies, and a beer she'd found in Jack's. She knew alcohol wasn't good for the baby, but neither was dehydration. Aside from a single sleeve of graham crackers, the food was gone. Her body was withered and gaunt.

And she smelled like death.

The severely frostbitten sections of her skin had turned black with necrosis and oozed foul-smelling green pus.

But there was nothing she could do.

She'd even been forced to make a corner of the tent her toilet...because of the animals.

Those goddamned infected animals.

Day and night, they circled her tent, enticed by the scent of her rotting flesh.

Day and night, the many legs on their tongues scratched against the thin nylon walls.

Day and night, she wondered when they'd get tired of playing and finally finish her off.

But it was the maddening scratches that bothered her the most. They taunted her—seemed to say, "You know you're going to die...but on our time." It haunted her, even in her dreams.

That incessant *scratch, scratch, scratch.*

...the last sound she'd ever hear...

MISS MOLLY, MISS MOLLY

TONY EVANS

9

MISS MOLLY, MISS MOLLY

By Tony Evans

"GOD*DAMN*!" SCOTT SAID, JUMPING as a loud crash of thunder shook the whole house. "Now 'at sounds like a storm!" He looked at Janet, who was sitting next to him, threw his arm around her, and squeezed. He could tell she was bored and that maybe she didn't like the storm, but he was also hoping that both of those factors would aid in accomplishing his ultimate goal for the night. He slid against her and squeezed a little tighter. "Looks like we ain't goin' nowhere tonight, baby. Not until 'is storm passes, anyway."

"Oh boy," she sighed. "Maybe it'll be quick." She hoped so, anyway.

"Oh, now don't you go worryin' about the storm. I ain't gonna let nothin' git ya, girl. Trust me." His smile was bordering on 'creepy old man' status, but it didn't surprise anyone. His intentions were obvious. He was, after all, a *guy*.

Janet smiled back. "Oh? What's gonna *git* me?"

"You never know, 'specially 'round 'ese parts. Whatever it is, though...you're safe as long as you stay right next to me."

Unphased by his poorly hidden perversion, she didn't seem to mind, pressing into him almost comfortably. Her boredom was evident, and, just like Scott and his perversion, she made no attempt at hiding it. She was from southern California, after all, and her Saturday nights typically involved more than just sitting in a house in the middle of nowhere with three people doing nothing during a thunderstorm. It wasn't really their fault, though, and she couldn't blame them.

They were supposed to have gone to a movie tonight, but the impending storm put a damper on those plans fast. It could be worse, she knew, but it could also be better. She liked her new friends, at least. They shared lots of similar interests, and usually they had a good time together, but she was still getting used to the slower life of small-town Kentucky.

Add a stormy night on top of that and things got even slower, *real* fast. She'd never been a fan of thunderstorms in general, especially bad ones. There was just something about them, something about the feeling they brought on that sort of spooked her. It was almost as if she could feel the change in the energy associated with them, and unfortunately for her, this one was supposed to be a doozy.

The local weather folks had been calling for the possibility of severe weather for tonight since earlier in the week, and as it turns out, it appeared that they got this one right. Some of the more energetic meteorologic personalities had even gone as far as to say that tonight's storm could be the storm of a lifetime, something unlike anything most of their viewers had ever witnessed; a storm unlike anything Pine Grove had seen for the last hundred years, maybe longer.

"Oh, shut up Scott. You're not scarin' her. She's not a baby," Kris said, shaking her head at his stupid attempts.

Janet chuckled. "She's right. If you're trying to scare me, it's gonna take a little more than that. I'm not sure a storm will—"

Thunder rumbled in the distance; a loud crack popped almost directly overhead, spooking Janet.

Kris glanced at her, a wry grin covering her face. "Is that right? Could've fooled me."

She chuckled nervously, embarrassed at how it had got her. "Really. I'm not scared. Thunder just kinda puts me on edge a bit. Not used to it, and if I'm being honest, it kind of reminds me of gunshots."

"Oh, yeah. I guess I could see that. Kinda makes sense, comin' from the city and all." Kris paused, considering the difference in the environments in which they'd grown up. Southern California had a different reputation than eastern Kentucky, at least that was what she'd assumed based on all the rap songs and television shows she'd heard and seen. They shot guns here, too...but it just wasn't the same. "Well, whatever it is, it'll be fine. It's just a typical summer thunderstorm 'round here. Nothin' outta the ordinary."

"I don't know about gunshots, but I'm not a fan of thunderstorms either, especially when they get like this." Her hands rubbing her arms, Rachel walked over to the window to get a better look at what was happening. The sun had set more than an hour ago, yet it was still oddly bright. The western sky had taken on a dark shade of reddish purple, almost as if backlit by the sun. Large, thick clouds engulfed the mountains as they forced over them from the head of Long Branch Holler. Her eyes widened; the swirling of colors almost hypnotizing as she gazed into the eerie darkness. It was almost as if she had to, almost as if she wasn't able to turn away.

She stared for a moment; the colors swirling together to form odd shapes in the clouds. Strange dark splotches mixed with the more vibrant hues almost making them look like they were dancing for her, almost like they were alive and begging for her attention. If she looked hard enough, just enough out of focus, she was nearly able to convince herself that there was something there. Something that wasn't supposed to be. Figures forming in the clouds, arms and legs loosely materializing to wave at and taunt her. For a brief second, she was almost certain that something was looking down at her, something alive, and that it was smiling.

What the...

She shook her head and squeezed her eyes shut, turning away from the window.

No. No, it's not...

"Whoa, now, girl! You okay?"

Startled, Rachel opened her eyes to see Kris standing in front of her. "Oh! Y-yeah. I'm fine. I just...never mind. It's stupid. I was just looking at the storm."

Kris cocked her head. "You sure? You seem a little out of it."

Rachel looked back at the sky. "Yeah, I'm sure."

"It's supposed to be a pretty big one. The storm, I mean. They're sayin' it's gonna be bigger than anything we've ever seen around here. I know you don't like 'em, so I just figured I'd ask."

"I know." She faced her friend, a slight grin, eyes squinted, looking almost confused. "Hey, Kris...is it just me, or does it look kinda...I don't know...strange out there?"

"Strange?"

"Yeah, like...it's nighttime, but it's still bright enough to see. I wouldn't even need a flashlight to get around if I was out there. It looks like dusk or somethin', not the middle of the night."

Kris leaned over and looked for herself. "I mean, it's a *little* brighter, yeah. Maybe it's the moon backlightin' the clouds or somethin'. I don't know. I ain't no weather scientist."

"The moon?" Rachel raised an eyebrow, skeptical of the probability of her friend's suggestion. "*Maybe*. The clouds do look a little weird, too, so maybe that's all it is. It's almost like I could see someth..." She caught herself, not wanting to draw any more attention. She already didn't like storms. Both Kris and Scott knew this, but they also knew why she was particularly nervous about bad ones."

"Do what?" Kris said, studying her. "Rachel...you know 'at stuff ain't real. They're just stories."

She nodded anxiously; a bit ashamed that she let the stories get to her so badly. "I don't know. I just thought I saw somethin'. I know it's crazy."

Kris looked at the sky for herself. The colors of the sky were magnificent. There was no denying that. Something was certainly different about this particular storm. "I don't see anything. It looks wild out there for sure, but I don't see anything like...well...you know."

Rachel shuffled her feet, wanting to believe her friend. Wanting to believe that she was just being a stupid scaredy-cat that let too many tales sink into her gullible brain. It *was* almost idiocy, after all...what she'd thought she'd seen. It was all just an old story people told to scare little kids in town. "Yeah, I know. It's stupid, but I just thought...you know what? You're right." She laughed it off, or tried to, anyway, until Scott caught wind of their conversation.

"Y'all ain't talkin' 'bout what I think you're talkin' 'bout, are ya?" He stood up, looking at them from across the room, a big dumb and cocky look. "It might not be so crazy. What you *think* you saw out there, I mean."

Rachel and Kris turned their attention. "Scott, stop it. She didn't say that. Hell, she wasn't even talkin' to you. Mind your own goddamn business for once, would ya?"

"Oh, come on now. Don't be a couple of babies. Besides, Janet ain't never heard 'bout her." He shot her a look, eyebrows raised. "I don't think, have ya?"

"No," Rachel started. "I didn't say a word, Scott. I was just sayin' it looked a little..." She took a quick look back at the sky. The air was still bright and colorful, but the swirling was gone. Just ominous and dark clouds pushing their way toward them. Nothing more than a storm. "It just looked a little weird, that's all." Her face was flushed now, slightly embarrassed.

"You *sure* that's all you was thinkin'?" he taunted.

"Yes. That's all. That stuff ain't real, anyway. Even if it *was* what I was thinkin'."

"Wait, what? Who haven't I heard of? What's not real?" Janet stood up and put her arm around Scott. "What are you all talking about?" She smiled, genuinely curious. It was obvious that the three of them knew something she didn't, which didn't surprise her. She'd only moved to Pine Grove six months ago, and the rest of them had been born and raised there. She hadn't had time to learn all the ins and outs of it, what to really say and not to say, or any of the local stories, even if it was a small as shit town.

Scott grinned. "*Yeah*! *That's* what we can do! *Hell* yeah! I don't know why I didn't think of it earlier!" He had a crazed look in his eyes, a mixture of arrogance and, oddly, horniness. Why not, though? They couldn't go anywhere, at least until the storm passed, and who the hell knew how long that would be? His girlfriend was bored out of her mind, that was obvious as fuck, and if he wanted any shot at finally getting in her pants, which was supposed to have been happening after the movie they now couldn't make it to, this was a prime opportunity to do it. It was one of the oldest tricks in the book. *Scare* her into bed! "Yeah, and this is the *perfect* night to do it, too!"

"Do *what*?" Janet said, eager to hear. "What am I missing?"

Kris looked at Rachel, eyebrows raised as she shrugged. She knew it wasn't going to set well with her friend, but if she were being honest with herself, it was better than doing nothing. She was bored, too.

Rachel, on the other hand, was anything but amused. She rolled her eyes, shook her head in dispute. It wasn't real, none of it was...it *couldn't* be. But there was always the question of *what if*?

"I'm up for it," Kris said, mouthing the words 'I'm sorry' to Rachel, hoping she wouldn't be too mad at her.

"Great," Scott announced.

"Up for *what*?" Janet said. "What are you guys talking about? Somebody tell me!"

"It's a game. Something folks around here play now and then when they're feelin' particularly brave."

"Oooo, that sounds fun! What kind? Like a drinking game?"

He shook his head slowly, attempting to build tension. "Nah, it ain't no drinkin' game. It's a scary one, and it's based on a story from around here. An old folk tale, you might say."

"Oh. Interesting. Well, I'm bored out of my mind, so I'm definitely up for playing."

They all looked at Rachel. She tried to ignore them, staring at the ground. They could tell she was nervous, but in Scott's eyes, that made it all the more fun. Made it better when somebody jumped scared her at the end.

"Well," Kris said. "How about it, Rachel? You down?"

She shuffled her feet a bit and looked up at them. "I...I don't know, guys. Y'all know how I feel about it and what they say about her. Especially during a thun—"

A rumble of thunder echoed in the distance and a sudden gust of wind rustled the dying October leaves.

Rachel jumped, her attention flinging to the window.

"Come on," Kris said. "It'll be fun! It's just a game, I promise. Besides, we've played before."

She walked to the window again. The sky was different now than before, a creepy sort of darkness. It was a darkness that somehow seemed to make the shadows almost pitch but left the open areas untouched, a darkness that seemed unnatural, almost as if the sun was shining through some kind of colored filter. "I don't know, guys. I'm up for about anything, y'all know that. I don't really like this though. I just think that maybe we should—"

A strong gust of wind rattled the house, causing a series of shifts and pops all around them. Lightning streaked through the sky and another crash of thunder sent vibrations through the floor. One by one, large drops of rain blew in on the wind, colliding with the glass as if begging for their attention. It was coming, and it wouldn't be long until it was fully on them.

"Oh yeah," Scott said. "This is gonna be *good*. As long as..." he glanced at Rachel, eyebrows raised. "You're good to play. You know we gotta have ya."

Turning away from them, Rachel huddled next to the wall. She didn't *want* to do it. It was stupid. But she didn't want to tell them no and make them upset. She didn't want to admit to them that she was scared, that maybe she saw something in the clouds earlier. She didn't believe it, necessarily, but she wasn't quite sure it was all made up, either.

Kris walked over and stood next to her, taking her shoulder and turning her around so they were eye to eye. "Come on, girl. It's just a stupid game, you know that. Just a way to pass the time. Besides, we *need* you to play. We gotta have four, remember? And I *want* you to play."

She scanned the room. Janet and Scott were both staring, hopeful looks in their eyes.

"How about it? We ain't got nothin' better to do. Storms gonna be too bad to go out for a while. Might as well see if we can make somethin' happen, right?"

"I just don't know. You know what they say about this kinda weather."

"I promise," Kris said, taking her hand. "Nothin' to be afraid of. You've played it before. We played a couple years ago at Aaron's party, remember? Nothing bad happened then."

Kris was right. They had played then, but it wasn't the same. There was no storm that night, but nothing had happened just the same. Rachel thought for a moment, then smiled, though it wasn't too convincing. "Okay. I'll play. I don't *want* to, but since the rest of you do, and you need four people, I'll do it. But just once."

"Fuck yeah!" Scott shouted. "I'll go grab some candles. Kris, can you get the matches from the second drawer, the one next to the fridge?"

"What can I do to help?" Janet asked, excited to finally have *something*.

Scott looked at her as he made his way across the house. "Just get ready to have some fun."

AS THEY ALL SAT down around a small circular table Scott used to play cards on, the wind began to pick up, stronger and more consistent, blowing from what seemed like every direction at the same time. With each gust they could hear the storm's breath howling at the seams of every window, almost as if it were prying at them with chilly little October fingers, desperately trying to get inside. Rain was coming down in sheets, the sound of it pelting across Scott's roof every few seconds in massive waves, drowning out nearly every other noise.

Scott struck a match and held it up to his face. The way the light darkened certain areas while accentuating others made him look creepy; the perfect look for what they were about to do. He lit four candles, placing one in front of each of them at the table.

"Okay. So, how's this work? What's the name of this game?"

He eyed them one by one for effect, then in a low, deep voice, he said, "the name of the game is Miss Molly, Miss Molly."

She pursed her lips, eyebrows furrowed. "Hmmm. Doesn't seem too scary to me. How do you play?"

"It's easy. You need four people in a circle, just like this. We all have to hold hands, close our eyes, and chant a phrase out. Pretty simple. The candles have to stay lit, though, or it won't work."

"Oh," Rachel said. "So, it's like Bloody Mary or something, is that it?"

"Kinda," Kris said, "but...kinda not."

Scott and her giggled. They were giddy with excitement.

"Well, I've played Bloody Mary a ton. We used to play it back in Cali when we were kids. Say her name three times in a mirror with the lights out and she's supposed to come for you, right?"

"That's how you play Bloody Mary, yeah, but you don't know nothin' bout ol' Molly Je—"

"Wait," Rachel said. She looked around the table, around the room, her eyes darting about, twitching like crazy.

"What is it, Rach? You see her already?" Scott laughed. "Hell, we ain't even started yet!"

"Be quiet, stupid," Kris replied, not wanting to make her friend feel any worse about her anxiousness.

"I just don't know that we should...I mean, with this storm and all, well...what if—"

Almost as if on cue, lightning flashed and the lights in the house flickered off, then back on again, several times.

Rachel screamed, startled by the thunder. "That!" she yelled. "What if the power goes out or something? Jesus Christ, w-we shouldn't be doing this."

"Wow," Janet said. "What's gotten into you? This must be some story, huh?"

"You don't know about her. You're not from around here," Rachel said. "People take it seriously. Scott, please. We shouldn't be doing this. You know what they say."

"It's okay, Rach. It's just a story, remember? Like I said earlier. It's just a game."

"Calm down, Rachel. Goddamn." Scott said, borderline scolding. "As I was *tryin'* to say before I was so *rudely* interrupted, it's a game based on a story 'bout a little girl 'at used to live up the holler here. Her name was..." He paused, looked around as if expecting to be interrupted again. He eyed Janet, staring at her with intent, and whispered the name. "Molly Jenkins."

They all fell silent for a moment, each of them exchanging glances with one another as the name rang in the air like a rotten fruit refusing to fall from the tree. It was one Scott, Kris, and Rachel knew, one they'd heard before, even if only in hushed whispers. It wasn't a name discussed often in Pine Grove, typically only used as a warning to those who dared venture in the wrong places, or by drunk or high teens tempting fate by playing the very game they were about to play while it was storming.

Molly Jenkins.

It wasn't that they really thought anything bad would happen, especially Scott or Kris, but they'd been conditioned with that name their entire lives, it was one that was as close to forbidden as you could get in their little piece of the world. Even the *thought* of saying it, the simple fact that Scott had uttered it out loud, was almost blasphemous. It didn't sound like anything out of the ordinary, yet...as it was spoken, goosebumps crept up their arms as a certain tension filled the room, a feeling that they'd started something there was no going back from.

Rachel swallowed hard. She immediately thought back to the color of the sky, the swirling clouds, the things she'd thought she'd seen in them earlier in the night. Figures. A particular figure, maybe? The stories. She shook her head, her breath still, nerves on edge.

No, she thought. *We can't do this.*

"Ooooo," Janet mocked, eyes wide as she laughed. "*Molly Jenkins*! What's so special about her?" She looked around the table, but nobody else seemed to be picking up on her attempt at humor. "Geez. Y'all *are* serious, huh?"

Scott nodded toward the window, his expression changing to a serious one. "Well, they's all kinds of stories 'round here, girl, but they ain't none of 'em like hers. You see, Molly was the youngest of four children...'at's why we need four to play, by the way...all of 'em used to live in a cabin way back up in the head of holler here. All her siblings were sisters, and they say 'at Molly was just a little *different* than they was."

"Different?"

"Yeah, you know, sort of off in the head. She had some kinda disorder, I guess. Probably ADHD or somethin' like 'at, but way back then nobody know'd what 'at kinda shit was. They say she was just *different.* That she talked to people 'at nobody else could see, all the time jerkin' and twistin' in weird ways, almost like bugs was under her skin and eatin' away at her brain. You know, just fuckin' weird. All her sisters used to make fun of her pretty bad, callin' her all kinds of names and just generally pickin' on her, takin' her stuff, laughin' and all 'at, especially the oldest. Boy, she didn't care too much for her from what they say, and you can figure how Molly didn't like it too much. She tried to stand her ground, but she was just too little, 'specially against all three of 'em."

"Aww, poor little thing."

"Yeah...*sure*! One day all four of 'em was out in the woods playin' around, gatherin' walnuts and such, when a big ol' storm blowed in outta nowhere. They say it was the worst storm Pine Grove had ever seen. Almost flooded the town 'at night, I reckon. Well, their parents took off lookin' for 'em, and 'bout halfway up the holler they heard a scream like nothin' none of 'em'd ever heard before." He gestured toward the window again. "They say everybody in the valley heard it, even over the hellacious storm goin' on. Some say it sounded like a mountain lion, others say it sounded like a woman. Some even said it sounded like some kinda monster, somthin' evil. Eventually, they ran up on the oldest girl. She was kneelin' on the ground in a puddle of mud on her knees a cryin' her eyes out. They tried askin' her what was wrong and where her sisters were, but she couldn't stop cryin'. Her momma hit the ground with her, tryin' to calm her down and get her to tell 'em what happened, where they were, but she just kept on sayin' the same thing."

"What?"

He took in a deep breath, pausing for dramatic impact, then let it out slowly. "All she'd say was 'at *He* took 'em."

"He? Who's *He*?"

Rachel shivered, standing to walk around the room as she shook her hands. "I don't like this story. It creeps me the fuck out. Especially—"

A rumble of thunder caught her attention over the pouring rain.

Kris jumped. "Tell me about it! I ain't heard it told 'is good in a *long* time, and the weather is making it even better!"

Scott nodded slowly, his eyes settling on Janet's. "Nobody knows who it is. Some folks believe it's Satan, but others reckon it's just a demon or warlock or somethin'. I don't know which one is more likely, but ain't none of 'em sounds too good."

"Wait...what happened to the other kids? Molly and her other two sisters, I mean."

A hard clap of thunder erupted, jarring the house again. Rain was falling harder with each passing second, the lightning flashing in rapid bursts, almost nonstop.

Janet's focus shifted to the window. She swallowed hard; the wind blowing at near gale force outside.

"'Round about midnight, right when the storm was at its peak, Mr. and Mrs. Jenkins heard they oldest daughter, the only one they'd found to that point, start screamin' from her room. She was hollerin', 'It's *Him*! It's *Him*!'. They took off to see what she was goin' on about, and when they opened the door, Molly was standin' there over her sister, soaked plum to the bone, both of 'em covered in blood, and Molly was fuckin' eatin' her sisters insides. They say she was holdin' organs in each hand, goin' at her like a starved savage. They screamed for her to stop, but when she turned around, they said it didn't look like Molly no more. Said her eyes was coal black and she was just grinnin' from ear to ear."

Janet's eyes widened. "Holy fucking shit. That *is* creepy."

"'Elp. Fuckin' *crazy* is what it is."

"What happened to her after that?"

"They say Molly jumped out the window and went off into the storm, cacklin' like some kinda animal or monster or somethin'. When they went out lookin' for her, they didn't find Molly, but they did find the other two girls on the ground below the window. At least they assumed it was them. They say they wasn't no meat left on 'em. Just a bunch of bones. Parents ended up buryin' the three daughters and leavin' town a few weeks later, and rightfully so. I'd imagine, 'specially back in them days, if somethin' like 'at happened, the whole town would shun you for witchcraft or some shit."

"And...Molly? I mean, how long could a little girl survive out in the wilderness like that all alone?"

Scott chuckled. "'At's the thing. A little girl, all alone, probably not too long, especially back then. But based on how 'at story goes, though, Molly was far from a little girl anymore. They say the storm brought somethin' with it 'at night, conjured up some kinda evil or somethin'. I told you, Molly was always said to be a little different, a little on the other side of normal. Some say she made a pact with the devil 'at night, some say she was possessed. Regardless, folks 'round here ain't too fond of bad storms, especially the older ones. They say that whatever it was 'at came in on 'at storm liked her. That it saw somethin' *different* in her and took her back with it. And still to this day, every now and then when we get a really bad one, they say 'at whatever evil it is comes on back, and they say it brings lil' Molly with it to take even more blood. They say if you look just right, you can see it in the sky, in the rain, smilin' at ya."

"Damn. I like this story."

"What can I tell ya, girl? They's just somethin' in the storms around here, somethin' different, like whatever was in Molly. And that's where the game comes in."

He looked at each of them sitting around the table. "Everybody ready?"

Kris nodded. "Let's do it."

Janet smiled, excited to see what it was all about. "I'm ready."

Rachel seemed hesitant but agreed, none the less.

"OKAY. EVERYBODY HOLD HANDS. We gotta make a complete circle."

Each of them took the hand of the person next to them.

"The point of this whole thing is to evoke the spirit of either Molly or one of her sisters. Again, 'at's why we need four people...'cause they was four of them. They say that if you can do that, you can find out what happened to her and who or what exactly it was in the storm 'at night."

"So, this is more like a séance, then? I see! Oh, this is gonna be creepy!" Janet shifted in her seat, ready to get the show on the road.

"Okay then. One at a time, we have to call her name. I'll go first and goin' to the left. Everybody needs to repeat after me. They's two phrases 'at we gotta say, and keep your eyes closed through it all. Got it?"

Everybody nodded. They'd all played before, except Janet, so they were familiar with the ritual.

"The phrases are 'Miss Molly, Miss Molly,' and 'What happened that night?'. And remember, keep your hands locked and keep the candles burnin'."

"Why?" Janet asked.

"Because," Kris said, an excited smile on her face. "If we break hands, they say she can possess one of us. Take us over."

"Just...don't let go, got it?" Rachel looked at Janet, dead serious.

Janet rolled her eyes. "It's just a game, but I got it."

"Okay, I'll go first, then repeat after me from left to right." Scott took in a deep breath and closed his eyes. "Miss Molly, Miss Molly."

There was a brief pause, then Kris chuckled. "Miss Molly, Miss Molly."

Rachel shook her head again, her voice low and nervous. "Miss Molly, Miss Molly."

Janet didn't hesitate. "Miss Molly, Miss Molly."

A massive wind blew another sheet of rain into the house, causing them to jerk. Kris laughed, followed by Janet.

"What happened that night?" Scott said.

"What happened that night?" Kris repeated.

Rachel cleared her throat and sighed. "What happened that night?"

Janet was jittery now, expecting someone to grab her or shout once she spoke the phrase, so she tried to mentally ready herself for the shock.

"What happened that night?"

A monstrous explosion of thunder sent a shockwave through the house, shaking every picture on the wall. The electricity flickered off, the only light remaining that of the candles burning. A strong wind rattled the door, almost as if someone were trying to knock it down.

Surprised, Janet jumped, letting go of both Scott's and Rachel's hands.

Before she even had time to react, before any of them could move, a cold sensation ran up the back of Rachel's neck, like fingertips dragging against her skin. There was a breath in her ear, icy and dark. Barely loud enough to hear, a voice whispered to her. "Let me show you."

The wind pushed harder, so much so the door gave way, bursting open. A sheet of rain covered the floor, soaking Rachel's back and extinguishing the candles.

"Holy *fuck!*" Kris shouted, jumping up to close the door.

"Jesus, that was fucking nuts!" Janet yelled with a laugh. "Goddamn! Really had me goin' for a second!"

Scott was doubled over with laughter. "That was perfect timin'!"

It was dark inside the cabin now, no electricity, no candles, the storm raging hard outside.

"You okay, Rach?" Kris asked. "I can't see anything in here."

"Hang on, I'll get some flashlights," Scott said.

"Rach?" Kris said again. There was no response. "Rachel? You okay?" She reached for her phone and pressed a button to illuminate the screen. She shined it toward Rachel's seat, but she wasn't there. "Guys, where's..."

She heard a noise in the corner of the room, barely audible over the storm. She felt gooseflesh cover her arms as her mind placed the sound. It was giggling, almost like that of a child. "Uhm..." she started, "Rach? Is that..." She turned on her phone's flashlight and shined it toward the noise. In the corner, there was Rachel, or at least what used to be Rachel. She was hunkered down in a ball, staring up directly at her, an unnaturally sinister grin stretched from ear to ear. Kris screamed, dropping her phone in the process.

"What?" Janet shouted, turning toward her friend. "What's wro...what the fuck is that?"

The way Kris's phone had landed showed the scene perfectly. She saw her friend lying on the floor, her legs and arms twitching frantically, almost as if she were having a seizure. But it was no seizure. On top of her was...something, someone...drenched to the bone. Whatever it was had its face buried inside Kris's neck, blood gushing onto the floor with every beat of her weakening heart. It looked up at her, stringy, wet hair draped to the sides, crimson liquid dripping from thin, pale lips. Its eyes were pitch black, haunting and emotionless, that same fucked up smile searing into Janet's brain.

"Scott!" she cried, staggering back into the wall. "Scott, please, help!"

The thing that used to be Rachel let out a cackle as it cocked its head sideways and scurried across the floor like a cockroach.

"Help me, please!"

Scott came rushing back into the living room, flashlight in hand, and shined the beam at Janet. "What's wro...holy *fuck*! Wh-what *is* that?"

It glanced toward Scott, the beam directly in its eyes. It didn't seem phased by the light, letting out another deafening laugh. It shot toward him instead, blood and slobber dripping to the floor as if it were a rabid dog. He glanced at Janet, who was still pressed against the wall and crying now, then back to Rachel, or rather to the thing she'd become, as it closed the distance between them. He turned to run, making it as far as the opening to the kitchen, but there was no escaping.

Janet watched as it jumped, leaping through the air like a wild beast, hands latching onto Scott's shoulders, feet kicking into his legs to force him to the floor. The flashlight flew from his hand and slid across the floor, it and Kris's phone the only sources of light in the place.

Janet was still from shock, tears streaming down her face like a busted faucet. The beam wasn't directed at them this time, but she could see their movements in the shadows. A hand rose and came down, striking Scott, almost in slow motion, the sound of his clothes tearing as claws tore into them, the sound of his flesh being ripped from bone amplified by the adrenaline coursing through her body. Snarls and gulps as whatever she now consumed him, piece by piece, bite by bite until the screaming stopped.

Janet placed a hand over her mouth, attempting to quiet herself. Her erratic breaths, the sounds of snot gurgling in her nose and throat, not helping to conceal her location, as if she'd ever been truly hid. A rumble of thunder erupted overhead, catching her attention, and she looked toward the door. She knew it was her only chance. She had to run, had to try. Across the room, she heard Rachel giggling, the sound of claws clacking against the floor as she moved. She caught a glimpse of a shadow moving. It was only a matter of time until it came for her, too.

Janet let out a scream and bolted for the door. Rachel ran for her, nearly catching her ankle just as she opened the door and pulled it closed behind her. She could hear clawing from inside as Rachel scratched away, doing her best to get out. The doorknob jiggled, the door itself rattling as she did her best to hold it closed, but the rain had soaked it, making it impossible to get a solid grip. Her hand slipped, and she stumbled backward, her feet trying to find purchase on the steps but failing.

She hit the ground hard, water splashing up and over her face on impact. Her hands found her eyes, rubbing and wiping away the mud. She rose and saw Rachel standing on the edge of the porch, crouched down on all fours, still smiling. She stopped, afraid to move. What if it was like a cat or something? What if it was waiting on her to move so it could pounce? As the rain came down in a torrential downpour, Janet watched as Rachel's focus shifted from her to something in the sky.

Pushing herself to her feet, she slowly turned around to see what was happening. The lighting was strange; it was night, but hints of red and purple brightened it just enough for her to make something out. There, in the sky in front of her, a figure began to take shape. It wasn't in the clouds, no. It was closer, almost close enough for her to reach out and touch. It was taking the shape of a person, almost as if the rain were falling over someone invisible who was floating there, breaking their silhouette. She wiped her eyes again as she tried to make it out, squinting and squeezing them open and shut, trying to clear them of water.

She shook her head hard, one final attempt at gaining better focus, and opened her eyes for the final time. The figure in the rain was standing in front of her now, an odd face taking form. Dark blotches in the place of eyes and mouth, the areas in between streaking water as if it were made up of the storm itself. Its arms to the side, it made no attempt to reach for her.

It just stood there, staring at her, staring through her. She looked at them for a brief moment, drawn in by something stronger than her own willpower. She wanted to look away, but she just couldn't. Her body and mind wouldn't allow it. For a moment, if she looked at it in just the right way, she thought she could see something in there, something deep inside those hollow eyes moving around. Little girls, maybe?

No...

Her heart began to accelerate even faster than before, and the figure began to laugh. "Miss Molly, Miss Molly," it hissed. "What happened that night? Show this young lady, won't you?"

Behind her, Janet felt a searing pain pierce her neck as Molly laughed.

WILDFIRE

KATE KINGSTON

10

WILDFIRE

By Kate Kingston

The line of slow-moving cars coming toward me has my hindbrain alarmed, and I'm fighting the instinct to turn around and join them. My heart keeps skipping beats, my arrhythmia triggered by this stress, and my vision keeps tunneling out. Driving through the orange haze of smoke is a thousand times worse than watching the evacuees trying to escape on the news, and my sense of self-preservation is flashing more red warning lights than my dashboard.

I know my engine is probably choking on the particulates in the air and I'm worrying about the same thing everyone going in the opposite direction is: what if the car dies before I escape? I'm the only person driving toward the fire, though. What if I am burned alive, here in my car, or gagging for a final breath on the pavement? I've spent more than enough time with my psychiatrist to know that I should not be doing this, but I feel like I have no choice. This is my last, my best, my only chance at finally healing.

Visibility is bad, as bad as the worst snowstorm or fog I've ever seen, and I'm driving faster than I should on the empty side of the highway. A siren wails behind me, its swirling red and blue lights cutting through the haze, and my heart drops into my stomach. I'm being pulled over. I haven't been pulled over in years, and I know I wasn't speeding, but I also know that I'm not supposed to be driving toward the evacuation area.

With one hand on my chest trying to calm my pounding heart, I ease my car to the highway shoulder and slow to a stop. My pulse is beating so rapidly that my ears are roaring. My hands are tingling. My fingers grip the steering wheel too tightly. I'm forcing myself to take deep breaths. I will not cry. I will not cry.

An officer taps my window and motions for me to roll it down. He is wearing a respirator, and all I've got is the flimsy blue face mask I left in my centre console after the pandemic for 'just in case' moments. I wonder momentarily if I should put it on, my panicked mind thrown back to those lockdown days when masks were required everywhere. It's 2023. You don't need a mask.

"You need to turn around. Ford Valley is under evacuation orders." He reminds me of Darth Vader, barking through his respirator, waving at the long line of traffic crawling along bumper to bumper on the other side of the grassy divide. The smoke is so thick that I can't make out any faces behind the windows. I can see flames in the distance, now that I'm focused in that direction.

My jaws clench and spit gathers in my mouth as I fumble for a response. I could just be reasonable and turn around at the next paved patch used for emergency vehicles and join the evacuees. That would be the sane thing to do. At this rate, they would be dead before too long anyway, but I wanted to be there to see it happen. I needed to. Something switched in my brain and I burst into tears.

"Please, officer! My grandparents are stuck in their house. I'm the only one who can get them to safety! They called me begging! I can't let them die!"

Where had that come from? I was quite a little actress when I wanted to be, but these tears felt genuine. The officer thought so too, because his tone changed to one with more compassion.

"I'm sorry to hear that, miss. Where do they live? I can have an officer ride out to pick them up if they're within a kilometer of the burn line."

I don't want an officer to save them. I want to watch them die.

"They're just off the next exit, actually, and they won't go with anyone else! They're usually under the care of a full-time aide, but they said she left to pack up her own family this morning. They were crying! Please, I can be quick–"

A loud crash across the divide pulls the officer's attention away and I see flames jump from the front of a car that has rear-ended the one in front of it. I wouldn't have guessed that they were traveling fast enough to cause such damage, but I see my chance and I take it. I press my foot down on the gas pedal and speed away, leaving the officer standing in the middle of the empty lane behind me. Praying there is no roadblock ahead, I push the engine to its limit, topping out at 180 km/h, faster than I've ever driven before.

I'D LIED TO THE officer; my grandparents live at the eastern edge of Ford Valley, just below the treeline of Mount Verna, where the wildfire is headed. I have no idea if I'll make it there, but I have to try. I skip the next exit and slow down, sure the officer is not following me. I take the next one and drive through the downtown core, which looks like something out of Silent Hill. A substantial layer of soot has already landed on every surface, turning everything deathly grey. I can taste the smoke in the back of my throat, and I realize I've been coughing since leaving the officer behind. The paper mask is wound around my gear stick, and I tug at it clumsily, hoping the ear elastics are still intact. Thankfully, they are, but I'm not sure it's going to help me breathe in this situation. I put it on, anyway, piloting my car with one hand, hoping for a little psychosomatic relief.

The shopping district ends abruptly in Ford Valley. I sail through the red light at the last intersection knowing there are no other cars around and begin the steep climb up Sydenham Road to my grandparent's subdivision. It's even harder to see through the smoke as I drive up the slope at the base of the mountain, and I start to worry that I'm already too late. Both of them are sickly. They have been for a long time. My grandmother has cancer again, in the bowel this time, and my grandfather has been on an oxygen tank for years thanks to a lifetime of cigars.

I remember sitting at the dinner table with him as a kid and watching the scab from his oral cancer fall off his lip and land on his plate of baked beans. He'd huffed a small laugh and continued eating without fishing the scab out, grinning while he watched my reaction. I was horrified, but I didn't dare cry. I knew better than that; I'd always known his behavioural expectations, and what his punishments were if he wasn't happy.

I hadn't been up this way since I was twenty-one years old, the year I started remembering things and separated myself from them. My mother had shut them out that year, too, her own memories triggered by the questions I was asking her about my childhood. I'd thought I was losing my mind at the time; anyone would if they were having memories like those, but years later, a psychiatrist confirmed for me that he'd treated seven other women in the area for the same abuse by the same people. The world wide web was just getting started then, so my online search for other evidence or survivors was fruitless, but I couldn't deny my memories after that doctor told me I wasn't the only one reporting the same things.

Approaching their street now, I feel the urgent need to pee along with a piercing pain between my legs. Body memories. Nausea rises quickly and I stop the car in the middle of the road and throw the gearshift into park. I take off my seat belt and open my door, leaning out just in time to avoid vomiting on myself. It splashes onto the silent pavement and smoke billows into my car, filling it quickly. I spit the last of the vomit out of my mouth and inhale deeply, which is a mistake.

The smoke chokes me and I cough hard, my eyes watering. The force on my diaphragm makes me throw up again, but I'm struggling to breathe at the same time and it dribbles down my shirt. I pull my door shut and turn on the air conditioner, thinking that maybe the air circulation will help, and it does help a little. It helps enough to allow me to get my bearings and put the car back into drive.

That self-preservation instinct is trying every trick to make me stop and turn around. My brain spits out one scenario after another, all of them ending with me burning in the approaching flames, unless I turn the car around right now. My head hurts. A tight band squeezing it from the base of my skull through to my sinuses. My chest feels like there is a fifty-pound weight crushing it. I know I need to make a decision and get out of this smoke. Before I can make that decision, I realize I'm already pulling up to their house. Every nerve in my body is on fire, and I know I'm bouncing back and forth, trying to escape my body.

One moment I'm fully aware of every tiny thing my body is doing, and the next I'm floating above myself, watching that body experience yet another panic attack. I've been told I'm lucky I learned how to do this, that it likely saved me a lot of pain over the years. It does feel good to float above, out of that body that I cannot control, and I've often wished I could just stay this way. That's probably one of the reasons I've attempted suicide so many times. Just like every other time it's happened, though, some unseen force draws me back into my body and I blink in confusion. It's jarring.

It only takes a split second to feel lucid again, and I'm surprised to see another car in the driveway. I'd made up the story about their phone call, but it looks like their aide is still here. I assume that's who the car belongs to, anyway. I haven't spoken to them in more than twenty years, but my mother allowed them back into her life a few years ago and is relentless with unwanted updates about their welfare. I have no idea why she forgave them, or how, but I never will. That is why I'm here.

After decades of therapy, I'm still a fucking mess. I am forty-three years old, have been divorced twice, have never held a job for longer than six months, can't stand looking at myself in the mirror, am broke, and have attempted suicide twelve times. Sure, some of those attempts were half-assed, but I've been hospitalized twice with close calls. I'm such a failure, I can't even kill myself properly. I consistently alienate friends, helicopter parent my adult children, and pretty much just hate myself every minute of every day. I am a waste of space. Or, as my grandfather used to say, I'm bad, I'm ugly, and I'm stupid. No one will ever love me because I'm unloveable, and if I try to tell anyone what he did, my mother will die and so will I.

MY MOTHER CALLED ME this morning, crying, asking me to turn on the news to see how close the wildfire was getting to their house, but she lives even farther away than I do and was freaking out, feeling powerless because she couldn't get to them in time. I consoled her but did not offer to try myself. When I hung up, she was supposed to be trying to contact the authorities in Ford Valley to tell them that her immobile parents were trapped, but I have no idea if she did so. Watching the news footage was enough to snap a fragile branch in my mind and get me into my car. They were finally going to die, and I wanted to be there to see it happen.

I park my car on the street and walk up the drive to their front door, but I can't make myself knock. I'm paralyzed on the cement porch, eyes watering in the smoke, my brain shutting down again. I'm thrown back to my childhood, and the smell of their living room invades my senses, the memory of it alive and well in the corner of my mind that makes me cower when triggered. Every home has its own funk, and theirs was distinct: a blend of dusty drapes, old wood resin, roast beef, and "old person" decay. We stayed with them for eight weeks during the summer of my twelfth year, so the smell is deeply etched.

My sister and I had shared a bedroom in the basement, but she was always out with our mother when my grandfather paid me his special visits. He'd been doing it for so long by then that I was already broken. The sickest part of it that summer was that my mother took my sister out to shop so he could have access to me. She knew it was happening and made it easier for him. Sure, they'd brainwashed her to comply when she was a kid, but it's still mind-boggling to understand how a mother's protective instinct could be so off-line.

I shake my head to clear the memory and open the door without knocking. Although the air inside is smoky, it's much better than the outside and I allow myself a moment to stand there, back pressed against the door, and just breathe. Feeling slightly refreshed, I can think again. I look around the dimly lit room and am stunned that nothing has changed. It's the same dusty furniture, the same Hummel figurines, and crocheted doilies, the same forest green carpeting. My grandfather's lounge chair looks a little worse for wear, but it's still pointing at the same old television with dials and bunny ears. I hear footsteps coming down the hall from their bedroom and my knees clench. I'm aware of the muscles in my back tightening and I can hear my heart thumping. My blood pressure is probably dangerously high.

A woman walks around the corner and frowns at me.

"Who are you?"

I put my hands up, palms facing her in the international symbol of "I mean no harm" and tell her.

"I'm Sandy, I'm their granddaughter. I'm here to evacuate them."

The woman, Rosetta, the personal aide my mother has talked about, I assume, looks too relieved to question me.

"Oh, thank goodness! I called for an ambulance three hours ago but who knows when they'll get here!" She's stepping from one foot to the other and flapping her hands like a kid who needs the bathroom, and I don't know if she's waiting for me to give her permission to leave or not but I offer it, anyway.

"Oh, thank you! Janet!" she calls down the hall from where she stands, "Your granddaughter is here, she's going to get you out of here, okay?"

I step aside to let her into the hall closet where her purse and jacket are hanging. "I live in Riverview, and we just got the evacuation order, too. I need to get my kids out of there! Bless you and be safe!"

Rosetta is out the door and in her car before I can respond, and I find myself frozen in place again. What am I doing? I'm not seriously going to watch these people die, am I?

"Hello? Rosetta?" I hear my grandmother's frail voice calling from down the hall. Her bed springs squeak, and I know she's about to put her slippers on and shuffle down the hall. She was already shuffling when I saw her last, bent over with osteoporosis. I don't know what I'm going to do yet; I haven't thought about how this will go down. Part of me is screaming to leave and run for my car, but there's some other twisted part that's been patiently waiting for retribution and right now it's stronger than any other sense. I put one foot in front of the other and walk toward their bedroom.

Family photos line one side of the hallway, pictures of my cousin and his children, but there are none of my mother or my family. On the other wall, there are oil paintings that my grandfather made years ago, of tall ships with billowing white sails and red-painted barns in pastures. They are quite good, and just part of his disguise as a 'normal person'. Anyone visiting this house would assume that my grandparents were good, God-fearing folk. He is a high-ranking Freemason. She bakes pies for church sales.

'It's really too bad,' they'd say, 'that their daughter is a bad egg. They'd worked so hard to provide a good home for her. It was unfair that she treated them so badly. My teeth grind with anger.

Their bedroom door is open and I pause, unsure how I'm going to react when I see him again for the first time in so long. I imagine him withered and weak, laying prone under one of their thin summer quilts. I listen, waiting to hear the heavy breathing that still haunts me. When I hear someone breathing like that, I go into panic mode, fight or flight. I get nauseous, I cry, I can't breathe, and my brain screams at me to get away, get away, get away—

I don't hear him. I've folded my lips into my mouth and I'm biting down hard, and I know I'm shaking. I don't have to do this. *Yes, you do.*

My body leans forward at the waist and peeks around the corner to find my grandmother sitting on the edge of her twin bed. The other one is empty and perfectly made. I blink but have no words. She looks so small, her face wrinkled like an apple doll, her white hair sparse and patchy. She squints at me, and I know she has no idea who I am. She seems unaware of what's happening outside as well.

"Who are you? Where's Rosetta?" Her dentures are clacking, too big for her mouth. I answer her without thinking.

"It's me, Grandma, Sandy. Marie's daughter."

Her brow furrows, and she shakes her head. "No, you're not. Sandy is dead. She died a long time ago."

That stings. This woman allowed them to torture me from the time I was two weeks old until I was five, and then let her husband do what he wanted to me until I was fourteen after the group decided I didn't have the powers they thought I would. She kept three kinds of ice cream in her basement freezer so I could choose what kind I wanted as a reward when he was done with me. Now to hear that she'd killed me off in her mind instead of showing any remorse—What had I expected, though?

"Well, then I'm back from the dead Grandma, because it's me." I'm trembling. "And I know what you did."

Had I just said that? My face feels numb, and my fingers are tingling again. I feel like I'm slipping out of my body, rising above it. An immense pressure is building behind my eyes, and there's a moment of pure darkness before the light comes back and I am again floating above my body.

Dissociation. My best friend in times of severe trauma. My psychiatrist said I wasn't just lucky that I could do it, but that it also explained why all of my memories were from the ceiling's point of view. Now I'm watching myself speak to my grandmother, but I can't control my words or my body. I've never said or done anything while in this state before, and the realization of what's happening, what has potentially been happening for a long time, has me terrified. Someone else is at the wheel.

"What-what do you mean? I haven't done anything!" Janet is clutching her nightgown fearfully now, the soft cotton material wadded between her gnarled hands against her chest.

"We both know that's a lie." I say, lowering myself to sit on the other bed facing her. I watch with enough detachment that it doesn't hurt, but I'm grappling with the idea that I may have other personalities that have been hiding in the deep, dark recesses of my psyche. I also have one eye on the window behind her where the smoke has gone from grey to black.

"I don't know what you're talking about." She says and tries to push herself up to stand. It takes a few tries, and when she's finally almost upright, I push her back down.

"Oh really? You don't remember letting him play with me in his special way? Watching Jeopardy while he gave me baths? Baking cookies while he took pictures of me in his den?"

Her brows furrow as I speak, and her mouth twists, lips pinched tight.

"How about what he did to Mom? All those things and more? And how about his secret club? He wasn't the only one who liked to play with little girls, take pictures, was he?"

A look of recognition flits across her face, and I know I've broken through her dementia.

"Ah yes, you do remember. I can see it on your face."

"You enjoyed it, Sandy. You loved the attention."

I watch as I freeze, eyes wide, shocked into silence. I'm still floating above myself, watching this unfold like a movie, and I gasp as I stand up and punch my grandmother hard in the face. Part of me wants to cry, the part that did have a few happy memories with her as a child. I remember going on shopping trips on the bus and picking out new clothes for school, and making microwave popcorn on sleepovers at her house when it was a brand new thing, but I know now that those memories are false. The emotions I attach to them are false, anyway. They are the emotions of the child who was blocking out reality and clinging to every normal moment she was dealt. My grandmother helped other people abuse me, even in her own home, and now she was saying I'd wanted it all.

I keep hitting her until I hear her cheekbone crunch, and then I hit her again.

"This one's for the time you came down to the fruit cellar for a jar of jam and found him force-feeding me a mason jar full of yellow spiders." CRACK!

"And this one's for the special tea you used to make me before sleep that knocked me out hard enough to make it easy for him to take me out of bed and put me in the back of his car in the middle of the night." CRACK!

I know I've passed the point of no return, but I'm not done.

"This one's for letting him do it to my mother!" CRACK!

Blood is gurgling in her mouth, and the right side of her face has caved in. I watch as I step back and let her drop on the bed. She's alive, but not for long. I snap back into my body and my eyes fixate on the window again. In my mind, her body is not there. It's an empty bedroom, and the fire is getting closer. I really should leave, save myself, but I know he's here somewhere. I turn and leave the bedroom to search the rest of the house.

I PASS THROUGH THE living room into the kitchen and flashback to holiday dinners prepared and eaten there. I can smell the roast again, and the gravy burning on the stove. People are laughing around me, enjoying each other's company, and children are squealing with excitement. It feels joyous until it doesn't. I walk through the kitchen to the basement door and open it, its creaking sound both familiar and ominous.

He's breathing behind me, snorting in air through nostrils lined with bushy white hair, exhaling through his open mouth. I can hear spit moving around in his mouth, dripping between his teeth as he smacks his lips. He's prodding me forward, but I don't want to go. I look down and see my little feet in white stockings, and then sideways at my chubby hand carefully holding on to the rail. The steps feel huge to my adult mind, but my body was so much smaller, then.

He steers me by the shoulders toward his workshop at the end of the basement hallway, its open door gaping in the darkness. I'm numb, and not paying attention. He nudges me through the doorway and closes the door behind us, leaving the room in total darkness for a moment before pulling the chain attached to the fixture in the ceiling. This is just part of his game. He loved scaring me. I'm huddled next to the washing machine beside the door, and he's moving toward one of the woodworking benches against the far wall. When he gets there, he opens a red toolbox and takes out a magazine.

"Come here, Sandy, you're going to love this one." I stay where I am, watching his back as he shifts his current project out of the way and takes his camera off of the top shelf. He removes the lens cap and checks the settings, and I can hear his snorting breath from where I stand. When I don't move, he turns slowly and growls. He sounds like a snarling dog, threatening, and it's my cue to do what I'm told. I move toward him slowly, and he turns back to the magazine, picking it up to flip through the pages. He groans when the centrefold flips out and slips one hand into his pants. I move like a robot, no sense, no feeling. He turns back to me, grinning, showing me a picture of a woman with her legs spread wide open, the tip of one stiletto heel partially inserted into her vagina.

"We don't have shoes like that, but this will do." He holds up a long wood file. "Come on, Sandy, you're going to look so pretty!" He picks me up and sits me on the bench in the space he's just cleared and pulls at the toes of my tights. Upstairs, I can hear my family laughing and talking, having a wonderful time.

Now, standing at the top of those stairs, I am filled with dread. I have so many memories from each of the rooms down here, and it's hard to bat them away long enough to focus on what I'm doing. I hadn't planned to kill my grandmother, and I don't honestly feel like I did. Someone else did. I just watched. I think I'd assumed it would be smokier in the house, and they'd both be almost dead when I got here. All I'd wanted was to watch the last wisp of life leave their bodies, but clearly, I hadn't thought it all through. What am I going to do when I find him?

I look in his den first, but he's not there. The old black filing cabinet is still tucked into the nook under the stairs, and I flash back to the day my mother and I broke into their house many years before, looking for proof of what we were remembering. We didn't think we'd find proof of the cult, but he had taken so many pictures that maybe he'd kept some hidden away to play with over and over again. We found them in that filing cabinet, in an old shoe box. Combinations of men, women, and children posed or performing lurid acts. It was all there. We didn't take the photos with us, but we never spoke to my grandparents again. Or I didn't, anyway.

On the other side of the hallway, there is a rec room, and it looks very different from the way it did the last time I saw it. My aunt, my mother's sister, lived with them for a few years and must have brought her own furniture. She lives out west now with her newest husband and must have left her furniture behind. It's mind-warping to see this one room differently after walking through the time capsule upstairs, and I pause to take it all in. A modern television is mounted to the far wall, and a newer L-shaped couch sits across from it. There are more oil paintings on the walls, but most of these are hers.

She got my grandfather's artistic ability. Just beyond the rec room is a small kitchen that was never renovated, and I can taste the Vernors' soda in my mouth. It was the only place we were ever allowed to have soda, and Vernors was my favourite. Behind that kitchen was a bedroom. The bedroom. The one my sister and I had stayed in for eight weeks when I was twelve years old. The one he'd played his games in so often that summer that I developed a raging urinary tract infection. There was no real door to the room, just a flimsy folding plastic divider that slid on a track in the ceiling. It's still there, cracked and peeling, and it's closed.

I give myself one more chance to stop, to turn around, and let the encroaching flames do their job, but I can't move. Panic forces me out of my body again, and I watch as I reach out to fold the divider back and look into the room. The room. It slides with difficulty, halting as though caught on something, but it does part to reveal a plastic sheet hanging from ceiling to floor. It's clear, and it crinkles when I touch it. Beyond the plastic I hear beeping, and I smell antiseptic. I push the plastic to the side and there he is, laying in a bed, attached to a hospital-grade electric blood pressure cuff. He's sleeping, his oxygen mask in place. They must have moved him down here when the smoke started to drift the month before, a safe space for the poor old man with breathing difficulties.

He's a lot smaller than I remember, too. In his prime, he was overweight, with a full head of black hair and eyebrows like caterpillars. He stayed large even after his bowel was removed in the late 80s, which largely contributed to his heavy breathing. Now, he's probably less than half his normal size, and he's bald. I barely recognize him. If we passed on the street, I don't think I would know who he is. Being this close to him now, even though he's asleep, all of my alarm bells are ringing. I may not be in my body, but the stress is so high that some of the panic is stretching through my tether and I desperately want to leave. Below me, though, I'm staring at him menacingly and my fingers are curling in and out of fisted balls.

I could easily push a pillow over his face and be done with it, but where's the fun in that? I watch curiously as I back out of the room and go into the old workshop, trailing myself like a ghost. I reach up and pull the chain light on without looking for it, and move toward the workbench on the far wall. I pull the red toolbox out from under the bench and blow the dust off of it before popping the silver latch and opening it. I lift out the top tray and move tools aside until I find what I'm looking for, the long metal file. I hold it in both hands for a moment, almost reverently, then turn back toward the bedroom.

His eyes are open now; I probably woke him up when I was digging through the toolbox. His gaze is fuzzy, and I wonder if he's on pain medication. He knows I'm there, but not who I am or what I'm doing. They're clouded with cataracts now, but that sliver of blue through his drooping lids is enough to send me reeling. I'm thrown back to my childhood, rapidly reliving everything he did to me.

I SEE MYSELF AS a toddler wrapped in my blanket, waiting at my kitchen door in the middle of the night for the car to appear. My mother is standing behind me, rubbing my arms through the blanket to help me keep warm. She woke me up when she got the call and led me down to the kitchen so we could watch together for the men to arrive. They always called when my father was on a night shift at the tire factory, carefully planning these excursions for when it would be easiest to take me. When the tan-coloured station wagon with wooden side panels pulled into our driveway, she hurried me out the door and down the steps, then opened the back door and watched as I got in. The men didn't speak to me as we drove away, they just chatted between themselves and smoked one cigarette after another.

I see myself another time, sitting in the back seat of that same car, watching a group of adults digging in the ground. We're in a cemetery, and I'm wrapped in the same blanket. I can see their clouds of breath in the night air and I shiver, wishing they would hurry up. When they finally come back to the car, they're carrying something heavy. They open the back hatch and dump it in, and it's heavy enough that the car bounces with its weight. I can smell dirt and something else, a stink that grows stronger when they close the hatch. I won't dare look, though. I'm supposed to be sleeping.

I'm in my body this time, laying on a cold stone floor, peeking out from under my blanket. I'm dizzy and tired, but I smell fire. I know I've been here many times before, but I can't remember anything else. There's someone else under a blanket beside me. I can hear their muffled breathing. From its steady pace, it sounds like they are sleeping. *Are they small, like me?* I see feet moving around, all of them covered in dress-up shoes and peeking out from just below white gowns. A familiar stink makes its way under my blanket, and I close my mind down. *Go to sleep, Sandy, go to sleep.*

I'm crying and gagging, but they're making me do it. The man smells bad, like dirt and rotten meat, and he's cold. There's something wrong with him. They say I have the power to wake this man up, but the way they're making me do it is horrible. His skin keeps slipping off in my mouth.

I'm standing under a tree and a cool summer breeze is making my night-gown sway, tickling my skin. There is thunder in the distance, and they're all standing around me in a circle, chanting quietly. I raise my arms and watch as the branches of the tree sway violently. The circle chants louder and the branches creak against one another. I feel like electricity is coursing through my veins, and I know I'm making the tree move, and that's what the people want me to do. I'm magical, and they worship me.

I'm laying on a table and I'm strapped down. My small arms and legs strapped down at each of the four corners. The men have all lined up and are taking turns.

I'm in my grandparents' garage, sitting on his lap, and he's lifted my shirt up. I'm only twelve, and he's touching me, telling me that my breasts are too small, they're ugly, and no one will ever want me.

I'm curled in a ball on my side, crying desperately, knowing that I'm worthless. I've embarrassed my grandfather. The cult has kicked me out, and now I'll have to pay for it with my skin.

I watch as I pull back his blanket, his colostomy bag full and needing changing, and remember going to see him in the hospital after his surgery. I'd been terrified, and my mother was crying, but when I saw that he was asleep, I relaxed. He wouldn't be able to look at me if he was sleeping.

I think I know where I'm going with that wood file now, but the man has no anus. It was sewn shut when they removed the last of his intestines and colon. The me who is down there with the file realizes this at the same time and grunts like an animal. I could slap him into full consciousness and tell him who I am, and why I am here, but I don't.

Rage takes control and I plunge the file into his chest. It's not sharp, but he's frail and I'm mad. The file sinks between his ribs and his eyes fly open in shock. He raises a hand to block me, but I'm faster and stronger and ready to pull him apart with my bare hands if I need to. I throw all of my weight into the next strike, and I hear his sternum crack. Blood bubbles out of his mouth and I stab him again, and again, and again, blinded by years of anguish and tears.

I stand over his bloody body, heaving for breath as my tingling muscles begin to give way, the adrenaline rush quieting before my thoughts can catch up with me. At some point in the attack, I climbed on top of him for better leverage, and now that I'm back in my body, I'm repulsed by what I've done. I look down at his face and feel vomit rising again, threatening to spill forth into the holes I created in his torso.

FLAMES LICK THE SMALL window above the bed, and I know it will only be moments before the thin glass panes smash inward under the pressure, and I will be consumed along with his corpse. I don't know if I blanked and more time has passed than I think, or if the fire was closer than I thought when I arrived. It's here now, and I don't know if I can escape.

I stand there on the bed, his body between my feet, and I weigh my options. I have been a waste of space my whole life, and the world would not miss me. I'm middle-aged. I've worked more than fifty jobs in my lifetime because I can't stay anywhere longer than six months before having a meltdown. I have no children. I drive a beat-up car, live in geared-to-income housing, have no friends, and I'm broke.

I can't stand looking at myself in the mirror. According to my psychiatrist, I'm the only one of his patients who was abused by this cult that has survived this long. The rest either killed themselves or went into prostitution and got killed. *Am I worth saving?* I don't have any power. Not the kind they wanted me to have, and certainly not over my own life.

Yes, you do, Sandy, you do have the power. We just hid it, so they'd leave you alone.

My heart stops for two beats, and I feel a flush of electricity flooding my entire body. It feels familiar. Part of me wants to disassociate again and fly free, but the others won't let me.

Stay, Sandy, feel it. Use it. You're strong. We're strong. Bring down the fucking house.

I raise my arms above my head, touch the ceiling with my fingertips, and howl. Head back, throat wide open, howl, and my fingertips begin to sizzle. I look, and I'm making black streaks on the paint, burning lines into it as I pull my fingernails across the plaster. I dig them in and howl again, directing the electrical charge coursing through them and into the house.

The window above the bed shatters and flames quickly eat through the curtains on either side of it, licking the ceiling just a few feet away from me. I charge myself again and send another bolt of power through the ceiling and into the house. I hear the structure screech in protest; wood, and nails grinding together under the unrelenting roar of the fire outside.

Flames jump to my hands and down my arms and I scream in pain, but I do not move. I throw my power over myself like a blanket and force it to spin. The flames engulf it and spin with it, but they don't touch me anymore. I'm standing in the eye of this swirling firestorm, and I'm controlling it.

I hear crashing above me and know that the roof has collapsed. Its thunderous demolition sealing my fate. I'm trapped with my grandfather's corpse unless I can hold the fiery tornado in place long enough.

A hand grabs my ankle, and I lose my focus, dropping my shield. My grandfather is grinning at me. His face is blistering in the heat. The oxygen mask held in his other hand. I feel the flames eating my clothes and skin and pop out of myself just in time to watch both of our bodies burn.

Above the house now, I'm rising ever higher until I'm looking down at the wildfire. The conflagration is massive, spanning more hectares than I can guess, and I don't see anyone fighting it. It doesn't matter to me now, though. Nothing matters anymore. I don't know where I'm going, but I'm finally free.

WOLF LIKE ME

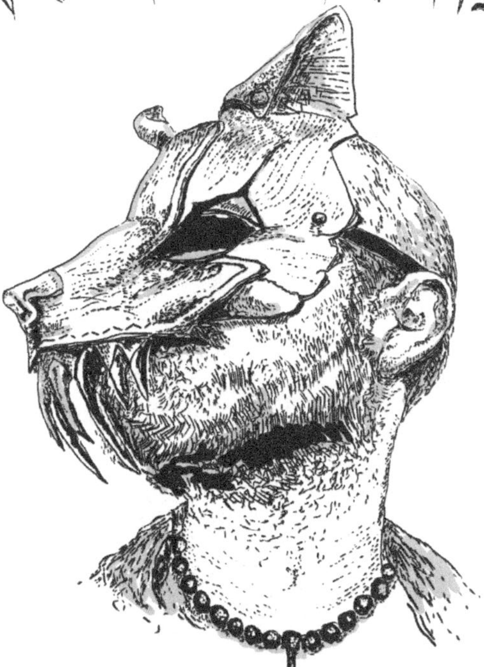

REBECCA ROWLAND

11

WOLF LIKE ME

By Rebecca Rowland

A THOUSAND NEEDLES FELL from the sky, each one seeming to embed itself in Howard's forehead as he half-ran, half-slid across Congress Street, the large brown envelope tucked under his arm like a papier mâché football. It was early November, too early for proper Boston snow, and so, in a cruel joke, the gray sky projectile-vomited a grab bag of rain, sleet, and hail, shellacking the streets with a half inch of clear ice that shut down the above ground trains for two days straight.

The storm was merely a nuisance for Howard, whose bachelor loft on Atlantic Avenue kept him detached from any reliance on the subway, or a car, for that matter. He walked to work, keeping his own hours since deadlines often stretched well past the last running train, and when the wind tunnel that shot along the wharf severed his spine each morning during the winter months, he found himself reminiscing about the days when the newspaper's offices were housed in Dorchester.

The bars were more pleasant on the South Side, full of townies who knew when to keep their mouths shut. The financial district, on the other hand, catered to a different clientele: yuppie twenty-somethings with cell phones permanently tattooed on their palms. In the warmer seasons, Howard watched them scurry across State Street, their necks bent forward like tower cranes, never glancing up, and he wished more often than he could count that a car would sideswipe one of them, just to teach the lot of them a lesson about entitlement and basic common sense.

In an act of morbid coincidence, a brown delivery truck shimmied dangerously close to Howard then cut suddenly toward the tunnels, the sharp change in direction threatening to topple its boxy frame before the vehicle righted itself and disappeared down an access road, its engine echoing off the cement skyscrapers in the stark silence. Howard stopped a moment and scanned the street. He was the only pedestrian in sight, even though the sun was hours from setting. If the truck had mowed him down, it could have escaped with impunity, leaving a smattering of Howard under its wheels and along much of Haymarket.

Howard shook the water from his shoulders as he stepped inside Hennessy's. In one fluid motion, he waved to the bartender, peeled off his overcoat, and tossed the package onto the bar in a wet thud. Although the rain had smudged some of the lettering, the newspaper's address and instructions to deliver only to Howard were still clearly visible.

Ernie, the bartender, turned the envelope a quarter clock and studied the writing. "*I know that after my departure, savage wolves will come in among you, not sparing the flock. Acts, twenty to twenty-nine.*" He frowned and pointed to the verse carefully printed underneath the return address. "What's this, now? Lancaster Correctional? Inmates sending you God from prison?"

Howard pushed his disheveled hair from his forehead, then grabbed a cocktail napkin from a nearby dispenser and mopped his face with it. "Guess the Second Coming doesn't translate well digitally," he quipped. Howard scanned the place; two patrons sat kitty-corner at the other end of the bar, and they both side-eyed him suspiciously before returning to their whispered conference. The tavern was a virtual ghost town, not unlike downtown since the storm began. Howard nodded politely at the two men and continued. "I have quite a following at Walpole, actually."

Ernie shrugged and poured a heavy hand of Maker's Mark over a pair of ice cubes in a rocks glass. "Who knew?" He rested the bottle on the bar and crossed his arms over his chest. "Looks like a bit more than a single page letter, there, though."

It was true. The envelope was heavy, solid. In the old days, a secretary opened all of his mail for him—a particular blessing when Howard had angered the mob or the police with one of his polarizing columns. Now, hand-written or physical correspondence was infrequent and Howard spent much of his mornings sifting through emails. "Mailroom guy caught me on the way out," Howard said. "I was too damn lazy to bring it back up to my desk." He ran his index finger along the meticulously arranged postage stamps running in three even rows.

Ernie wadded up the bar towel and tossed it into an unseen bin near his feet. "The suspense is killing me, Howie," he deadpanned. "Open that sucker up. Here—" He ran his hand under the cash register, pulled out a box cutter, and offered it to the writer, who took another swallow of his bourbon before accepting the blade.

Inside of the packaging was a stack of yellow legal pad paper. A quick thumbing through revealed that each piece was covered—on one side only—with writing: large, even block lettering in bright blue ink. On the first page, the author had noted the date exactly one week earlier. Howard patted his shirt pocket and placed its contents, a well-worn pair of drugstore reading glasses, on his nose, then cleared his throat and began to read out loud.

Dear Howard:

I apologize for the familiar tone, but I feel like we know each other already despite having vastly different starts in life. I was born in Danvers, just a stone's throw from the ocean. You, on the other hand, are from the western half of the state, along the New York border, if I'm not mistaken? And yet, we both landed in the big city, opposite sides of the same coin.

I've followed your work for some time now. As you're well aware from the return address, I'm an inmate at Souza-Baranowski Correctional. In here, most guys have a radio or sack out in front of the common area television for much of the day, but me? I'm a reader. Every morning, I line them up and knock 'em down: *The Globe*, *The Herald*, even the *Worcester Telegram*. Every night, it's the Good Book. When you have all the time in the world to go looking, it's easy to find Jesus: Turns out, he *was* hiding under the bed the whole time.

I wish I could say that my block mates were as literate—or as in touch with the concept of a Higher Power—as I am, but that isn't the case. We're in here for the long haul: lifers without parole. Do not pass 'Go', do not collect two hundred dollars. Talk of eternal life isn't always so interesting when you're smack dab in the middle of an eternity, I suppose.

The guards call us guys on Block 5 the Wolf Pack. I read somewhere that dogs—you know, the kind you keep as pets—used to be wild like wolves. That's kinda what society does when it throws men in prison: a kind of...forced house training. Up on Block 5, though, each of us is a wolf to the core, a special kind of predator that can never be domesticated. We're fascinating to study from afar; you should see the fan mail some of us get. Every year, there's a roll call of graduate students from the psychology programs at Clark or Suffolk requesting interviews. Every year, it's the same chorus line of broad smiles, the same hostess gifts of fixed stares and firm handshakes. They try to deceive me with their false flattery, but I won't be swayed. Each autumn when their Birkenstocked militia comes bearing questionnaires, I think of Matthew, chapter seven: "They come to you in sheep's clothing, but inwardly they are ferocious wolves."

If there's one thing I know, it's that you can't out-wolf a wolf.

For instance, for a while, there was a guy on Block 5 named Samson. He was a deaf-mute, but that's not what got him caught for his crimes. He was too easy to pick out of a lineup, I think. Samson had a scar, a long, deep one shaped like a bird's leg, snaking along his right cheek. None of us spoke sign language, mind you, so in order for Samson to be understood, he kind of pantomimed what he wanted to say, often waving his arms dramatically to get his point across.

Samson's neighbor in the next cell was a man named Dennis. He was chatty enough for the two of them, plus a couple of stragglers. Dennis also had a mean temper and a short fuse, and one afternoon, he snapped, held Samson down and tried to saw the man's hands clean off. It was a full seven minutes before the guards pried Dennis off of poor Sam, splayed like a rag doll on the linoleum, one hand flipped backwards one hundred-eighty degrees, his wrist gaping open like a puppet mouth frozen in silent scream.

After that, we gave old Dennis the nickname Delilah. We never did find out where he'd gotten the blade, but he spent a month in the hole for the assault while Samson recovered in the infirmary, his heavily bandaged forearms thrust out in front of him like an offering. Delilah had managed to sever the nerves to one of Samson's hands. From that point on, Semaphore Sam was one flag short when he talked. No matter. Within a week after returning to the Block from solitary confinement, someone jumped Delilah in the showers and cut out his tongue in repayment. Samson wasn't a made guy or anything, but everyone liked him well enough, and pack members take care of their own. We'd all gotten frustrated with his frantic arm-waving at one time or another, but the thought of Delilah silencing him for good, well, it didn't sit quite right with any of us, so as far as we were concerned, Delilah's tongue had simply fallen out on its own.

I used to visit Samson when he was holed up in that ward. When I told him what happened, he watched my lips carefully, then kind of smiled, crinkling the edges of the deep crease stenciled along his cheekbone. A few years later, they opened the cage for old Sammy, let him out on parole. Compassionate release, they called it. Delilah, however, is still here. Sometimes, when he wants us to know something, he waves his hands around like a chorus boy in one of those old timey musicals—

"WHAT DID THIS GUY do, send you the rough draft of his sappy memoir?" Ernie interrupted. "Who is he?"

Howard put the letter down and checked the return address on the envelope. There was no name in the upper left corner, only an inmate number. He flipped back the pages of the yellow paper until he reached the end of the correspondence. "It's signed Daniel. Another damn Bible verse, then *Yours in the Lord, Daniel*," said Howard.

Ernie picked up a glass and began to polish away a lipstick mark that had escaped the dishwasher's tongue. "What'd ya do to piss this one off?" he asked. "I mean, you've mentioned some of the hate mail you get."

Howard tapped his index finger against his glass. "This reads differently. I get all sorts, you know? Manifestos from the nuts, sticky adoration from the incel fanboys. This is neither. This is—" He frowned, then flipped back to where he had stopped reading. "Something else."

HOWARD, I REMEMBER WELL the series you did on the Catholic priest scandal back in the late 90s. I still have a few of the clippings taped to my wall. They're yellowed and frayed in places, but one can't help the ravages of time. I've been on Block 5 for more than three decades: I, too, am yellowed and frayed in places. It takes a bit to get acclimated to a cell. Today, I'm grateful for the slice of daylight that streams through my frosted window each morning. In the beginning, I teetered in and out of solitary, and for a time, the warden fixed his gaze on my inhabiting the hole permanently, what with my fits and starts—but I am a quick learner.

And one must learn patience and self-control to get along. Zephaniah, chapter three, states, "Her judges are wolves at evening; They leave nothing for the morning." As a young pup, I thrived in my anger, let it well up inside me, and unleashed my rage unfettered, but all it earned me was a ten-by-seven pen. That doesn't mean that my thirst has dried up; I've simply learned to bottle my wrath until an appropriate time.

After high school, I wavered between odd jobs and hopped around moth-eaten bedrooms. I didn't mind the transient life; I imagine you, Howard, have come to appreciate it as well. With no family to answer to, it's easy to live out of a satchel slung over your shoulder. Sleeping on a couch at the office, sleeping on a stranger's sofa: they aren't much different. I never wanted to be tied down to anything. I've never owned a car. At twenty-three, I was still hiking or hitching. It's what landed me in this cell in the first place.

I needed to get west, head out to a buddy's place in Fitchburg, so I hoofed it to Waltham and tried to thumb my way down Route 2. It wasn't long before a guy in a brown Chevy pulled over. He was an average-sized guy, doughy in that dad sort of way, with a hefty paunch choking to death under the strain of his belt and two-day-old beard stubble scuffing up his cheekbones. "Name's Rolly," he said after I slid onto the bench seat next to him. "Rolly like a cinnamon roll," he added. "I have a bit of a sweet tooth."

I shrugged, not sure what to say to that, but I sure appreciated the ride, so I nodded politely as we sped down the two-lane highway and the city disappeared, swallowed by pine trees with tips that tickled the sky and rest stops designated as scenic areas. Rolly talked the entire way, showed me pictures of his family: his thin, blonde wife and equally thin, ghost-eyed daughters, all of them too old to be wearing pale pink from head to toe but doing so anyway in an endless montage of holiday photos.

We were almost to Leominster when he suggested we pull over. I didn't understand at first; I was only a few miles from my destination. Couldn't he wait just ten more minutes? "I have a hankering for something sweet," he said, and I felt an invisible finger trace the center of my spine. He parked in the furthest spot from the road, under the shade of a thickly leaved elm, and as the engine cooled, it made a ticking sound, a subtle drum beat to accompany the whistle of the wind.

"Relax a little," Rolly said, unbuttoning the top of his collar. "Let's just take a minute to enjoy the day." He turned around, reached his hairy arm over the scratchy upholstery, and fumbled for something in the back seat. When it didn't emerge immediately, Rolly turned back to me and winked.

He winked.

I knew what that meant. I had no money to pay him, no drugs or party favors to barter with, and like they say, it's gas, grass, or ass. The Book of Habakkuk talks of being "keener than wolves in the evening." I was keen to what he wanted, but I wasn't going down without a fight.

Before Rolly could reposition himself, I wrapped my hands around his stubbly neck and squeezed for as long as I could hold him. I had taken him by surprise, and while instinct clamped his meaty hands atop mine as we struggled, a pungent wet stain grew in the crotch of his khakis. When at last his body went limp, I released my grip and fumbled for my knife. Since high school, I'd carried that switchblade, though I wasn't careful enough to keep it clean and dry, and the edges were slightly rusted in patches.

It took me hours and a couple of rounds of fisticuffs with my driver when he awoke screaming, but I managed to flay the skin off most of Rolly's body. Each time I peeled a strip, I threw it in the back seat until I overshot a handful and had to lean over to retrieve a wet piece stuck to the back window. It was then that I saw the box of doughnuts in the back foot well.

In the end, Rolly looked ridiculous: a wolf shorn of its fur. The state police found me wandering down the interstate, blood-soaked and exhausted. It took me years to come to the Lord after that, but once I did, He showed me a sign in the form of Father James.

I'd been at SB-C for fifteen years by that point. I'd grown used to the smell, so much so that when they let me out for my time in the yard each day, I began noticing the subtle shifts in scent that wafted through the outdoor air: the clean smell of winter approaching, the slight musk of the first spring day. The day they brought Father James to the facility, the air smelled like a storm was approaching: not the earthy, warm petrichor of a summer rain, but something slightly sharp—crisp and humid simultaneously. The sky was a light gray, without a wink of blue, and the light that shone through the clouds made everything appear slightly muted, like an image on an old television set.

We'd known Father James was coming; everyone followed the case in the papers, and I, for one, had a vested interest in his fate. You reported on it yourself, Howard: more than one hundred and thirty documented cases of sexual misconduct—and those were the ones for which the Church kept records—but only one tried. The jury found him guilty in a matter of hours. Another wolf, it seemed, had been trapped by the net.

And yet.

Father James wasn't placed on our cell block. No, the defrocked priest received only an eight- to ten-year sentence, a slap on the nose with a rolled-up newspaper. He'd be home, curled up by the fireplace, before the decade was over.

And yet.

Father James didn't smell like the inmates outside of Block 5. He smelled like us. That's how I knew what I had to do. That evening, as we gathered in the mess hall at dinner, the rain increased in ferocity, changing its theme music from a monotonous tap to a lunatic's ranting. The temperature plummeted, transforming the precipitation from water to slush and ice. It clung to the ground with sharp claws, turning the nearby interstate and access road into a makeshift hockey rink.

We gathered around the television in the common area, watching the news reports of pile-ups and road closures, overextended hospitals and warming shelters. Travel was nearly impossible, we learned, and the guards on day shift crew would be forced to stay until DPW salting trucks could catch up and their replacements arrived. It was a "perfect storm" of sorts—not the infamous one in '91 just north of you in Gloucester, but one of divine omen just the same. Something pushed me back to my cell, instructed me to open the Bible the missionaries had sent me on the first week of my sentence. I opened the book at random and peered down at the words. It was Ezekiel, chapter twenty-two: "like wolves tearing the prey, by shedding blood and destroying lives in order to get dishonest gain." Father James had preyed upon children. He had not merely maimed them but killed a part of their souls, permanently altering the trajectory of their lives forever, and the Lord told me what I must do in vengeance.

I found him sitting alone in his cell, thumbing through a magazine. I wish I could tell you it was something with dramatic resonance, like an issue of *Boy's Life* or the NAMBLA membership newsletter, but it was more likely *People* or *Vanity Fair*. I recall Ben Affleck staring blankly up at me from his resting place on Father James's blanket when they dragged me from the cell twenty minutes later. When Father James saw me enter, his expression did not change, as if he had been expecting me. He removed his reading glasses and hung them on the lip of his sink. Before he could say anything, I closed the cell door and wedged beneath it the heavy doorstop I'd purloined from the infirmary.

When I turned back to face him, the former minister was on his feet. Father James was old—elderly, really—but alone in that cell, he crept nimbly like a cat, as if an invisible puppeteer had pulled the gaunt and crooked husk of a man to rigidity rivaling that of a spry Marine. I pounced on him, and he fell backwards against the toilet. I wrapped my hands around his neck. The skin there felt loose, crepe-like, and I almost expected it to peel from his musculature like a Halloween mask. I pressed my thumbs deep into his throat, feeling his arterial pulse pound against my own. Father James's arms flailed wildly, slapping my face and scratching my skin, and I pulled him forward and threw him to the ground.

The old man coughed, a wet sputtering sound like gravel through a playground slide after a heavy rain. I stopped to catch my breath, to listen for what the Lord wanted me to do next, but no instruction came. Instead, the guards began to bang against the cell door, ordering me to open it. I looked back at Father James, still lying prone on the ground, and that's when I saw it. The slight grin tipping from the corners of his mouth. To this day, I don't know what generated that countenance, what the man possibly could have been thinking about to warrant such an emotion, but it was the signal for which I had been waiting.

I sprang with both feet onto Father James's torso, landing squarely on his ribcage. I jumped again and felt the bones crack beneath my feet. I repeated the action, stomping and crushing, again and again, as red and black blood spouted from Father James's mouth, his hard shell melted into soft pulp, and my feet made wet, squishing sounds with each landing. When the guards—

"Holy shit!" Ernie yelled. "This is from the guy who killed that pedophile priest in prison?" He grabbed Howard's empty rocks glass and filled it with fresh ice. "What'd that guy get? Another life sentence? Claimed insanity, if I remember right." He filled the empty space around the cubes with bourbon and slid the glass back to the columnist. Behind him, the two men at the other end of the bar were suddenly silent. One checked his watch, then fished a dark cap from his jacket and wrestled it onto his head.

Howard accepted the glass and drained a healthy swallow. "Yes," he said. "Yes, that's what this appears to be." He frowned and let his eyes skim the rest of the sheet he was holding.

"Well, don't stop now," said Ernie. "I gotta know what this guy wants. Maybe he's angling to have you write a book about it. Now that would bank some serious cash."

Howard looked up from the pages and held the glass up in a mock toast. "Since after retirement, Social Security won't be enough to cover my tab, I'd say we'd both profit from that kind of deal." He took another sip, but something dug at the back of Howard's mind. His intuition scratched at him, but he smothered the itch with a third swallow of the alcohol.

The patron wearing the hat tossed a fat wad of cash onto the bar and nodded at Ernie before exiting, his companion in tow. The bartender thanked them and began to clear their abandoned area, stacking their empty glasses into the dishwasher and wiping a rag over their corner. Within minutes, every trace of his only other visitors to the bar had evaporated.

Howard flipped quickly through the remaining pages. "There are only a few more left," he said. "Top me off and I'll finish it for you."

Ernie did as he was instructed, and Howard cleared his throat and continued.

EVERYONE KNOWS THE MOST famous aphorism: "I am sending you out like sheep among wolves. Therefore, be as shrewd as snakes and as innocent as doves" (Matthew 10:16). It always makes me sad to read that piece of the New Testament. Sheep are one of the most docile of all the animals on Earth, and perhaps that's what makes them the most vulnerable. Maybe that's why what Father James did bothered people so deeply. He fed upon the prey that came to him willingly. Then again, that is its nature: "the wolf will dwell with the lamb" (Isaiah 11:6).

I hadn't known about the wolves until I was fifteen.

I was a decent kid up to that point. Never drank or did drugs. I didn't steal or give much grief to my parents, though, truth be told, they weren't around often enough for me to bother. School was never easy for me, however, and I was too shy to make many friends outside of the ones with which I'd been forcibly shuttled in yellow bus seats. One January morning of my freshman year, some older guys in my neighborhood told me they were ditching class to head down to Somerville, maybe play some games at the arcade in Davis Square, and they asked if I'd like to come along. As soon as we got there, though, the two picked up a couple of girls they knew, and I was the odd man out.

They had driven us down to the city, but I didn't mind hoofing it home. I could always catch the bus at North Station, I reasoned. The day was cold, and it was clear, but, Howard, you and I have lived in Massachusetts our whole lives: we know where that story ends. The old adage *Don't like the weather in New England? Just wait a minute!* doesn't do the area justice. The weather isn't simply transient; on some days, it's damn near schizophrenic. A day or two of eighty-plus temps in November will trick rosebushes to re-bloom only to be suffocated by a frost the next morning. While a snowstorm rages in one town, just over the city line, it's sunny as a spring wedding. Unsurprisingly, as soon as I made to Medford, it began to sleet.

I'd worn a hooded sweatshirt, but the precipitation only increased in velocity, and soon, I could feel a cold wetness grow heavy on my head. The wind picked up, and a laminate of ice began to form on fire hydrants and sidewalks. I fumbled in my pockets, running my fingers over the coins there. I could not afford a cab, and the commuter rail would be a stretch if I needed to pay for a bus to the station.

And then, as if summoned, he appeared.

The 1970 Monte Carlo, with a diamond shine paint job of indigo black, its hood long and curvaceous as a college cheerleader, pulled up beside me just as I passed the Italian deli on Main. I didn't pay much attention until the driver rolled down the passenger window and yelled for me to come closer. He wasn't much older than me—twenty, maybe twenty-two years old at most—with shaggy blond hair and an oversized incisor that was painfully visible when he smiled.

"Hey, you need a ride?" he called, stretching from behind the wheel his lupine body over the long, gray bench seat.

I glanced down the street in front of us. In the distance, the sky was even darker, a sure sign that the storm would only worsen as the day progressed. I pushed my hands deeper into my pockets so that the knuckles met over the bump of my coat's zipper. "Where're you going?" I asked in response.

The man turned his head to look through the windshield, then returned his focus to me. "I'm headed home. Got me a few six-packs and some girls waiting there, but I'm afraid I can't handle all those women at once. You want to help a guy out?"

I laughed self-consciously. I'd never even had a date with a girl, never mind acted as an overflow ditch for a deluge of them. And the most beer I'd drunk was a couple of sips of PBR from my uncle's can at family holidays. "Me?" I clarified.

The man shrugged. "Sure, sport. Hop in." He flashed that game show host grin again, the fang seeming to grow even longer.

I lifted the silver door handle and climbed inside. As I furiously rolled the crank to close the window, the man tossed a can of beer into my lap. "Chug-a-lug, partner," he said. I expected him to start driving, but he simply sat there, staring at me, until I pulled back the tab on the beer and began to drink. The rain continued to pound on the roof, and soon, the view out of the windshield turned slightly distorted as the rivers of rain slowed and froze drowsily in place.

We stayed parked there until I finished my can; then, he handed me a second and cracked one open for himself. "Let's motor," he announced, then put the car in gear and drove off, despite the building layer of ice obscuring much of his vision. His apartment was nearby, on the second floor of a two-family in Winter Hill, but by the time we arrived, I had finished the second beer, my legs had grown wobbly, and my head danced.

"This is it," he said, pulling up on the emergency brake and shutting off the engine. He pretended to pause in thought and opened another can. "One more before we head up. You know, to lighten the load." He handed the open can to me, and I gulped down my third beer as he sipped coolly from his first. By the time I followed him up the rickety driveway toward the house's entrance, I'd polished off the rest of the six-pack. The world had wandered away from its axis and was spinning ever so slightly, and I had to hold on to the man's shoulder in order to keep upright while negotiating the slick terrain.

He slipped his key in the lock and half-guided, half-pulled me inside and up the narrow hardwood staircase. When we finally reached the top, I was strangely exhausted. All I wanted to do was lie down and take a short nap, and before I could stop the words from gushing forward, I told the man exactly that.

In response, he did something I've never been able to wipe from my memory. He winked, a small smile leaking out from the corners of his mouth.

There were no girls in his apartment. There never had been.

And by the time I was allowed to leave, there weren't any sheep left, either.

I never told anyone what happened in that apartment. By the time I got home that night, it was late, nearly midnight, but my parents had gone to bed without an inkling of concern over where their only son might have disappeared. And that *is* what happened: I disappeared, a magician's sly trick. I climbed into that shiny Monte Carlo as Daniel, but I emerged from that apartment as someone, something, very different indeed.

HOWARD HASTILY SHOVED THE yellow papers back into the envelope, crushing the pile into an angry origami mess. The reading glasses slipped from his nose and toppled to the bar. He reached for another cocktail napkin and wiped the condensation on the side of his glass, then pressed it to his forehead. The room spun.

"Hey, there was something written on the back of the last page—" Ernie began, reaching out toward the bloated envelope.

Howard pulled the parcel out of his reach and stood up, awkwardly tugging on his coat. "I'm not reading any more of this horseshit. I'm packing it in for the night, Ernie," he groused, pulling out his wallet from a side pocket. Instead of bothering to count out the bills, he folded it back up. "Mind adding it to my tab?" he asked.

Ernie nodded. "Careful out there, my friend. Weatherman says it's not set to melt until at least tomorrow."

Howard tucked the envelope inside his coat and held it in place with his free arm. "I'll take it slow, Ernie. Thanks."

Outside, the sun had set, leaving the streetlights to glimmer like holiday trimmings against the sheen of the frozen landscape. Howard took a careful step forward onto the sidewalk and felt his gait slide a bit. He took a second step, carefully redistributing his weight so that he would not topple forward. With the additional drop in temperature, the reduction in light, and, of course, the generous sloshing of bourbon in his bloodstream, the trek proved more treacherous than it had been earlier. Howard was concentrating on staying upright and focused his vision on the ground in front of him, so when the two bar patrons appeared around the corner, he did not see them until their shoes came into view.

Howard stopped and stared at the two men. One was nondescript, of average height and weight, with a dark winter cap covering his hair. The other was taller. He tilted his face slightly to the left so that it was perfectly visible in the gaze of the streetlight. A thick scar that branched like a bird's leg covered his cheek.

Howard turned to run, but his feet slipped out from under him, and he dropped like a stone on the pavement, his kneecap cracking like an egg as it struck the ice. Before he could scream, the man in the wool cap was upon him, holding one hand over his mouth while he pinned Howard's upper torso to the ground with the weight of his body.

The deaf-mute's left arm hung lifeless by his side, but with the other, Samson reached nimbly into his coat and removed something from an inside pocket. Howard watched in horror as the former inmate lifted the cleaver high above his head before slamming it down onto Howard's left forearm, severing the bone. Howard screamed, the muffled screeches pouring down the slick streets like water, then echoing as they sloshed along the empty alleyways. Samson repeated the motion, driving the knife through Howard's right arm. Red arterial blood gushed from the abbreviated limbs, forming crimson puddles that mingled with the melting layer of the ice below as the disarticulated hands lay completely still mere inches away.

The man in the wool cap stood up, leaving Howard writhing in agony on the ground. He pulled a large handkerchief from his jacket pocket and wiped the spray of blood from the side of his face, then cleared his throat. "Daniel asked us to tell you, *If your hand causes you to sin, cut it off*," he said, his voice even. "*It is better for you to enter life crippled than with two hands to go to hell, to the unquenchable fire*. Matthew, chapter five, verse thirty."

He wiped his hands on the cloth and held it out before the man holding the knife. Samson twirled the soiled cleaver around the handkerchief, efficiently wrapping the weapon, and gingerly placed the bundle into his inner pocket. He nodded wordlessly to his partner, and the two men walked slowly away, disappearing into the darkness of a nearby side street.

The world turned black as the sky spit slivers of frozen rain onto the columnist's shivering face. And Howard continued to scream.

PS: As I WRAP UP this letter, I have noted the weather forecast. It's a good chance by the time you receive this, Howard, a terrible storm will be walloping Boston, and who knows? Maybe it will be an ice storm, one just like the day that car stopped me on my walk toward the bus in 1980. Just like the day Father James and I had our last tussle. Be careful on your well-trodden path down to Hennessy's Tavern...or to your loft on Atlantic Avenue.

You ask yourself how I could possibly know your routine. Like I noted earlier, Block 5 has quite the fan club, lots of pen pals salivating at the chance to chat with one of the wolves, admirers more than willing to provide the kind of information only those on the outside can provide. Not to mention debts to be paid.

Wolves beget wolves, they say, and it's true. "For everything in the world—the lust of the flesh, the lust of the eyes, and the pride of life—comes not from the Father but from the world" (1 James 2:16). You're a wolf like me, Howard. May the Lord bless you and keep you. You made me what I am, and for that, dear columnist, I owe you a debt I intend to pay in full.

I hope you accept it with gratitude.

NO SHELTER

KRISTOPHER RUFTY

12

NO SHELTER

By Kristopher Rufty

Brianna Troutman could feel her father's elbow digging into her ribs. Grunting, she tried to scoot over, but the closet didn't grant her the room she needed.

Why couldn't we have a storm cellar? Or a bomb shelter?

A room with space to take shelter in. And snacks. Maybe a generator.

That'd be awesome.

She was half tempted to go out into the house like her grandfather.

"Why do we have to hide in here if Grandpa is staying out there?" she asked.

A pale shape that she figured was her mother shifted in the tight space. "Because he's stubborn, and we're not. This is the safest place."

"And he has that big air tank," said Dad. His breath was hot and smelled slightly of coffee. He'd been drinking a cup when the power went out right after a loud lightning crash.

Hurricanes sure are fun.

Brianna almost started to cry. She was fifteen and was about to start school again in two weeks. Being hit by a massive hurricane at the end of her summer break was not how she wanted to spend the little bit of time she had left.

"He could go a little while without the air tank," said Mom. "It's his *stubbornness.*"

"Where would we have put him?" Brianna asked.

Nobody had an answer for that.

In the silence, the wind sounded like a train rushing by close enough to shake the structure. Even this far inside the house, she could hear the tree branches outside groaning under the consistent, heavy gusts.

"It's about to hit," said Mom. "Should we pray?"

Brianna rolled her eyes because she knew her parents couldn't see her.

"I told you we should've cut those damn branches," said Dad.

"I like the shade," said Mom.

"Still..." Dad huffed. "I keep waiting for one of those big limbs to crash through a window or break through the roof. The way that damn wind's blowing out there."

"They're not *that* close to the house."

"Well, they're close enough. I can hear one tapping against the house right now."

"It's not ta—" Mom stopped talking.

Now Brianna could hear it too—a faint, steady rapping sound from the front of the house. Didn't sound like the noise a branch might make against the house.

"What *is* that?" Mom said.

"It's a branch. Probably snapped on the tree and is scraping outside."

"Would it stop and start like that?" asked Brianna.

They listened some more. There was no tapping now.

She heard her father take a breath as if he were about to speak, then stopped when the tapping started again. It went on for a couple seconds, then stopped.

"Someone's at the front door," said Mom.

"Somebody's out there!" Grandpa's voice boomed from the other side of the door.

Brianna jerked, nearly squealing. She hadn't even heard him wobble up to the door.

"Are you sure?" asked Dad.

"Yes, I'm sure. I may be old, but I'm not senile. I can still tell when somebody's knocking on the front door!"

"I'd argue against that," said Mom, under her breath.

Dad sighed. "You've never liked my father."

"You've always known that. Why so surprised?"

Brianna didn't want to be stuck in the middle of one of their stupid arguments, especially cramped together like this.

"They're still out there!" Grandpa said. "Sounds like they're asking for help."

"Oh, for the love of it all," said Dad, getting to his feet.

"Where are you going?" asked Mom.

"To see what's up."

"But the hurricane..."

"Doesn't matter if I'm in here or out there."

"It'll matter if the windows blow out! Just stay in here. They'll go away, eventually."

Ignoring Mom, Dad opened the door. Though there was no light on in the hallway, it was still brighter than the cave-like darkness inside the closet. Brianna squinted against the dim luminosity as she got to her feet.

"And what are you doing?" asked Mom.

"Stretching my legs." Brianna still wore the shorts she'd slept in with a T-shirt she'd kept from her ex-boyfriend after he'd come over to swim in their pool. It was baggy and comfortable and reached almost to the bottom of her shorts. It was a good thing the windows hadn't exploded, as Mom had feared because she was barefoot.

Grandpa was already halfway up the hall, with Dad right behind him, moving slower to keep from mowing him down.

"Well, I'm not staying in here by myself." Mom got up and stepped out, exhaling a deep breath. "I can breathe again."

"It was your idea to go in there."

"The emergency message said to get to a safe area immediately. *Immediately,* Bri."

Brianna stared at her mother. She was very pretty, even with her hair a mess like it was now. People always complimented Brianna about how much she looked like her mother. She hoped so.

"What?" said Mom.

Smiling, Brianna shook her head. "Nothing."

"Can I help you?" Dad's voice resounded from the living room.

"Guess we better go see what this is about," said Mom.

Brianna walked with her mother into the living room. It was usually a comfortable area that opened into the kitchen. Now it was gloomy and gray, with the soft writhing of orange light from the candles on the mantle stretching over the walls.

Their door had an oval-shaped window in the center that nearly filled the whole space. Strange designs spread across it, making it impossible to see in or out. Other than a dark, squiggly shape, she could tell nothing about the visitor on the front porch.

"I need help," said the person outside. He was male and sounded young.

And familiar.

Brianna noticed the frown on Mom's face as well, as if she also recognized the voice.

"What kind of help?" Dad asked. He stood off to the side of the glass, a shoulder against the frame. "What happened?"

"My car went off the road. I was trying to get home but got caught in the storm. I'm stuck in a ditch. Can't get my phone to work and you're the only house out here."

Other than some farmland and *a lot* of woods, there was nothing at all on this road. Brianna liked it because she could lie out in the sun without fear of a car driving by and seeing her. Plus, they were off the road, tucked away from almost everything.

"I'm sorry to hear that," said Dad. He looked back at Mom, shrugging.

Mom shrugged in response. Brianna wasn't sure how, but they'd somehow communicated an entire conversation through simple gestures.

Even Grandpa seemed to understand. He stepped over, blocking Brianna from the door. Feeling annoyed that she couldn't see anything, Brianna moved over closer to Mom, who had a good view.

The shape outside shifted. She saw hair, tangled sprigs bouncing with the movement. "I appreciate it. But if I could just borrow your cell phone..."

"Ours aren't working, either."

There was a pause outside, then a subtle movement. "Do you have a landline I can use? Please?"

"Sorry."

"How about a bathroom?"

"Our power's out, pal. I wish I could help you, but I can't. Your best bet is to go back to your car and wait for one of the road crews to come by."

"No power?"

Dad rubbed his eyes. "No. Sorry. We can't help..."

Dad was interrupted by a clacking sound from outside. Brianna had heard similar sounds before, but only in movies right before somebody shot a gun.

The voice outside gave an eerie laugh. "That's what I wanted to hear."

"Get away from the door," said Grandpa, reaching for Dad.

Brianna heard a click right before she saw a flash of light. At first, she thought a lightning bolt had cracked through the air and hit the glass, causing it to explode and pitch shards all over. But the boom that accompanied it *did not* sound like thunder.

Grandpa flew back, arms thrown high. Blood jumped from his chest in a thick cloud that coated Dad's face in sticky red beside him.

Mom's screams sounded as if they were coming through a funnel.

Brianna only stood there, ears ringing as she watched her grandfather hit the floor, sprawled on his back. His chest was a deep cavity filled with blood.

A scream tried to leap from Brianna's mouth but was lodged in her tightening throat, strangling her. She heard the *clacking* again and whipped her head toward the door.

Dad was running toward her and Mom, arms held out as if he'd planned to escort them away from the madness. Then another boom resonated from behind him. His stomach blew open, shooting out blood and strips of intestine.

Now it was Brianna's turn to be splashed with blood.

It felt sticky and warm.

And knocked the scream lodged in her throat loose, shrieking as her father dropped to his knees in front of her. A third boom blew his head apart and threw him to the floor.

Still screaming, Brianna looked at the door. A young man was stepping through the broken window, holding a shotgun. The barrel was short, probably sawed off, and he held it in his hand like a pistol.

He jacked the pump. A shell shot out, bouncing along the floor with a hollow clamor. He looked at Mom and smiled. "There you are," he said. His dark hair was plastered on his head, dangling wet strands in his eyes. He was young, probably around twenty. She wasn't quite sure, though she'd seen him many times at the grocery store.

Mom, sobbing, pointed at him. "Garret!" She wiped her eyes and shook her head.

Brianna saw him in her mind, helping them with their emergency supplies this morning. He'd stood in the parking lot, talking with them as the storm was just starting to roll in.

Mom sniffed once more, but the tears had stopped. "You're not supposed to be here. We didn't talk about this."

"I couldn't wait. And plus, it's better this way. Don't you think? I figured the storm would provide a great cover story. But with the power out? And the phones not working? It's as if it was meant to be today."

Brianna looked at her mother. "What's he talking about?"

Mom sniffled and straightened her posture. She looked at Brianna. "We've been seeing each other for almost a year now."

Garret laughed. Nodded. "Oh, and what a year it's been."

Brianna's knees felt like they might fold on her. She looked down at her father, her grandfather, and the bloody mess Garret had left them in. "I don't...understand."

"We were supposed to plan this out more," said Mom. "Together."

"It's perfect," said Garret. "The cell towers are down, so we don't have to worry about phones being tracked! The alarm isn't working because the power's out! And..." He shrugged. "You can say a madman wandered up to the house and killed everybody, and that gets you in line to get all the money. And...I just really wanted to see you."

Mom put a hand to her chest and another to her mouth. "You're the sweetest..."

"But I didn't want to shoot again and risk hitting you, babe."

"You *do* care."

Garret nodded. He made kissy sounds with his lips.

Brianna had no idea what the hell was happening right now. It felt as if she'd woken up in a bizarre universe that was the exact opposite of her own. Her mother had been sleeping around with...the grocery store clerk?

And they'd planned...?

Brianna shook her head. "No. This..." Brianna's eyes filled with tears, making her vision look as if she were watching them from underwater. Wiping away the tears, she sniffled. "You killed Daddy? And Grandpa?"

Mom laughed. "Daddy? You haven't called him that since you were nine."

The woman standing beside her no longer resembled her mother. The voice was the same, but the pretty appearance that she'd envied for years had taken on an almost roguish quality, one that made her look evil.

"Babe?" said Garret.

"Huh?"

"You want to come over here with me? Don't want to hit you with the buckshot."

Mom sighed. "It wasn't as hard watching them die as I thought, but it'll probably hurt a little to see it happen to Brianna."

Brianna began to tremble. Why wasn't she running? She should be moving as if rockets were strapped to her shoes.

My mother's going to let him kill me?

"Just stand behind me," said Garret. "Don't look."

Mom sniffled again. "You're so good to me." She took a couple steps toward him, pausing at Dad's corpse. She raised her foot. "Better than you ever were!" She was about to kick him.

"Wait!" said Garret. "It'll look weird to the cops if you kicked him."

Nodding, Mom lowered her foot. "You're smart." She looked around. "But what about our footprints?"

"We'll clean that up."

Smiling, Mom pranced over to the younger man. She wrapped her arms around him and pressed her lips against his. Keeping the gun trained on Brianna, Garret kissed her back. Their tongues rolled over each other's mouths with gross smacking sounds.

Watching the pornographic display nauseated Brianna.

Garret pulled away. "Don't look, babe."

Giggling, Mom turned, putting her back to Brianna.

"Muh-mom?" Brianna's voice had turned thick and bubbly. "Why are you doing this?"

"I've turned my ears off, Bri," said Mom.

Tears slid down Brianna's face.

Garret lifted the shotgun with one hand, the short barrel pointing straight at Brianna's face. "Say "hi" to your dad for me," said Garret, smiling.

"Too far," said Mom. "Don't be a prick."

Garret shrugged. Then he squeezed the trigger.

Brianna jerked, expecting the boom to be loud. But there was only a click that somehow seemed just as deafening.

"Shit," said Garret.

Mom turned around. "What's wrong?"

"I forgot I shot Pops twice."

"So?"

"It only holds three shells!"

Garret shoved his hand into his jacket pocket and pulled out a couple of red tubes that were capped with gleaming copper.

He's out of ammunition!

Brianna's legs felt as if the invisible chains holding them finally snapped. Spinning on her heels, she dashed into the kitchen.

"She's running!" Mom yelled.

Brianna made it to the back door, pausing as she reached for the knob. The wind blew so hard out there that it made the rain look like wet sheets that smashed against the house. Tree branches bent and swayed while the trees they were attached to looked on the verge of cracking in half.

I can't go out there.

But there was no other choice. She couldn't go back through the house or upstairs to hide. She'd never make that far. Besides, there was no place she wouldn't be found. Mom knew the house just as well, if not better, than Brianna. She always found her when they played hide-and-seek, when Brianna was little.

Brianna nibbled on her bottom lip, then twisted the deadbolt to unlock it.

Behind her, she heard the squeaky stomps of Garret's wet feet on the kitchen floor.

"Ha!" he said, pumping the gun. Brianna could hear the ammo entering the pipe.

She didn't wait another second and jerked the door open. The wind tried to snatch it out of her hand, but she managed to hold on to the knob long enough to run outside. Behind her, the door banged shut as it was sucked back into the frame.

She rushed down the wooden steps of the back deck, gripping the railing to stay up. Her T-shirt folded around her. Her hair flapped and slapped her face as heavy rain stung her eyes. More drops pelted her thighs, feeling like rocks as it caused a flurry of bites all over her skin.

Reaching the ground, she looked around for a moment, trying to decide where to go.

The woods.

That's a terrible idea!

But it was better than being out in the open. Wiping the hair off her face, she started running toward the great wall of trees that made up much of their property. Their house had been erected on a flat patch in the middle of the thick woodland.

The wind seemed to be screaming at her as she ran, its invisible hands shoving at her to keep her away. Even the storm seemed to be telling her to go back inside. She felt safer out here, though she knew it was probably even worse.

Reaching the woods, she turned sideways and ran into the darkness of the trees. She ducked behind one, daring a look back. She expected to see Garret struggling against the storm as he pursued her. But she was shocked to find he was already almost to the woods, while her mother was a short distance behind him. The rain had turned her white shirt translucent, molding the soggy fabric around her breasts. She looked feral, as if she'd just come from dark waters meant for demonic sirens.

Brianna let out another squeal before turning and rushing into the woods. The ground felt soggy under her bare feet, like running through oatmeal. Every couple of steps, something sharp poked or jabbed the bottom of her foot. Branches lashed her arms and face. Once, her toes hit a protruding root. The pain that shot up her leg had nearly made her fall, but she kept going on.

She ran for an undetermined amount of time, thinking she'd gone pretty far into the woods. But as she reached the top of a steep hill, she paused to look around.

She was nowhere near as deep in as she thought.

Brianna screamed when she spotted Garret coming up the hill. The rain slashed through the sky, pounding against him so hard it had flattened his hair and made his clothes look like sodden weights dragging with him.

But the shotgun beamed in his hands.

He saw her watching. A smile pulled the corners of his mouth wide, making it appear way too big for his face. "Almost there!"

She scanned the woods for her mother but couldn't locate her.

Garret was even closer now, moving up the hill with an ease that was terrifying. How he could do so against the hard winds that felt like rushing trains, she had no idea. But she couldn't wait around to ask him. She had to keep moving.

Brianna put her back to him and took a step. Her bare foot came down in the mud. It shot out from under her, throwing her sideways. She hit the mushy ground and started tumbling down.

Thankfully, the ground was soft.

Maybe I'll be okay!

A tree stump appeared just to prove her wrong. Her hip struck the coarse bark first, folding her, but the momentum carried her over. The jagged wood scraped her belly through the shirt, igniting fire on her skin.

Now she was in the air, still spinning with nothing beneath her. She saw branches jutting from the ground—broken and dropped from the trees above, their speared tips pointing up.

God, save me!

Her shoulder came down on the wet ground first, digging a rent into the soil until her legs folded over her back, flipping her one more time.

She came down on her rump; the speed turning her around like a water slide until her back finally smashed against something hard, immediately stopping her.

The air blasted out of Brianna's lungs. Her throat felt like hands were squeezing it as she tried to breathe. Whatever solid object was behind her was scratching her, raking her skin.

Had her shirt been torn? Probably. Was it another tree stump? Probably.

Didn't matter either way. She was hurt and wasn't going anywhere.

It's over. I'm dead.

Garret was sliding down the hill on his heels like a snowboarding Terminator. He held the shotgun above his head while he hooted into the sky. The wind slammed him, throwing his jacket behind him like a ruffling cape. The wind had torn down trees but couldn't knock him over.

He reached the bottom of the hill just as Mom appeared from behind the trees.

"Where'd *you* go?" he asked.

"I told you there was a trail." She looked at him and winced. "You're fucking filthy! Look at all that mud all over you!"

From the knees down looked as if he'd been stomping around inside a pigpen. He shrugged. "Not much I can do about that now."

"You could've taken the trail and caught her just as easily."

"This way was more fun."

Brianna took a deep breath that hurt her inside. She wasn't sure, but she thought she had a broken rib or two. "Mom?"

Mom looked down, her hair hanging in wet tangles all over her face. She looked even crazier than before, less like her mother and more like some unknown creature.

"How can you do this?" She sniffled. She was sure she was crying, but the heavy rain washed it away. "How can you...?" Brianna let her head rest on the hard object. A stump, most definitely.

Mom shook her head. "You just don't understand. You never did. Your father and I haven't loved each other in a very long time."

"He loved you."

Mom rolled her eyes. "Okay, fine. I haven't loved *him* in a very long time. And I found out that his father, your grandpa..."

"Dead grandpa," corrected Garret.

Mom giggled. “Right. He changed his will. His fortune wasn’t going to us. It was going *you,* soon as you graduated college. I thought your father would talk him out of that, but he was fine with it. Said we had enough money.”

“No money,” said Garret, “is enough money.”

“You understand me so well, baby.” Mom reached out, caressing his wet cheek. “So, Garret and I got to talking and, well, we decided it would be best to kill Grandpa and Dad. *And* you. See, with all three of you gone, I get *everything.*”

“*We* get everything,” said Garret.

“Right. But we have to be patient, honey.”

Nodding, Garret began to laugh. “So much fucking money!”

Now Mom was laughing with him. “Free to do whatever we want. Millionaires!”

Brianna couldn’t believe this was the same woman she’d just been cooped up in the closet with not even a half hour ago. She’d cooked breakfast for everyone in the house. They’d played Scrabble together last night, drinking coffee and listening to the storm slink in.

For years, Brianna had looked on her mother as not just a parent, but as a friend she could truly confide in. There’d been many nights they’d stayed up late, talking about various things going on in Brianna’s life.

She’d trusted her mother with secrets she hadn’t even told her friends.

And now she’s going to kill me. Over money.

“You’re a bitch,” said Brianna. “A damn bitch.”

Mom shrugged. “Can’t argue with that, kid. I do feel bad that you have to die, but I knew you wouldn’t go along with all this. And even if you did, you’d somehow fuck it all up. Or you’d feel guilty and blow it.” She shook the wet hair out of her face, sighed. “There was really only one option, honey. You have to die.” Mom smiled as if she’d just explained how paying taxes worked. “Okay, Garret. Do it.”

“Are you going to turn around?”

Mom considered this. “Not this time. It almost went to shit the last time I did.”

Garret shrugged. “Fine by me.”

He turned sideways, holding the gun with one hand.

“Do you have to do it like that?” asked Mom.

“Like what?”

“Like you’re *John Wick* or something.”

“Wick’s cool.”

"Just hold the gun right."

"It's fine, babe."

Sighing, Mom shook her head. "Fine! Whatever. Just do it. We have to figure things out."

Garret laughed. "Yep. Then it's a life of luxury."

"That's right."

Garret shuddered. "I'm so hard right now."

"Don't be gross."

"Sorry."

"Shoot her."

"Fine."

Garret focused, settling the gun on Brianna's face. The rain formed around the barrel, streaming to the sides as if it were a rock in a stream. A big rock that would make a very big hole in Brianna's head.

So this is it.

Brianna sighed. She wasn't scared. Heartbroken, yes. But not scared.

Garret's finger began to squeeze the trigger.

Okay. Maybe I'm a little *scared.*

Just as the shotgun began to fire, Mom produced a knife that Brianna recognized from their knife rack in the kitchen. The blade flashed before vanishing into Garret's side. Flinching, the shotgun tilted and boomed. The recoil threw it back, clacking the hard barrel against Mom's face and sending her backward.

The tree stump beside Brianna's head exploded into a mist of splinters. She felt the sharp fragments nicking her face, slicing into her nose and forehead.

"You bitch!" Garret yelled.

When Brianna looked at him now, she saw he was on his knees. The hilt of the knife stuck out from his side like a switch. Blood flowed from the wound, thinning in the rain.

Mom, sitting on her ass, held a hand to her nose. Blood leaked from a split over her left eye. "You messed this up, Garret! Showing up like this? Letting Bri get this far? I had to improvise! So now, you have to die, too. And I'll be the lone survivor, as always."

"I'm going to *kill* you," said Garret.

Mom laughed. "You'll be dead in a minute. I got you in the liver. You're already dying and don't even know it."

Garret straightened up, lifting the shotgun. Though he was shivering, he managed to keep the weapon aimed at her. "You're going with me, babe."

For the first time, Mom looked worried. "Baby. I didn't *want* to do it. You left me no other choice."

"I did this for you. I killed them all...and..."

"Bri's still alive," said Mom. "So you're a failure. And I'm gonna have to finish her."

Garret glanced at her, then back to Mom. "Who cares?" Holding the gun with two hands, he angled the weapon, so the barrel was now trained directly on Mom. "Am I holding it good enough for you now?"

"Don't do this, baby!" Mom said, holding up a hand. Blood kept running into her eye and she blinked it away. She managed to feign fright a bit longer before laughing. "You're such an idiot."

"What's so funny?"

"You." Mom laughed harder. "You're a great fuck, but stupid in the head. How much longer before you bleed out? Jesus, this is taking forever!"

"Shut up!"

Brianna watched them go back and forth like this for a while until it became too much. "Stop it!"

They looked at her.

Brianna took a deep breath. "You're an idiot because you haven't done the..." She lifted up her arms and mimicked the action of pumping it to fire.

"Bri, you little bitch," said Mom.

Garret smiled. "Oh. Guess that's what getting betrayed does to me. Makes me forget." He jacked the shotgun with purpose, the ratchet-like click reverberating through the woods. "Now I'm ready."

Mom shook her head. "Baby. Don't do this. B—"

Garret shot her in the face. The buckshot created a massive hole where her nose was, making a much larger exit hole that sent skull shards and brain gunk out behind her.

Garret managed to laugh a few times before dropping onto his side. He was alive for a couple minutes before going still. Though Brianna couldn't see much through the thick layers of rain, she figured he was dead.

Her leg was definitely broken. The pain she felt in her thigh when she tried to move it told her that. Plus, the grating sound of broken bones grinding together was loud enough to be heard over the howling wind.

She was stuck out here.

The sky was the color of ash; the clouds swirling like smokey waves. The rain never let up and only seemed to be getting heavier as it poured down, feeling like hail as it pummeled her. All through the woods, she could hear the ghostly cracks of tree limbs snapping or the loud crash of a tree tipping over.

And there's not a damn thing I can do about it.

If a tree came down on her, that would be all she wrote for Brianna Troutman.

But she wasn't worried about it.

After all she'd gone through, the hurricane felt almost more like a nuisance than a dangerous threat.

About the Authors

BRENNAN LAFARO — Brennan LaFaro is a horror writer living in south-eastern Massachusetts with his wife, two sons, and his hounds. An avid life-long reader, Brennan also co-hosts the Dead Headspace podcast. Brennan is the author of the horror western, *Noose*, the story collection *Illusions of Isolation*, and the *Slattery Falls* trilogy. You can read his short fiction in various anthologies and find him on Twitter at @brennanlafaro or at www.brennanlafaro.com.

JUDITH SONNET — Judith Sonnet is a very sad girl. She writes gross and disturbing horror books, and she collects old paperbacks as well as 70's action movies. She grew up in Missouri, but now she lives in Utah. She's trans, asexual, and is an abuse and suicide survivor. If you want to know more about her, check her out on Facebook . . . or contact her through your nearest Ouija board.

MICHAEL MOORE — Michael J Moore's books include *Highway Twenty*, which was short-listed for the 2019 Bram Stoker Preliminary Ballot, the bestselling novel, *After the Change*, *Secret Harbor*, the middle grade series, *Nightmares in Aston*, and *Cinema 7*. Follow him at https://www.facebook.com/michaeljmoorewriting.

LUCAS MANGUM — Lucas Mangum is a horror author living in Central Texas. He's a father, husband, and a fan of trashy movies. When he's not working on a book, he's co-hosting *Make Your Own Damn Podcast* with bizarro legend Jeff Burk or walking in the woods. His newsletter, posted every Monday, can be found at LucasMangum.com

CAITLIN MARCEAU — Caitlin Marceau is a queer award-winning author and illustrator based in Montreal. She holds a Bachelor of Arts in Creative Writing, is an Active Member of the Horror Writers Association, and has spoken about genre literature at several Canadian conventions. Her work includes *Femina*, *A Blackness Absolute*, and *This Is Where We Talk Things Out*. Her novella, *I'm Having Regrets*, will be coming out later this year and her debut novel, *It Wasn't Supposed To Go Like This*, is set for publication in 2024. For more, visit CaitlinMarceau.ca or find her on social media.

TIM MEYER — Tim Meyer dwells in a dark cave near the Jersey Shore. He's the author of more than fifteen novels, including *Malignant Summer, The Switch House, Dead Daughters, Limbs,* and many other titles. When he's not working on the next book, he's usually hanging out with his wife and son, shooting around on the basketball court, playing video games, or messing with a new screenplay. He bleeds coffee and IPAs. His newest novel is *Lacuna's Point,* out now through DarkLit Press. You can learn more about his books at timmeyerwrites.com.

ANDRE DUZA — Andre Duza is an actor, stuntman, screenwriter, martial artist, and the author or co-author of over 10 novels, a graphic novel (Hollow Eyed Mary), and the Star Trek comic book Outer Light. He has also contributed to several collections and anthologies, including Book of Horror Lists; alongside the likes of Stephen King and Eli Roth.

BRIDGETT NELSON — Bridgett Nelson is a registered nurse turned horror author. Her first collection, *A Bouquet of Viscera*, is a two-time Splatterpunk Award winner, recognized both for the collection itself and its standout story, "*Jinx*." Her work has appeared in *Counting Bodies Like Sheep, Dead & Bloated, American Cannibal, A Woman Unbecoming*, and several volumes of the *If I Die Before I Wake* series of anthologies. Bridgett is working on her first original novel and has been contracted by Encyclopocalypse Publications to write a novelization of the cult classic film *Deadgirl*. She is an active member of the Horror Writers Association and the co-chair of HWA: West Virginia. She was a 2022 Michael Knost "Wings" award nominee, won second place in the '22 Gross-Out contest at KillerCon in Austin, Texas, and third place in the '23 Gross-Out contest.

TONY EVANS — Tony Evans is the author of *Sour, Wicked Appalachia, Better You Believe, The 11th Plague,* and *A Bad Case of Tinnitus*. He has also authored over two-dozen short stories that have appeared in various print and online horror and dark fantasy magazines and anthologies. Tony was born and raised in the Appalachian foothills of eastern Kentucky and his fiction is largely influenced by the folktales and legends he grew up listening to. Tony's ability to retell and put his own spin on those old folktales while keeping their Appalachian roots intact is what sets him apart from others in the field, and his storytelling is unmatched.

KATE KINGSTON — Kate Kingston has been writing scary stories since childhood. As the lead psychic investigator for a local ghost tour company from 2000 to 2010, Kate spent many dark nights in forbidden places that most people are never permitted to see. She was featured on 6 episodes of Creepy Canada and on many other tv/radio shows where she was asked to sense and communicate with the dead. While some of her work reflects those experiences, she has more recently focused on splatterpunk and revenge horror, written for fellow survivors of childhood abuse. Kate also established the Hamilton Book Crawl, a monthly outdoor venue for local authors to sell their books free of cost, and the Greater Hamilton Writers' Association. She dreams about owning a haunted old bookstore where she can sell indie horror authors' books and chat with ghosts about the world going to hell in a handbasket.

REBECCA ROWLAND — Rebecca Rowland is the American dark fiction author of two fiction collections, one novel, a handful of novellas, and too many short stories. She is the curator of seven horror anthologies, including the best-sellers *Unburied: A Collection of Queer Dark Fiction and American Cannibal.* Rebecca is an active member of the Horror Writers Association and snagged a Godless 666 gold medal for her novella *Optic Nerve*; her speculative fiction, critical essays, and book reviews regularly appear in a variety of online and print venues. The former acquisitions and anthology editor at AM Ink Publishing, Rebecca owns and manages the small, independent publishing house Maenad Press. Her latest release is *White Trash & Recycled Nightmares* (October 2023) from Dead Sky Publishing. In her spare time, she pets her cat, eats cheese, and drinks vodka (sometimes simultaneously). Follow her dark tomfoolery at RowlandBooks.com or on Instagram @Rebecca_Rowland_books.

KRISTOPHER RUFTY — Kristopher Rufty lives in North Carolina with his three children and pets. He's written over twenty novels, including *ALL WILL DIE, THE DEVOURED AND THE DEAD, DESOLATION, THE LURKERS* and *PILLOWFACE.* When he's not spending time with his family or writing, he's obsessing over gardening and growing food. His short story *DARLA'S PROBLEM* was included in the Splatterpunk Publications anthology *FIGHTING BACK*, which won the Splatterpunk award for best anthology. *THE DEVOURED AND THE DEAD* was nominated for a Splatterpunk award. He can be found on Facebook, Instagram, and Twitter. For more about Kristopher Rufty, please visit: www.kristopherrufty.comFor signed copies of books, please visit www.kruftybooks.com

Acknowledgements

Uncomfortably Dark would like to thank this incredible group of authors for taking part in this year's anthology, as well as the many readers, authors, and reviewers that took time out of their busy schedules to help support this project.

Special thanks to Patrick R. McDonough for writing the foreword.

Massive "Thank You" to Clay McLeod Chapman, Jill Giradi, and Nikolas P. Robinson for taking time to blurb the anthology. Deeply appreciated by all.

Special thanks to Christina Pfeiffer for her unwavering support and assistance throughout the project.

To the Uncomfortably Dark team: Mort Stone, Darcy Rose, Chaz Williams, Rachel Schommer, Sonja Ska, Christopher Besonen, and Christina Pfeiffer. I could not do what I do without each one of you on my team. You are a valuable part of the Dark.

Also By Uncomfortably Dark Horror

ANTHOLOGIES

Uncomfortably Dark presents The Baker's Dozen-2021 Dark Dozen anthology & the 2022 Splatterpunk award-winning extreme horror anthology. Published by Uncomfortably Dark.

Uncomfortably Dark presents Trapped-2022 Dark Dozen anthology that explores themes of horror focused on being trapped in an unspeakable situation. Published by Uncomfortably Dark.

The Generator-quad collaboration anthology featuring Candace Nola, Eric Butler, M Ennenbach, and Nikolas P. Robinson. Published by Uncomfortably Dark.

Made in the USA
Middletown, DE
23 December 2024

68098891R00136